DR. CEO

LOUISE BAY

Published by Louise Bay 2023

ISBN – 978-1-80456-012-9

BOOKS BY LOUISE BAY

The Doctors Series

Dr. Off Limits

Dr. Perfect

Dr. CEO

Dr. Fake Fiancé

The Mister Series

Mr. Mayfair

Mr. Knightsbridge

Mr. Smithfield

Mr. Park Lane

Mr. Bloomsbury

Mr. Notting Hill

The Christmas Collection

The 14 Days of Christmas

The Player Series

International Player

Private Player

Dr. Off Limits

Standalones

Hollywood Scandal

Love Unexpected

Hopeful

The Empire State Series

Gentleman Series

The Wrong Gentleman

The Ruthless Gentleman

The Royals Series

The Earl of London

The British Knight

Duke of Manhattan

Park Avenue Prince

King of Wall Street

The Nights Series

Indigo Nights

Promised Nights

Parisian Nights

Faithful

ONE

Kate

My toes still tingle with excitement, even after all these years of opening the tea shop on the Crompton Estate. I genuinely look forward to every new day—and really, how many people can say that about their job? I unlock the door and flip the sign on the window to "open". Today we'll serve tea, coffee, cakes, and flapjacks, not to mention Sandra's soup of the day, to hundreds of smiling visitors. Buoyed by a tour of Crompton's gorgeous gardens, they'll pop in for a short break before continuing their tour of the gardens or driving home.

The magnolia outside the tea shop has just burst into flower, and I just know people will push open our door while remarking on the flowers that grow as big as my head and the sweet scent that tells me it's the middle of May. It's the same every year. It will put everyone in an especially good mood today. How could anyone not be in a good mood when visiting Crompton? It's impossible.

The opening bars of "I Feel Pretty" from *West Side*

Story filter in my direction. My smile widens and I twirl to face Sandra, who's turned the speakers on and begun to sing. I join in while twirling back towards the counter.

"And I pity every girl who isn't me today," I sing.

I haven't got a *great* voice—even if I'd wanted to, I could have never made it in the West End—but I can sing well enough for the Crompton amateur dramatics production of *Frozen* we put on last year. I was Elsa, and Sandra, even though she's thirty years older than me, was Anna.

"How's Granny?" Sandra asks. Everyone calls *my* granny "Granny". She's lived and worked on this estate for thirty years and is as much part of it as the cottage on the grounds where she lives.

"Good. Her cold has completely cleared up now." I'm flicking through the comments on the Crompton Instagram page. I manage the official account, and receive a small uplift in my café salary to cover the additional work it takes. "You like this one?" I turn the phone and hold it out so Sandra can see the picture of the magnolia I took as I arrived.

"They're all pretty," she says.

"That's the problem. There's so much beauty all around us, we get spoiled. We don't realize how lucky we are."

"There's no danger of us forgetting," Sandra says. "We've got you reminding us all the time."

I laugh. I am unabashedly enthusiastic about the place where we live and work. Not only do I not wonder if the grass is greener on the other side of the estate's many hills—I know for a fact it isn't.

"I'm posting it. I'll put the others up on our stories."

The bell above the door tinkles and I step around the counter and turn to face the first customer of the day.

What I expect to see is a retired couple wanting to

warm up with a cup of tea before they start their self-guided tour of the gardens. Or perhaps a group of Japanese tourists who want me to explain the map.

The absolute last person I expect to find coming through the door is a man so tall he has to dip to make sure he doesn't catch his head on the lintel—a man who's rolled his white shirt sleeves up to reveal his forearms in a way that seems almost provocative. He comes to a stop directly in front of the counter, looking at me like I'm a slice of Sandra's Bakewell tart and he's going to devour me.

It's safe to say the man in front of me is not Crompton's typical customer.

I manage to hold my smile in place as I greet our new customer, despite the fact I'm almost positive I'm blushing just from looking at him. "Good morning. How can I help you?"

An amused expression crosses his face. I absolutely do not want to know what he's thinking. Because from the way the corner of his mouth twitches and his eyes widen, I just know whatever it is, it's *filthy*.

"Tea? Coffee?" I suggest, a little unnerved. "We have cartons of orange juice in the back fridge." I wave towards the unit that holds the cold drinks.

Sandra shuffles towards us and I see her out of the corner of my eye, placing the chocolate gateau on the counter. We'll do a sweepstake later of what time the first slice will be eaten. It's always the last to be ordered, but once the first slice has gone, it's like Black Friday—nonstop orders until it's gone. Before that, homemade granola bars and carrot cake comprise the bulk of each morning's business.

"Aren't you a handsome chap?" Sandra says to the perfect stranger in front of me, who hasn't even told me if he wants tea or coffee yet. Sandra puts her hands on her hips and steps towards me, and therefore the stranger, as if she's inspecting him, making sure he's as good-looking as she first thought. There's no doubt about it. The dark brown glossy hair, the full lips, that jaw ... even the hint of a crease between his eyes adds an intensity to his handsome face.

The customer's mouth curls up in a quarter smile. "Thank you."

"And American!" she says as if she's just been introduced to a zebra. We see Americans every day. Or most days anyway.

Sandra nudges me. "He's American."

I can't help but smile. Sandra is unintentionally funny at least forty percent of the day. The other sixty, she's singing, which makes her the perfect colleague. Plus she has no filter, a talent for baking, and I've known her since I was born. Sandra is family.

"Carrot cake?" I suggest, trying to ignore Sandra and focus on my job—the job I dreamed of growing up, and started when I was sixteen.

"A black coffee," he says.

Instead of actually fixing the customer a coffee, while I take the payment, Sandra leans on the counter. "You live in America?" she asks. "You over here on holiday?"

"That will be one pound fifty, and the questionnaire from Sandra is entirely optional."

He chuckles and my thighs flame. It's true there aren't many good-looking men who wander onto the Crompton Estate. And I don't often leave the estate, other than to pop into the village if I need to go to the post office or the supermarket. I don't cross paths with many men my age who look like the man opposite me, but my body is having such a visceral reaction to him, I'm quite thankful it's been a while since I ventured farther. Maybe I've had some kind of hormonal shift and I'd start convulsing on the floor if I was to visit Cambridge, stumble around a corner and find myself opposite an entire group of men.

Although a dozen men put together are unlikely to have the confidence of the one opposite now. It oozes from every pore of him. In just a few seconds of interaction, I can tell he's a man who knows what he wants.

A man who *gets* what he wants.

"It's not a questionnaire," says Sandra. "I'm just making small talk. I like people. What can I say?"

"At the moment I live in the States," he replies.

I'm about to ask him whether he wants to pay by cash or card when he lifts his phone in answer to my unasked question, nodding when I offer him the card reader.

"I have family over here. I'm meeting them this morning to tour the gardens."

"Lovely," I say.

"A family man," Sandra says in confirmation. "Are you married?"

At this, the man chuckles. I'm not quite sure if it's all the questions or the personal nature of this specific question.

"I'm not." His gaze slides to mine and then back to Sandra.

"I'll bring your coffee over, if you want to take a seat. You have a choice of tables." I want to hit my forehead with my palm. Of course he has a choice of tables. He's the only one here. It's not like some are reserved for VIPs.

"Thanks," he says before turning to go.

I watch as he sits, unfurls his legs under the table and pulls out his phone.

"He's gorgeous," Sandra says as we both stare at him.

He looks up abruptly, catching us as we ogle. Embarrassment creeps up my neck and I glance down at the till in front of me as if it's a laptop and I'm doing important work.

Did he hear Sandra?

"You're going to get us both in trouble," I whisper.

"You need a little trouble in your life. A little excitement or adventure."

"I like my life just fine as it is," I reply. The Crompton Estate is adventure enough for me. I'm happy here. That's what counts.

"Twenty years ago, I would have climbed that man like a tree," Sandra says.

"You were happily married," I remind her.

She shrugs. "But you're not."

"I'm happy." I've known adventure, which is why I like it here, in the coffee shop, singing show tunes and serving up carrot cake.

The stranger glances up from his phone and our gazes lock. He doesn't look away and neither do I.

TWO

Vincent

Jacob and Sutton aren't late. I'm early. I wanted to take in the place before I got distracted by anything—the tea shop, the pink gingham tablecloths, the show tunes being belted out by the two women behind the counter. I want to look around, get a feel for the gardens, the way the house looks when it's not swarmed by tourists. I need to be able to hear what my gut is telling me. I'm a fan of data, but even if the numbers look good, when I'm making an investment, my gut has to give its approval too.

"Okay by me in America . . ." The older lady behind the counter starts to sing along to the next song coming through the speaker. I smile. She sure is happy.

The sound of approaching footsteps makes me look up. "Your coffee," says the younger employee.

"Thanks," I say, twisting the mug around so the handle is the opposite way.

"Oh, another leftie," she says, beaming. She's wearing a pink striped uniform with a frilled collar and white apron.

It really shouldn't be as alluring as it is. It just looks so damn innocent.

"Your friend likes to sing," I say.

"We both do," she replies. "I wouldn't be able to work anywhere you couldn't sing." She says it deadpan, and I'm not sure if she's being serious until her face cracks into a wide smile.

She's dazzling.

Her blue eyes almost sparkle and her hair is swept up in a ponytail that bounces as she walks ... and I imagine when she's doing other things as well.

"Can I get you anything else?"

I narrow my eyes. "Nothing on the menu."

She blushes, and I mentally chastise myself for not being more of a gentleman. "I'm good, thank you."

The bell over the door chimes and in walks Sutton. And Parker—I wasn't expecting her. Closely followed by Jacob and Tristan, Parker's fiancé.

I push away from the table and stand.

"We've come as a foursome," Sutton says. "I need to see as many friends as possible on my days off."

"The more the merrier," I say, pulling Sutton into a hug. The bigger the crowd, the more it looks like a typical family day out, which is exactly how I want it to look. My family are unwitting players in my game today.

Everyone is pulling out chairs and peeling off sweaters and I glance over to the counter and catch the younger woman's eye. Without me saying anything, she picks up a pad and comes over to the group.

"Good morning, everyone. Welcome to Crompton. Can I get you anything?"

I watch as she studiously writes down each order, recapping to everyone what they just said. In between each order, her eyes slide to mine, as if she's checking I'm still here.

Then the bell tinkles again and my aunt and uncle burst in.

"I'm bloody freezing, Carole. That's why I'm wearing two jumpers and a coat."

My aunt ignores my uncle's complaining—she's used to it—and gets engulfed in hugs from her son and his soon-to-be wife and their friends.

I glance up at the counter and my friend is headed over here again.

"Two cups of tea and a carrot cake for John," I say.

"He's getting two cups of tea?" she asks. Then she shakes her head and realizes what I meant. She stares at my aunt and uncle as they twist out of their layers. A small smile curls at the edges of her lips. She flips her pen toward Carole and John in a movement no one but me would have caught. "Your parents?"

I smile. It's not just the older lady who's full of questions.

I move a couple of steps to the edge of our crowd and she follows me.

"What's your name?" I ask.

"Kate."

I take in her face—the dark waves that escape her ponytail, the three freckles she has on her left cheekbone, and I enjoy the blush crawling up her neck. I don't mean to embarrass her. "They're my aunt and uncle," I explain. "Jacob's my cousin—Carole and John's eldest. Sutton's his soon-to-be-wife."

"Fiancée," she corrects me.

I grin and push my hands into my pockets to stop myself

from doing anything else with them. "Then Parker is Sutton's best friend and Tristan is *her* fiancé."

She nods as if she's satisfied with my answer. "Big family vibe. Lots of fiancés."

I chuckle. "Not for me." I meet her eye. I don't know why I'm flirting so hard. It's not like I'm going to get her number or take her to dinner. But there's a pull to her I can't quite explain.

"We're expecting Nathan too. Another cousin. I have five. Nathan's wife is tied up at work, so won't be joining us."

She sighs, turns to me and puts her hand on my arm. The gesture is entirely too familiar, but feels completely right. "Have a wonderful day." She says it with such sincerity, it takes me by surprise. Then she turns and heads back to the counter.

"Thanks, Kate," I call after her.

A familiar tune starts to play and then I hear the opening lyrics—it's "Good Morning," from *Singing in the Rain*.

"Don't make them like this anymore," John says. "Great piece of music. None of this Andrew Lloyd Webber nonsense. *Singing in the Rain* is a proper musical."

"*The Dueling Cavalier*," Carole says.

John laughs. "Is now a musical."

Then it's Carole's turn to laugh.

It's good to see them happy, even though I have no clue what they're laughing about.

"You okay there?" I ask.

"I'd be better with a cup of tea," John says. "Do we need to go up and order?"

"No," I say, "One is coming."

"You're a good chap, Vincent. Unlike my lot."

I smile, but the prickling on the back of my neck intensifies.

Kate returns with a tray of drinks. "Can I get you anything else?" She turns to look at me.

"Maybe when Nathan arrives," I say.

"Until Nathan, then." She smiles at me and then turns back to the counter, singing as she goes.

"British women are the way to go," Sutton says.

I turn to her and it's clear she was watching me, watching Kate.

I chuckle. "Gorgeous women are everywhere, Sutton."

"Have you ever been in love?" she asks.

I really don't want to get into this. I guess it's normal that couples who are newly in love want the same thing for everyone they know, but I'm not built like that. I'm a rolling stone, uninterested in finding "The One" to be with for the rest of my life. I'm not interested in *anything* for the rest of my life. "I love life," I respond. Lucky for me, the café door opens and Nathan enters, arm in arm with a woman who's at least sixty years older than him, which puts her firmly in her nineties.

"Here they are, Gladys. I told you they'd wait for me. Now, let's get you a seat." Nathan glances up and nods at me. "Vincent, can we arrange a cup of tea for Gladys? Let's make that two cups of tea and an orange juice. Her daughter and granddaughter will be back from the loo in a minute."

I move towards the counter to place Gladys's order. Kate seems to have disappeared, but the door behind the counter opens and she's back.

We lock eyes before she sees she has more customers.

"Gladys!" Kate calls. "Didn't see you last week. Everything okay?" She rounds the counter and takes over from Nathan, escorting Gladys to the table nearest the counter.

She and Gladys talk, but I can't make out what they're saying because of the noise from our group greeting Nathan. I sit, taking a sip of coffee and looking at the gaggle of people in front of me having at least twelve different conversations at the same time.

"Are we all here now?" Carole asks from beside me.

I nod. "As far as I'm aware, there are no more Coves due."

She pats me on the knee. "It's nice to see you again. You've not been over for months. Perhaps you'll stay a bit longer this time."

The prickling on the back of my neck almost disappears and I place a kiss on her cheek. "I come when I can," I say. "But I have to say, I miss the place when I'm gone."

"So what is it we're doing here?" she asks. "I don't believe you've brought us just for a day out."

My aunt has had an extremely distinguished career as a surgeon. She's the sharpest member of our family by far. Nothing gets by her.

"*No one* believes you've suggested coming here for a day out," John says.

I check to see if anyone—namely, Kate and the older woman who works in the café—is listening. "Can you just suspend disbelief for a couple of hours while we're here? I'll fill you in when the time is right." The last thing I want is to be overheard by Kate and the older woman. They might overhear and jump to conclusions.

"Of course we can. As long as you're okay," Carole says.

I get regular texts or emails and calls from all my cousins and even my uncle, but it's always Carole who checks in to make sure I'm okay. She's done it since I was a kid. I used to fantasize about missing my plane back to the States after a summer spent in England with Carole and John. I guess that's why I came to university here. And why I studied medicine. I wanted to be just like them.

Have a family, just like them.

"More than okay," I reassure her. "You know how I like to track down a good investment."

She raises her eyebrows but says no more. I'll fill them in later. I'll only buy this place if the earl accepts the price I'm willing to pay. I'm just not sure what that price is and figuring it out is what today's all about.

John coughs and peers over at the counter. "That chocolate cake looks jolly nice, Carole—"

"No, John. It's five past ten and you've just eaten carrot cake."

He grumbles and takes another sip of his tea.

I smile and lean back in my chair.

It's good to be back.

THREE

Vincent

In the parking lot, after three promises that I'll go up to Norfolk before I fly back to New York, I stand by my car as my family leaves.

Them being here was a cover, but it was good to see them.

I check the time and head over to the house. Only the grounds are open to the public, but if I'm going to buy the entire estate, I need to see the house as well.

As instructed, I make my way through a small black gate in a wall at the back of a property, where I find the realtor waiting for me.

"Brian," I say.

"Vincent. So pleased you could make it. Sorry about not being able to see the gardens with you. But I can show you around the house no problem."

He doesn't need to know I've already visited the gardens. And while scoping out the land around the house, I was able to see the state of things from a distance. The roof needs fixing, if not replacement. There's paintwork peeling in certain places that aren't immediately noticeable. And there are weeds growing out of the guttering. The decay isn't obvious unless you're looking for it—and I'm looking. Not only because I want to know how much I'm going to have to pay to get the place into shape, but I also want to know how desperate the earl is to sell.

"Lead the way," I say.

"Let's start at the front of the house, as if you'd come through the entrance. You'll really get a feel for the grandeur of the place."

I follow him from the back of the building, taking in the cracked walls and curling wallpaper of the small, cramped rooms we move through, until we reach the entrance hall, which looks very different.

"You can imagine being a visitor here, the double-height ceilings, that sweeping staircase—it makes an impact as soon as you walk through the doors."

I push my hands into my pockets and look up and around. Brian's right, the entrance is impressive and it could be grand. It just looks a little tired and unloved. The carpets running up the stairs are worn and there seems to be an emptiness about the space. It's as if the art and furniture that should adorn the walls and fill the rooms are more conspicuous for their absence.

"Has the owner moved out?"

"Absolutely not. But since the countess died, the earl has lost his love for the place."

"She died about five years ago?"

Brian nods. Brian is the earl's broker, not mine. Apparently, I don't have to have one in the UK. It means I save money, but at the same time, I think he might be more open if I was represented.

"So he's looking to move on."

"It pains him, but yes, he doesn't want the upkeep anymore."

"Understandable. It's expensive and time-consuming caring for a place like this."

"Let me show you the library," he says.

We turn left into the book-lined room. A couple of wing-backed leather chairs sit either side of a small table. But other than the books, it seems empty. "Has he gotten rid of furniture? And art? There seem to be gaps."

"I think in readiness for the sale, he's given a number of pieces of furniture and artwork to family members."

Whether that's true, I'm unsure. Maybe the earl has sold them to keep the place up and running.

"Does having the gardens open cover the costs of running the place?" I ask.

"Would you look to keep the café open?" he asks. "And the gardens?"

"I've made no decisions yet," I reply. He didn't answer my question, which means the café and the gardens *don't* cover the upkeep of the house. And he knows it. Which means the earl has told him, which means he and the earl understand they're in a weak bargaining position.

Of course, there's no way I'll be keeping the gardens open to the public. If I transform this decaying old house into a five-star hotel, it will be exclusive. Luxurious. It won't have a back garden full of carrot cake and buses full of retired ramblers.

Brian pulls in a breath. "If you were to close them, planning might be a battle due to the loss of local jobs. Some of the people have worked in the estate for generations."

"It's a huge gamble," I say. Obviously, I've already looked into planning approval. I have a team of people to assist me making decisions, and although there are risks to acquiring a home like this without planning permission, I've taken bigger. Planning authorities understand that unless these huge stately homes are given new life, they will fall into disrepair. People will be left out of work and communities will crumble with holes at their heart. But Brian doesn't need to know any of that.

"Indeed," he says. "And you've come up from London for the day?" he asks. "Or are you based in the US?" I'm not sure if Brian knows he's doing a terrible job of not showing me how desperate the earl is to sell this place.

"I'm staying in the village," I say. "At the pub on the edge of the estate."

"Oh, the Golden Hare? Lovely place. Heard the rooms are great."

I nod. I haven't checked in, so I don't know what the rooms are like, but it's true that I'm staying there tonight. "I heard a rumor the earl has been trying to sell for a while."

Brian's brow furrows. "There's been a certain amount of speculation since the countess died."

We're both dancing around the real issue—namely, is the earl prepared to make the price appealing to me?

If he's not, I'll walk away, but I confess I like the place. I need a new challenge. New York doesn't seem to hold the same appeal to me as it did when I moved there. Moving to a different area of the city hasn't tempered my boredom, either. I need more than a change of scenery, and the Crompton Estate might be just the ticket.

"I can imagine. What's next?"

"The library leads into the morning room."

This room looks like something from a costume drama, with a huge chandelier hanging from the ceiling, ornate gold console tables sitting behind sumptuous lavender-blue couches. Art hangs on every wall, portraits of well-dressed men and women from the past and landscapes that look like they belong in museums. The rugs are soft and everything looks cared for.

"This is a nice room," I remark.

"The earl uses this as his drawing room. It's in daily use. But the formal drawing room is quite lovely."

He leads me back into the hallway and this time to the back of the house.

"This is my favorite room," he says. "The long room."

Three pairs of windowed doors open out into a court-yard garden, and three chandeliers hang from the ceiling opposite them. At each end of the room, there's a stone fire-place, intricately carved with what looks like animals, but I'd need to get closer.

Flaking paint on the windows has been roughly covered with a fresh coat, though no one took the time to scrape away the old stuff. Lipstick on a pig—and not even very nice lipstick.

"It would make an excellent function room or dining room if someone was to open a hotel," Brian observes, the hint of a question in his tone.

I smile, having no intention to answer. He doesn't need to know my plans.

"It's a lovely room."

We continue through another, smaller lounge, which he refers to as the parlor, and another he calls the dining room, though it has no table.

"Shall we go up to the first floor next?"

I nod back to beyond the dining room. "I'd like to finish this floor first. What about where we came in?"

His lips pull into a thin, straight line. "Very well."

We go back to where I first came in and it's clear why he

didn't want me in here. The walls are practically crumbling in the warren of four or five rooms that seem to make up a billiards room and maybe another sitting room. It looks like it's been abandoned.

"Obviously, it needs some work," he says.

"Obviously," I say, and he leads me out, back to the main hallway. "Have you had much interest in the place?"

We start ascending the stairs, which sweep up dramatically, just like you'd expect in a stately home. They take up a huge amount of space, which isn't ideal, but it's unlikely we'll get permission to get rid of them.

"We're marketing to a very small number of people," he says.

I let out a half laugh. Not because he's funny, but because he's so obviously not answering my questions. If he was a little more open, I might feel like I was in a weaker position, but I can't help assuming the worst if he's not prepared to say anything at all.

There's no point in asking anything more. We wander from room to room for a few minutes, taking in the bedrooms that don't look like anyone's modernized them for at least sixty years. On the top floor, it's more of the same.

The place is crumbling. The earl is desperate to sell. And I need a new challenge.

The stars are aligning over the Crompton Estate.

FOUR

Kate

I tie the straps of my green apron around my waist and put my hands on my hips. "I think we're ready to open," I call out, surveying the tables, which all have their zinc buckets containing knives and forks wrapped in napkins and their condiments tray. I wiped each table down with the anti-bac, despite them all being clean.

George, the owner of the Golden Hare, appears in the doorway. "Good job, because we're opening whether or not you're ready."

I grin widely at him, even though I know he's not joking. He's just so crotchety, it's funny. "You stick to the drinks, George. I've got the food sorted."

He grumbles. I know he's grateful I made it in tonight. There's a bug going around and Meghan, who was meant to be on shift, called in sick. We're a waitress down, but I can handle it. It's a Monday. Nothing ever happens on a Monday. Although we did have the tall, gorgeous American come into the tea shop today. He was mouth-wateringly good-looking, but it was his confidence that sealed the deal. He just had a way about him that made me want to shimmy out of my knickers.

I sift through the menus by the till, checking they're the right way around and adjust the ones that have been put back incorrectly. Then I grab a pad and a pen and put them in the pocket on the front of my apron. I glance around again, checking I haven't missed anything, when I spot something I haven't seen before on the oak shelf that runs around the room, about thirty centimeters below the ceiling. It's filled with small pictures and trinkets from the estate—a horseshoe, a brass box, earthenware vases filled with dried flowers that do nothing except collect dust. Every now and again, when we're quiet, I'll pull each thing down and clean it, so I know exactly what's up there. But today, what looks like a yellow plate has found its way into the mix.

"George," I call. "What's the yellow dish on the shelf?" It's not a big deal and really it's none of my business. It's just, for the five years I've had this job, nothing new has ever just *appeared* up there.

There's no response from George, so I pull out one of the chairs and place it underneath the shelf. I want to get a better look.

It seems like a plain, yellow dish. What's that doing there? It stands out against the time-worn items that have been there forever. Why would George put it up there? The beamed ceilings are low and I can just about touch the back of the shelf if I stand on tiptoes.

I grab the plate, and as I do, a voice booms behind me, "It's you again."

All my instincts fight each other. I want to turn to see who's talking to me, but at the same time, I want to keep my balance and make sure I don't smash the plate.

But all my instincts fail me and I don't manage to do any of those things.

Everything starts to blur and I lose my balance at the exact same time as my fingers fumble and the dish slips from my hand. Time slows, and as I fall backwards, I try to picture what I'm going to land on, and whether I'm going to end up missing my shift tonight because I'm going to have to go to hospital with a head injury or a broken leg. I wonder if I'll still be able to make my shift in the tea shop tomorrow, and whether Sandra will be able to hold down the fort without me. Tuesdays are busy. We always get at least two coach parties.

Falling is so inconvenient. But I close my eyes and brace for impact.

I don't hit the ground like I expect to. It's like someone's pressed a pause button, and I stop midair.

It takes me a beat to figure out someone's caught me.

I open one eye and realize I must be passed out and dreaming about the handsome American stranger from the tea shop—the one who gave me a knicker allergy. I shut my eyes again and realize if I'm consciously opening and closing my eyes, maybe I'm not unconscious.

Heat floods my body and I open my eyes in a flash.

"You caught me," I say.

"I did." His voice is deep and sonorous and I can feel it vibrate between my thighs. "Are you napping or can you stand?" he asks.

"I'd like a nap," I reply, gazing up into his eyes. "Unfortunately, I can't do that until after my shift ends. I suppose I should stand." I'm acutely aware of his hands on me—at the top of my thighs and under my back. He's big, like an adult-sized cradle. It's almost as if he were made for catching me.

"We can give it a few minutes, if you'd just like to rest." He grins at me.

"Awww, thanks. Maybe just until the first customer arrives. You are extremely . . ." I try and find the right word. Sexy? Yes, that would work, but a tad inappropriate given he's a stranger and a man I'm likely to serve up a burger to within the hour.

"You mean the second customer arrives," he says.

"Oh I suppose so, if you're counting yourself."

"I was hoping to be a customer, but I'm happy to wait until after your nap."

The situation is already weird and it's not going to get better until I let him put me down, despite my very real desire for a nap in his arms. Or frankly, *anything* in his arms.

"Actually, I already feel refreshed. Thank you." I shift and he sets me down.

"Anytime."

I grimace. "Not something you should say if you don't mean it. I very much like to nap—on or off the clock."

"Oh I mean it," he says, and just like before, he looks at me like he's hungry and I'm a Golden Hare special. "Anytime you want to rest, just let me know."

I think we might be flirting. I have such bad flirt radar, it's hard to tell. But he doesn't seem upset I landed on him. I'm not sure if that means he's flirtatious or chivalrous or neither. Or both.

"I'll be sure to," I reply with a smile that matches his. "In the meantime, would you like a table? And will Nathan and the crew be joining you?"

This time he full-on laughs. "It's just me. My family have all gone back to . . ." He trails off, gesturing vaguely with his hand. "I'm staying." He lifts his chin to indicate he's in the rooms George rents out.

"Oh," I say. "That's great. An extended stay." It is great. But it's also a little weird. The guests who take rooms here are usually families who rock up in pristine Range Rovers from London, or couples who also arrive in sparkling-clean Range Rovers. Basically, we cater to people who think they're country people but live in the city.

This guy is a city guy. He's not even pretending.

"Did you drive up here in a Range Rover?" I ask as I show him to my favorite table, under the watercolor of Cambridge's Mathematical Bridge.

"No. Is that a requirement?"

"Of course not," I say. But it would make more sense. Except, he still wouldn't fit. He would need a wife or a girl-friend with him. Why would he come on his own? "Will anyone be joining you?"

"Not unless you'd like to come sit with me," he says. "You've been on your feet a lot today."

I tilt my head, trying to commit his cheekbones to memory. Could I achieve that with contouring? What am I thinking? The few times I've ever tried to contour, I've come out looking like a monkey's backside. "Mondays are actually my least busy day. In terms of customers. Things start to heat up on Tuesdays."

He holds my gaze and it's like he's set me alight. Someone could toast marshmallows on me.

"Heat up? Tell me about that."

This guy is trouble. And I want no part in it. Scratch that. I want *all* parts in it, but I'm on shift and I need to take his dinner order before George comes out and shouts at me. Which he will do anyway, but I'd rather not be guilty of anything worth shouting about. "It's all about the coach parties," I say, raining all over his flirtatious parade. "I can tell you about our specials in detail if that works?"

"Not what I was hoping for, but let's go with that," he says.

"The salmon with homemade hollandaise is incredible. And of course, it's an oily fish, so you'll be getting your omega-3s. Or there's the buttermilk chicken burger." I wince. "Considerably fewer omega-3s, but honestly, it's delicious and there's a nice dose of tryptophan in there."

He looks me dead in the eye and it's like he's put me in a brioche bun and has just added a slick of mayonnaise. I swear the guy wants to eat me. And I'm not sure I don't want him to. "I'll take whatever's delicious."

I narrow my eyes at my order pad and studiously narrate as I write, "One buttermilk chicken. Can I get you a drink? Sides? Broccoli to fend off the mild heart attack?"

He chuckles. "Do you always hand out nutritional advice with the menu?"

"Not always. But you're American. You might not understand how things work here in the UK."

"Because salmon doesn't have omega-3 in it in the US?"

I shrug. "Probably not. But I wouldn't know, because I've never been." I pause as a full-body shiver passes through me at the thought of going to America. Or really anywhere abroad or. . .far away. "I'm erring on the side of caution. Broccoli?"

"Sure," he says. "And I don't suppose you have a tequila, do you?" He says it like he knows it's a long shot.

"I want to kiss you on the mouth right now." I say it before my brain can override my mouth.

"Because I ordered tequila? Or was my drink order incidental to your sudden desire to kiss me?"

"Both," I say, before I bellow, "George! I just got a

tequila order." I turn back to. . .I can't believe I don't know his name. "I convinced him to buy some tequila last month. He doesn't think anyone will order it."

Gah, this guy is the gift that keeps on giving. He saved me from a hospital trip tonight and I get to say "I told you so" to my cantankerous boss because of him. Plus the flirting? He's making me feel like I'm Adriana Lima sans angel wings. I should get him to fill out a lottery ticket for me.

"Glad to help," he says.

"I'll get you some sparkling water, too," I say. "On the house. What with you saving my life, offering to let me nap and then letting me get one up on George."

The front door opens and the Radcliffes file in. It's their daughter's fourteenth birthday tonight.

I glance back at the American. "I'll be back with your drinks."

I wave at Carly Radcliffe as I approach. "I have your table for you. Happy birthday, Ilana!" Ilana turns puce with embarrassment.

I show the Radcliffes to their table and grab some menus for them. They must know what's on offer back to front by now and they'll order what they had last Wednesday anyway. We only change the menu twice a year, from summer to winter. Then about every eighteen months, George adds a new dish and takes one away, at which point Meghan, Peter, and I moan constantly for at least six weeks until we've gotten used to it. We just added a Cobb salad that no one ever orders. I do wonder why George doesn't consult with us first before he does these things.

I glance back over at the American and feel my knickers tugging, trying to free themselves under my skirt. He's so freaking gorgeous. And those hands? Those shoulders?

Even his eyebrows are hot. How is that even possible? And he's cute to talk to. Easy. Doesn't take himself too seriously. Doesn't mind when I fall into him and just sit there awhile.

"How are you all this evening?" I ask the Radcliffes. "Shall I bring a jug of tap water and the cheesy garlic bread for you all to nibble on?" That's what I always do for the Radcliffes. No doubt, George will shout at me for bringing out the bread before they've placed the order, because he'll tell me people should be hungry when they order or they'll order less, but I know that's crap when it comes to the Radcliffes. It wouldn't matter if I ordered them a cheesy garlic bread each. I know Carly will order the chicken, Dave will order the rib eye medium rare. Joe will order the lasagna or the pizza and Ilana will have the chicken burger and only eat two bites.

"Thanks, Kate," Carly says and I head back to the till to place the orders.

When I finally pour the American's tequila, because George refuses, I take a tray with the lowball and the sparkling water over.

"Tequila and sparkling water," I say as I set the drinks on the table. "You wanted it neat, right?"

"Absolutely," he says. "Thanks."

"My pleasure," I reply.

He raises his eyebrows. "Is it?"

A wave of lust races up my spine and I suppress a shudder, but I hold his gaze. "It is."

"I like that," he replies.

I turn and head back to the kitchen before my mouth can override my brain again. I'm at risk of telling him I'm one hundred percent attracted to him, and whatever he wants to do to me with those pouty lips and large, strong hands, I'm down.

FIVE

Vincent

I didn't expect to enjoy dinner at the Golden Hare this much. Seeing Kate here was an unexpected surprise. She's fun. And flirty. And a breath of the fresh air I'm so desperately craving right now. I've watched her flitting from table to table, taking orders, making small-talk, delivering plates and drinks and more plates and more drinks.

"Oh no!" Kate says as she approaches my table. "You didn't like the buttermilk chicken? I've never known anyone not to like it."

"The chicken was exceptional," I reply.

She glances from my plate up at me and then back down at my plate. "It doesn't look like you thought it was exceptional. What about the tryptophan you're missing out on?"

I wonder if she interrogates any guest who doesn't finish their food, or has she saved that just for me? "I think I might go for a run later. I just don't want to overeat."

She narrows her eyes at me as if she's deciding whether or not I'm telling the truth.

I want to see what Crompton House looks like in the dark, and I want to confirm what I already know: I'm going to make an offer on the estate. I need to get an architect, surveyor, and team of people in to look the place over, but I'm confident we can make it work.

For the right price.

"Run?" she asks as if she must have misheard me.

"It's like walking but faster," I explain.

She doesn't smile in appreciation of my joke. Instead she still looks confused. "As if you were catching a bus?"

"I wouldn't know. I've never caught a bus."

"Because you don't like buses?"

"They don't make it into the top ten of things I like most in the world."

"Hmmm." She presses her finger to her lips as she thinks and I can't tear my eyes away. If feels like her lips are pressed against my dick and her sounds are vibrating in my balls. "You have a list?" she asks.

"Don't you?"

"No, but I could put one together in a rush."

"I like to be prepared," I say around my grin.

"I like you," she says, her mouth curling into a smile.

"I like you too. You want to join me on my run?" I take a sip of my tequila, wondering if she's interested in taking this back-and-forth somewhere she's not on the clock.

"Absolutely not." Disappointment lurches in my chest. She's fun and I need more of that in my life. "But if you're around when I finish my shift, I'll have sex with you."

I half swallow, half laugh and end up yelping like a dog.

Slick, Vincent. *Very* slick.

"That is, if you're back from your run," she adds. "I have

a couple of pictures to upload to the Crompton Instagram account, which I manage, and I have no other plans. You want dessert?" She offers me the menu in her hand and then snaps it away from me. "No. Don't want you sluggish. Another drink?"

I don't formally accept Kate's offer of sex, but she's confident enough not to need my confirmation. I order another tequila, thankful for the Brit's small measures, and divide my attention between my phone and watching Kate. She seems to know a lot of the customers. She's either worked her a long time or they have a lot of repeat customers or both. I do the mental calculations of how much a place like this makes. It can't be a lot. I looked into buying a chain of pubs in Norfolk once, but I couldn't make the numbers stack up, even though I liked the idea.

Kate glances over at my table every now and then, and maybe it's me, but heat seems to be growing between us with every passing minute.

My phone buzzes and I field a message from my assistant about timeframes for my team getting to Crompton. I turn my phone facedown on the table just as I remember Kate mentioning an Instagram page.

I bring up the app. I had my assistant create a profile for me a while ago. It's entirely anonymous, of course, and has no followers, but it allows me to search for Kate's Crompton estate page. It takes me by surprise. The house and gardens look beautiful. Not that they're not beautiful, but Kate's photographs seem to capture them at their *most* beautiful. Maybe it's the time of day—the light she captures. Or perhaps it's the way she manages to show the exceptional while artfully excluding the peeling paint and cracked walls. I'm pretty sure she's not a professional photographer, but it's hard to tell.

My phone rings in my hand and I dart out to take the call. The US are still at their desks and I want to make sure my assistant is lining up a team in the UK to come and see Crompton House over the next couple of days. I want to be in a position to act quickly if the opportunity is there. I'm a risk taker, but I'm not a gambler.

As soon as I step back into the pub, I lock eyes with Kate. I retake my seat, and next time there's a break between tables, she comes over.

"I thought you left."

"No."

"Where did you go?" she asks.

I laugh. "No" would be enough for most people in my life. They wouldn't expect further explanation. That's not true of my family. And apparently it's not true of Kate. "I stepped out to take a call. The US is still working."

"And you work in the US?"

"A lot of my work is US-based, yes."

"Right," she says. "You didn't leave."

"And pass up sex with you? Absolutely not."

It's her turn to laugh. "You don't need to hang around here if you have other things to do. Your run or whatever. I can come up to your room when I'm done."

I've abandoned the idea of a run. I can see the house at night another time, and besides—I think a far more enjoyable workout might be waiting for me at the end of Kate's shift. "I like watching you." I've tracked her all around the restaurant this evening. She's relaxed, like this place is home for her. And she greets everyone like they're an old friend, even when some people are clearly new to her. She's tactile, pressing her hand against her customers' upper arms when they talk, or patting them on the shoulder when they leave.

She likes to touch. But since I set her on her feet earlier, she hasn't touched me. Yet.

"I like you watching me," she replies. The air between us thickens, and for the first time since I met her this morning, Kate shifts from one leg to the other, like the thought of enjoying my attention is uncomfortable for her.

She turns and immediately someone calls her over. There are only two tables left, and one has just asked for the bill. I check my watch. I figure we'll be out of here soon. And then I get to have her.

I continue to watch her as she sees the final customers out, locks the door behind them and starts to fill the little tin pails that sit on the tables and hold the cutlery. She occasionally talks to the guy behind the bar or the chef or whoever is around the corner I can't see. I watch as she diligently wipes down every table, careful not to miss a square inch, then tucks in all the chairs and disappears behind the bar.

She reappears a couple of minutes later, her hands behind her back as she unties her apron.

"I'm done," she says, folding her apron and setting it down by the cash register.

I can't help but smile. "Am I next on your list?"

She laughs. "My list is complete. The rest of the night is . . ."

"Mine?"

"I was going to say *mine*. But maybe you can have some."

I'm beginning to think I might like all of it.

SIX

Vincent

She twirls as we enter the room, and for a moment, I think she's going to break into song.

"I don't like to complain, but I was a little disappointed in the lack of show tunes tonight. Is that strictly a daytime thing?"

She lies on the bed, her elbow propping her up, her hand under her head. "I suppose it is. George hates music in pubs, so I have nothing to sing along to."

"So there's a daytime Kate. And an evening Kate. And now I get to see after-hours Kate." I stalk over to her and pull her to her feet.

"After-hours Kate definitely doesn't sing."

I tilt my head a little to the left. "But does she scream? My name, specifically."

She laughs. "You don't lack confidence—but I'd have to know your name to scream it." She holds a finger to my lips. "Don't tell me. I want to guess. Brad?"

I take her hands and thread my fingers through hers. "Vincent."

She tilts her head, gazing at me, and it warms me from the inside. "Okay, I can see that."

"I'm pleased you approve."

She pulls a hand free and trails a finger along my jaw. I have to suppress a shudder. Under her fingers, I feel like a cat with the urge to stretch out and let her run her fingers across my entire body.

"I do," she whispers.

I cup her neck and hover, my lips almost touching hers. I want to prolong this moment for as long as possible—the moment before we shift gear. I've enjoyed the push and pull, her warmth, her humor, and I don't want the next minute to be less than all that. It's unusual for me not to want to race to the next stake in the ground. I don't like to be still, but right now, I have no rush to be anywhere but right here.

The breath between us heats and my pulse pounds like it's a dog straining to be let off the leash. Her lips are ripe strawberries and I swallow at the thought that so soon I'll be sinking into the taste of them.

She lifts her finger and strokes over my Adam's apple. "Even your neck," she says.

I narrow my eyes. "My neck?"

She lifts a shoulder in a half shrug. "It oozes out of every pore." She says it like that's meant to be an explanation I can understand. Tearing her gaze away from my neck, she looks up and must see confusion on my face. She adds, "Confidence. Charisma. Whatever it is, you have it."

"Back at you," I say. I've met a lot of people in my life, and there's nothing more magnetic than someone who is comfortable with who they are. Like Kate is.

She lifts up onto her tiptoes and we crash together. Our mouths fit like a key in a lock, and I groan at the relief that this moment wasn't a disappointment. She feels better than I expected and tastes sweeter. I circle my arm around her waist, pulling her closer to me so her body slots into mine. She feels like she did when I caught her before she hit the floor: soft in all the right places.

She kisses me like she needs it, like she's been waiting all night to taste me. I kiss her back the exact same way.

Smoothing her hands down my sides, she pulls my shirt from my pants, sliding her fingers underneath and over my skin. Sensation washes over me and it's difficult to place. Desire, yes. Lust, yes. But also a core-deep sense of this being right where I'm meant to be. It feels ten times more satisfying than good, but it's also a little disconcerting because I can't remember the last time I felt like that.

I push past it, dig my fingers into her hair and deepen our kiss. She fumbles at the button to my trousers and I push her hands away, pressing the small of her back towards me. She's not going to undress me. Not yet.

"I want to feel you," she says. Her hand rounds my backside and she looks up at me, pleading.

I want to enjoy this.

I step back and take a seat on the bed. "I want to watch you."

I kick off my shoes, stretch back, and relax. She doesn't move for a couple of moments, like she's considering what to do next. She gives her signature half shrug before her fingers go to the buttons of her white shirt. "So, you've been watching me all night," she says. "At what point did you think this was going to happen?"

"I think the bit when you said you'd have sex with me was probably a turning point."

She lifts her gaze to mine and smiles. "Well, wasn't that what you were asking me, in a roundabout way?"

"Maybe?"

"So I just cut to the chase." She shrugs the shirt from her shoulders to reveal perfect, flawless skin.

"You certainly did."

"Women must proposition you all the time," she says as she peels off her jeans. She's making no effort to tease me or seduce me. It wasn't a question, so I don't offer an answer. I figure we have limited time and I'd rather not miss an opportunity to watch her without talking.

I grin as she hops on one foot to remove her jeans.

"There's no sexy way to take off a waitress uniform," she informs me as she discards her pants on the chair behind her and stands in her underwear. She's unselfconscious, but not in a naïve way. More that she knows who she is, and more importantly, who she isn't. It's compelling, like a movie you can't tear your eyes from, or a piece of music you want to play over and over.

"Oh, I disagree. I've never seen a strip-tease quite so sexy."

She closes her eyes in a long blink and gives a small shake of her head before stepping towards me and straddling me, a knee either side of my hips. "Well, if that's the truth, I'm going to blow your mind tonight, so get ready."

I laugh and sit up, bringing us face-to-face. I reach around and open her bra with a flick of my fingers. She lifts her arms and her breasts shift up, perfectly aligned for me to capture a nipple in my mouth. I work my tongue, flicking and swirling, grazing her with my teeth, burying myself in her scent of fresh flowers. Her fingers thread through my hair and she moves against me. Then I shift to the other breast, while my fingers pinch and pull at the nipple that's been warmed by my mouth.

God, I love breasts. And I love how most women don't know how sensitive they are. I mean, they know, but they don't *really* know. Her hips begin to lift a little and she tries to coax my head away, but I won't be moved.

We have all night. There's no rush. She's come into this room thinking she's going to get a quick fuck and then forty-five minutes later she's going to leave and go home and find her vibrator to finish herself off because I'm some poor schmuck who can't make a woman come. But none of that's going to happen.

"Vincent," she says on a sigh. "I want to feel you."

I respond by flipping her to her back, settling down beside her and continuing my exploration.

"Do. You. Have. A. Ahhh. Oh god. A. Nipple. Fetish?" She arches her back as I press my teeth around her.

I slide a palm down her stomach and into her panties, down, down, down, into her wet heat. It's not me getting off on what my mouth's doing.

Okay, it *is* me. I like being able to get a woman drenched when I haven't touched her pussy. I like being able to get a woman so worked up she's ready to do anything for me. Absolutely anything.

But I have nothing to prove, so without taking my mouth from her breast, I work my finger back and forward through her folds.

She twists her hips away from me, like she's trying to escape.

"Vincent."

I bring my thigh over hers to keep her in place and slide two fingers inside her, circling and pulling and pressing while I flick and bite and tongue.

She bucks underneath me, like a horse that wasn't expecting the saddle. She suggested this. But she wasn't expecting *this*.

The thought has my cock pressing against my fly, desperate to fuck.

She releases a tiny whimper, and a groan escapes my throat like it's been stuck there for years. She's so warm and soft and wet and perfect.

Her fingers curl around my wrist and she chokes out, "You need to stop right now or I'm going to come."

But I'm not going to stop now.

And the way I feel right at the moment, maybe not ever.

I push my fingers deep and I clasp my teeth around her nipple and bite. Hard.

She screams, her legs shaking, I don't know if it's her sounds, her movement, or her orgasm that vibrates up *my* spine. Her pleasure and my pleasure are inextricably linked, winding around and around us, binding us together.

I lift my head as she covers her face, and I pull at her wrists. She turns her face away from me.

I press a kiss to each nipple, her fingers find the back of my head again, and she sighs.

"You okay?" I ask as our gazes meet.

A small crease appears between her eyebrows. "I'm not sure."

I press a kiss to the side of her head. "Tonight's not what you expected."

"No," she says.

A minute passes, she links her fingers through mine and she sits up. "You're good."

I laugh, but I nod. If Kate doesn't do false modesty, then neither do I.

"I'm a little freaked out," she says. "But also . . ." For a moment I think she's going to make some kind of confessional about how she's seen God or something, but I should know better. "Horny."

I laugh.

She pulls me over her as she falls back onto the bed.

"You smell so good. What is that?" she asks in between kisses.

"I smell of you," I say. It's all I can smell. Fresh summer flowers.

I kneel up and strip off my shirt, then slip off the bed to take off my pants. I grab a condom from my wallet.

"We might as well just get it out of the way," she says. I have no way of knowing what she's going to say. It could be anything from a confession of virginity—although that's unlikely—to her saying she's strictly no anal.

I raise my eyebrows in anticipation.

"Your body's insane," she says. "Like, wow."

A smile curls at the corner of my lips. I kneel between her thighs, circle my hands around her waist and pull her toward me for better access to her pussy. "You're perfect." I dip my thumb inside her, finding her tight and wet and sweet, pulling out and circling her clit. She tries to move away again and I'm not quite sure why.

"Why do you do that? Like when you're really enjoying something, you try and escape?" I put my thumb in my mouth and lick her off me, then slide my body over hers, caging her head with my hands, waiting for an answer.

"I don't know," she says. "What you do. . .it kind of takes me by surprise."

"And you don't like surprises?" I say, sliding my dick over her panties.

"I haven't given it much thought. I guess it feels. . .different. And my basic human instinct is to protect myself when things aren't what they usually are."

Is that a basic human instinct? I don't have time to answer my own question because she wraps her legs around my waist, grinding my cock against her.

I grin at her. "I wasn't expecting that, but I can't say I want you to stop."

I roll to my side and strip her underwear off, then reach for the condom. She tries to sit up. Our gazes meet and I shake my head.

"I can't go on top?" she asks with a little pout that is fucking adorable.

"Not yet."

"When?"

"When I say," I reply.

"You don't want a blow job? To get you hard?"

"Do I look like a need a blow job to get me hard?" My cock is pointing at the ceiling, rigid and desperate for release. She watches as I roll on the condom. "You okay?"

She exhales, her expression a little worried. "Yeah."

"Are you sure?"

"I'm sure."

"There's nothing to worry about. It's going to be good." I slide over her and press a kiss to her neck.

"Too good," she says.

I push into her, clenching my jaw, watching her as she bites down on her bottom lip and her eyes fall closed. I move slowly and her arms come to my shoulders.

She opens her eyes. "See? Too good."

She's right. She feels incredible under me. The feeling is all concentrated pleasure and thoughts run through my mind like, is it possible to stay in here a little longer? In

Crompton, but also right here. Because I never want to stop fucking this woman underneath me.

Her nails digging into my shoulders interrupt my chaotic thoughts and her knees coming up either side of my hips, allow me deeper, oh so deep.

"Fuck," I spit out.

Her breaths are heavy, half panting, half moaning with every movement I make. A look of fear crosses her expression and it's like she wants to flee. I bend and press a kiss to her lips. She can't not want to do this. Because this feels as good as it gets.

I reach underneath her, push one leg up and over my shoulder and the change of position makes her tighter somehow. I glance down and see her glistening on my cock, and I have to squeeze my eyes shut because it's so fucking glorious and I'm going to come and it's all going to be over so quickly.

"Vincent," she calls out.

I still. I don't want this over for either of us. Not yet.

She looks up at me. Desperate.

"Breathe," I say. "Deep breaths." Our skin is hot and slick with sweat, and even though it feels like I've only been inside her for a few minutes, it also feels like it's been this way for hours.

Her chest heaves and I bend and lick at her nipples, careful, because they'll be tender from all the attention I gave them earlier.

My breath steadies, but underneath my skin is a buzz that won't go away.

"You okay?" I ask.

"I'm not sure," she says, "but don't stop."

I groan and start to move into her again, the buzzing pressing through my skin, and I can't hear for the *boom,*

boom, boom in my veins. She lifts her hips to meet mine and we crash against each other, both yearning and desperate. Something explodes in my chest and I realize I'm about three seconds away from coming.

I can't stop it.

I don't want to.

But at the same time, I want these three seconds to last for as long as humanly possible.

I push into her so hard, I drive her up the bed. Her body twists and shakes as she comes apart underneath me and I piston up, up, up and fuuuck.

All I see is white light and summer flowers.

I can't open my eyes for minutes, hours, maybe it's fucking days. I've lost all track of time.

"I need to pee," she says from under me eventually. She's holding my waist, and I'm still inside her.

I move and take off the condom while she heads to the bathroom. I'm exhausted and maybe even dead, but neither of those things can stop me watching her ass as she moves across the room.

She doesn't shut the door and I can't see her, but I hear her pee. I laugh and scrub my face with my hands. I don't think a woman has ever peed with the door open. I hadn't realized it until now.

I hear the faucets go and then she re-appears. She heads to the minibar and pulls out two bottles of water. "You want one?"

I sit up and nod. She hands it to me and I pull her back onto the bed with me. She sits cross-legged opposite me, completely naked and I laugh again because I one hundred percent appreciate the view.

"What?" she asks, before taking a swig of water.

"Your body is incredible."

"Thanks," she says, screwing the lid back on the bottle. She's so adorable.

I take a swig of water and then put the lid back on the bottle and toss it onto the floor. Then I take her bottle from her hand and throw it so it follows mine, and pull her onto me so she's straddling me where I lie.

"So now it's okay for me to be on top?" she asks.

"Maybe for a bit."

She shifts in place a little and the slick feel of her wakes up my cock immediately. Jesus, five seconds ago, I was so spent, I wasn't sure I'd ever walk again. How am I ready to fuck again so quickly?

I settle my hands around her waist, my thumbs slotting under her hip bones.

She lifts up her breasts. "My nipples are a little sore," she says.

"They'll be tender for a few days after tonight."

"I didn't realize I liked that." She's started moving over me, sliding up and down my cock as we talk.

I nod. "You're very responsive."

"Like now?" She tips her head back as she picks up her pace and gasps. "I'm so wet again. I ache, I want you inside me so much."

Fuck, this woman knows just what to say to me.

"Yeah?" I ask. "You want me deep like before?" I feel the throb underneath her skin as she moves against me.

"So deep," she whispers. "So, so, deep."

"How did it feel, Kate?" I can barely get the words out. My throat is all brambles and tequila and I want to fuck this woman so badly, I can barely breathe.

She whimpers and she reaches her fingers to her clit, but I push her hand away. She's not making herself come. Not on my watch.

But I've got to get inside her. I move us to the edge of the bed, so my legs are on the floor and I grab a condom. Kate circles my neck with her limp arms, drunk on need for me.

I rip the foil with my teeth and roll the condom on in a second. "I'm ready for you."

Lifting her hips, I pull her onto my cock, savoring deep and desperate breaths. "Vincent," she calls out, half sigh, half moan.

She's deep like this, impaled on my almost-too-hard cock. Her hair is wild and untamed, and I like the way I've been able to peel back her layers today, from waitress with a penchant for ponytails and show tunes to undone temptress who aches for me inside her.

I lift her slightly and we start to move together, her body so fluid and perfect. It's like we're wheels on a track that have been running for years. She curls her fingers around my neck and our foreheads meet.

"Kate." My voice is guttural and rough. I bring her down onto me with more force now, needing to understand if this feels as good for her as it does for me.

"Just like that," she breathes out. "Oh god. Oh god. Oh god."

The speed is perfect, her skin is perfect, each vowel she moans into my mouth is entirely perfect.

It's intense like this. Touching like this. Our breaths mixing as we give and take and push and pull, like we're both trying to uncover buried treasure. We're both working to the end goal: bliss.

Gold-plated, fucking bliss.

She tenses, and now I recognize her instinct to run— she's close. So close. Her legs start to shake and I tighten my grip as her rhythm falters and her shoulders shift up.

Everything tightens, and a roll of thunder from deep inside me rumbles in warning.

You can't stop me, it whispers.

This time she doesn't try and twist away, and the thought of her submission to her orgasm, to her pleasure, to me—it's all too much.

The thunder picks up pace and I'm fucking helpless. All I can hear is the thudding of my blood in my veins and I just want to be closer. I want longer, faster, more.

I take her mouth in mine in a wild, groaning kiss as our orgasms rip through us like a lightning strike.

SEVEN

Kate

Everything aches. Muscles I didn't even know I had ache. But it's a good ache. It's the very personal brand of tattoo Americans called Vincent leave on your body. Thankfully I get to sit down for the next thirty minutes while I'm on break. I really shouldn't. I should stay standing and not give the adrenaline a chance to seep away, but my legs are about to give out, so I collapse on a bench outside the tea shop' kitchen. From here, the visitors to the gardens can't see me, but I can see the sweeping lawns at the front of Crompton House, down to the trees on the other side of the driveway.

I pull out my phone and see I've got a text from Granny. It just reads "milk". I smile and reply I'll bring some back with me. She lives in the cottage right next door to mine and has been there for the last forty years, well before I occupied the second bedroom from the age of seven. And for the years since I moved into the cottage next door.

I stretch out and swear I hear myself creak. I wonder if Vincent is feeling as delicate as I am. Probably not. That man was pure steel. Or he certainly felt like it. I've never had sex like it before. It seems almost like the sex I've had before last night was amateur warm-ups for Vincent. Being with him was effortless and comfortable, but it was also the most I've *felt* for a long time.

Everything was just. . .more. His scent, the way his muscles moved under his skin, the way he seemed to understand my body like we'd known each other our entire lives. The way he seemed to be able to control my orgasm, the way he decided *when* I could feel. It was all more than I've ever experienced with a man. I doubt I ever will again. The thought is a dull ache behind my breastbone. I press my knuckle against my chest to try and release it, without success.

I never got around to asking Vincent what he was doing here. I don't even know his last name. But I know every inch of that body of his. God, he was delicious.

Sandra pops her head out of the door. "Here. Someone just broke into the chocolate cake," she says and shoves a plate of cake at me.

"I can't eat cake. It's practically breakfast time."

"It's gone ten thirty. By the look of you, you need some sugar."

"I'm fine," I say. But I take the plate and the fork anyway. Sugar *might* help. I haven't told Sandra about Vincent. Of course I haven't. Not because she'd judge me. She'd be thrilled. She, along with the rest of the staff on the estate, are always telling me I need to have fun, asking me if I'm dating—or "courting" as the older staff say. They don't accept I can have fun without dating or husband shopping or even going to the cinema in Cambridge. I have plenty of fun at Crompton.

Case in point? Last night. No dating involved. Vincent

and his magic penis will be long gone by now and it will be like he was never here.

Suits me fine.

I wouldn't have hated it if he'd stayed an extra night, although probably best he didn't—I checked—as my body might have seized up if there'd been a repeat performance.

I open the Crompton Instagram page and check the notifications first. A few of yesterday's visitors tagged us in photos. There's one of the magnolia outside the tea shop that must have been taken just as we opened because there's a long shadow of the person taking the shot underneath the flowers.

My stomach lurches as I wonder for a second if Vincent posted it. I check the handle and it's just a picture of a mountain. It wouldn't be him, would it? He's not the kind of man who takes pictures of pretty flowers and posts them on Instagram. He's the kind of man who looks at you like you're a slice of cake and kisses you right into summertime. I click on the profile anyway, even though I know it's definitely not Vincent, just because, if it is, that's something I'd like to see. What would a man like Vincent's Instagram account look like?

But it's not Vincent's Instagram account. I scroll up and down the grid and figure out it's probably the couple from Harrogate that came in just after Vincent's cousin, Nathan, arrived. I repost the picture on our account, adding a tag for Crompton's gardens.

Nathan was the one whose wife or girlfriend wasn't with him. But he didn't look like the typical Crompton visitor either. I suppose they were having a family get-together of sorts, but it still doesn't make sense why Vincent stayed over. Couldn't he have gone back to London when the rest of the family left?

I'm over-thinking it. Why he was here doesn't matter.

The crunch of gravel catches my attention and I look up. Meghan is coming toward me, carrying a can of full-fat Coke and wearing sunglasses and a puffer jacket, despite the fact it's a balmy twenty degrees.

"Hey, sorry about last night." She hands me a Freddo—a chocolate frog. "Have this. I've had two already today."

"A two-Freddo morning. Must be bad. How's the migraine?"

"It's actually fine. I took the medication early, so I've escaped lightly. Sorry to drop you in it last night." She takes a seat on the bench next to me.

My stomach swoops at the thought that I almost missed Vincent entirely. If it weren't for Meghan and her migraine, we would have been like ships passing in the night. "It wasn't busy."

"It was Ilana's birthday, wasn't it? Anything interesting happen?"

"What sort of thing?" I ask, then realize I'm being defensive for no reason at all.

"Taylor Swift drop in?"

"If she did, I didn't notice her," I reply. "George was in a foul mood. We. . .we had a guy eat in who was staying upstairs."

"On his own?"

"Yes, I can definitely testify to the fact he was by himself."

"Up from London?" she asks.

"I guess." Did he say whether he was staying in London while he was in the UK? He can't have been staying with family because they left without him. "He was very handsome. Good tipper. Great in bed." I sigh wistfully as Meghan splutters and chokes on her Coke.

She looks at me as if to ask if I'm being serious. I just shrug.

"I really wish I'd made it in now," she says. "Did he leave this morning?"

I shrug again. I don't want her to know I checked the reservations book as I'd left. When I'd gone to leave this morning, he'd pulled me back to bed for a final kiss before I told him I had to go.

He was a great kisser. I want to give up my job and kiss him all day. I can still feel his stubble against my cheeks and his fingers in my hair, hear his low moans that vibrated across my body.

He was a good everything-er.

"There must be something happening to the moon. Or something," she says.

"The moon?"

"Yeah. Like ... you're having sex, Basil told me he thinks the estate is up for sale. I'm chomping Freddos like they're edamame beans. Change is afoot."

Basil was one of the more senior gardeners and a renowned curmudgeon. Every year he thought the magnolia wouldn't flower, the lawns would never recover from visitors' footsteps, and at least one of the old oaks in the circle of trees on the far side of the estate would die.

In my twenty years living on Crompton, he had never been right, but it didn't stop a wind of uncertainty blowing through the staff when Basil started muttering about the estate being sold, which he did from time to time.

"Because you're overdosing on sugar? And for the record, it's not like I never have sex."

"Oh, I forgot how you regularly date. There's a positive trail of your conquests throughout Cambridgeshire."

I wince a little at her words. Not because they're true, or

because she's hurt my feelings ... more because my lack of a social life obviously isn't as inconspicuous as I thought. Truly, though—I don't need to date. I have everything I could ever want in my life. I don't need a man. "I didn't say it was regular, but the fact I had sex last night isn't reason to think the moon has been thrown out of our orbit or something."

"Maybe. But do you think Crompton is being sold?"

I try and give an unbothered laugh but end up snorting. "No," I say, with a dismissive wave. "Of course it's not. There are always rumors."

"There are always rumors because the earl clearly can't afford the place. Rio says he had to attach plastic bags to the roof of the orangery last week because there was a leak."

"So?" That sounds like a practical solution to the problem. "I'm sure it's just a temporary thing until they can bring someone in to fix it. Rio is a handyman, not an orangery specialist."

Meghan unzips her jacket. "If it did sell, it wouldn't affect the pub, would it? I heard it's got a long lease on that land."

"Crompton is not for sale. No way would the earl part with it."

"He's not going to live forever. Even if Basil's wrong this time, eventually the Crompton Estate will be sold. There's no heir. No children for him to pass it down to."

The idea turns my blood to ice. I can't bear to think about Crompton being owned by someone other than the earl. Crompton is my home. My life. The culmination of all my childhood dreams. I like things just how they are.

Basil is just being Basil.

Crompton hasn't changed since my grandmother and grandfather started working here forty years ago. Even through the seasons, the shifts are gentle and expected, blending into each other like the watercolors of a painting. Life at Crompton is an immoveable rock that weathers every shift, every obstacle, and comes out looking just as it always has. It's part of the reason I love it here so much—the consistent reliability, the expectedness of everything, the lack of change. Basil can spout all the doom and gloom prophecies he likes; the Crompton Estate isn't going anywhere.

EIGHT

Vincent

Working remotely, all participants in a meeting on the screen in front of me, isn't something I started during the pandemic. I've always worked this way. Yes, I have an office in New York and some staff are based there. But I work wherever I am. And at the moment, I am in London. That means my office is in London as well.

I have a view of Hyde Park from my preferred penthouse suite at the Four Seasons on Park Lane, which makes a perfect backdrop for any meeting. It's a little different from my room at the Golden Hare in Crompton. Flashes of memory from the night I spent there with Kate cross my mind. She was beautiful.

"What I want at the end of this meeting is first to understand if Crompton is financially viable. And if it is, I want to know what our opening offer is," I say to Jason, my chief financial officer. I know from experience he's sitting at the board table in the New York office, his team around him so we can make a quick decision. He knows I don't want to have to wait for him to check x, y, and z with his people. I'm going to want the answer during this meeting.

"We've had numbers in from the team overnight," he says. "Although the architects have a huge range, depending on our instructions. The same goes for the building surveyor and the head contractor."

"That's understandable," I say. "I just want you to run a sensitivity analysis to understand our best- and worst-case scenarios."

Jason falls silent, which is what he always does when he thinks I'm not understanding what he's saying. But I do understand.

"I get the profit numbers depend on the number of rooms. And that impacts the building costs."

"Yes," he says. "You need to make a decision on number of rooms today. Without seeing the final drawings from the architect."

"But we need square footage of each room before we can decide," I say. "And these guys are the best. They've worked with all the five-star hotel brands around the world. Let's get them up on screen. I want to hear what they've got to say. Let's bring the designer and the contractor into this too."

While my assistant brings more people onto our call, I bring up Instagram and go to Crompton's page. When I see a new image on the grid, my heart thuds against my chest.

Over what? It's a damn photograph.

But I know who took the picture. And besides, it's beautiful, with the red brick of the house lit up in the dark and trees shadowing the background. Kate's got a talent, whether she knows it or not.

I click on the comments and add, "Beautiful." Part of

me hopes she smiles when she sees it. Another part of me wants her to know it's me who posted it.

Before I look away, I get a notification. She's liked my message.

Kate's online now. I wonder if she's at the café, show tunes in the background, checking her phone between customers. I think about her pink striped uniform and sliding my hands under its skirt, my skin against hers, again.

Another notification appears. I have a message. It must be her. Right? My heart picks up speed and I click on it.

Yup. Just as I thought.

"I'm so pleased you like the images of Crompton. Have you visited?"

It's like adrenaline has been poured into my veins and I can feel it racing to my heart.

Does she message everyone who comments on her photos?

I glance up at the screen. People are muted while we wait for additional team members to arrive. I stand and move away. I'm not sure if I'm hiding or if I want privacy. For what? Am I going to message her back?

"Sure," I reply. "I loved it." *So much, I'm going to buy the place,* I don't say.

"It's a very special place," she replies. "I've lived on the estate since I was seven years old. There's nowhere else I'd want to call home."

The adrenaline turns to ice and I press the button on the side of my phone, turning the screen black. She lives on the estate? She must be in one of the staff cottages. The ones that I'm planning to turn into additional accommodation if I buy the place. She's going to be forced to call somewhere else home.

I close my eyes, trying to push down that familiar

feeling of dread that swirls in my stomach from time to time. She'll be fine. We'll figure something out. Something just as good as the place she's in at the moment. I'll make sure of it.

I take my seat. Back to business.

"So," I say, "if we want at least four-fifty square feet in each standard room, where does that leave us?"

Peter, who I've brought on board to advise me about hotels, chips in. "We want between fifteen to seventeen percent of the rooms to be suites, with floor space of between ninety and one hundred and thirty square meters. The outlier is the Royal Suite, which should be about two-twenty. If we take the suites out, how many standard rooms does that leave us with?"

He's asking the architect, who starts lifting the drawings she has in front of her. "Taking out the suites would leave one hundred and twenty two standard and executive rooms. Plus the rooms in the converted staff cottages."

That was the answer Jason and I were hoping for. Jason's tell is he doesn't react at all if he gets the answer he wants. He learned it from me.

"So one hundred and thirty-three rooms in total," Jason says.

I know he's done the math, and at that number, the house is viable as a business. We just need to know what I can offer the earl, which depends on building and refurb costs.

Jasons speaks again. "Preston and Frank, you can give us your numbers now that you have number of rooms, right?"

"I can give you a range," Preston, the designer, says.

"I don't want a range," I interrupt. "You know how many rooms. You know how many beds to buy. I want you to tell me budget requirements."

I find people can do things even they don't think they can. You just have to push them in order to find their real limits. People will never work at their boundaries or beyond them if they don't have to.

After additional discussions, Jason and I get our numbers, and one by one, everyone leaves the meeting until it's just Jason and I remaining on-screen.

"This is a big investment," Jason says. "One of your biggest. You're looking at nine figures."

"But it works. WACC exceeds twelve percent?"

"It does."

I hear the caution in his voice. He's worked for me for far too long for me to be dismissive about it. "Tell me how I get out," I say. I always need an out. In all my investments I make sure there's an open door for me to exit when I want to bolt. I'm bound to nothing.

"We can structure it a number of ways. If you want to keep the debt simple, lease before the refurbishments start. Grant a twenty-year lease to the Four Seasons or whoever."

"So I'm just landlord?"

"Yes. Or you could do a sale and leaseback if you wanted to release the capital. Or you can just leverage the entire project."

"That doesn't get me out."

"No, it would just release your cash."

"I suppose that's a start. When don't the numbers work?"

"You can't overpay the earl for the estate. And you've got to get planning permission."

"I'll get planning permission." I've already had fireside chats with the planning department. I prefer to deal with areas of greatest risk personally. The committee members I spoke to knew the earl was going to sell, just as they knew the house isn't sustainable as it is.

"It's a risk," Jason says.

The risk itself doesn't concern me. "I think from what you're telling me, there's very little downside."

Jason laughs. "I think it's a big project that's going to take a lot of time and attention. And. . .I just don't know if it's you."

"It's me because it's going to make me money. Don't worry. I'm not planning on becoming the new earl. I'll put someone in there I trust, like I always do. It's not like I'm going to stick around and check guests in at reception. It's an investment. I'll need to be on the ground for a few weeks and then I'll leave it to the team. Just like any other project like this we've done."

"The WACC is fourteen point two percent so long as you pay less than ten million and you get planning permission," Jason says. "That's better than best-case scenario when we ran the numbers on the back of an envelope. And what do we think the earl will take to sell?"

"He's clearly motivated," I say. "I just think it comes down to whether he has any other buyers."

My gut tells me we're the only interested buyers. I also suspect the earl likes me and would be happy to sell to me. I managed to run into him at a charity dinner this week, shortly after I visited the house.

"Don't go higher than nine," I say. "Call me when it's done."

I hit *leave meeting* and take out my phone. It's still on Crompton's Instagram page, the comment from Kate left without a response from me.

I start to type. "I bet it was a beautiful place to grow up."

It's also a great investment. One I'm not willing to pass up.

NINE

Kate

It's rare the staff of the Crompton Estate are summoned to a meeting with the earl. In fact, I can't remember a time when it's happened before, but from all across the estate, people are making their way towards the house, where we've been asked to assemble in the long room. The gardens have only been closed fifteen minutes, but in that time, I've been able to finish clearing up at the tea shop and race home to get Granny.

"Just take it steady," I say to Granny, who's charging ahead in the June sun. "We have plenty of time."

"I know," she says. "I just want to get a seat at the front."

"You think they'll have set seats out in the long room?" I ask. "Seems like an awful hassle to me." Granny presses her lips together in a way that indicates she's not telling me everything. "You think people will be upset and need to sit down? Do you think the earl is ill?"

She waves her hand in front of her like she's shooing

chickens. "That man will live until he's a hundred and ten. He's fine."

"You think he's going to announce redundancies?" I ask. That was one of the rumors Sandra suggested. Another was that the staff cottages were getting an overhaul and we'd have to move out temporarily. Then of course, there's Basil's conspiracy theory that the earl is selling the estate.

"Darling, look at the place," she says. "There's a plastic bag covering a hole in the orangery's roof. There are weeds growing out of the cracks in the walls."

"There are not," I reply. "The house looks great. But what are you trying to say?"

"I mean the staff cottages."

"You're exaggerating. Maybe the earl is announcing bonuses for us all." I don't think that's a real possibility, but I don't think it's less of a possibility than any of the other suggestions I've heard today.

"Believe me, I've seen it for myself. A daisy flowered just above Basil's skirting board last week."

"You should have said. I would happily . . ." I pause. I'm not quite sure what the appropriate fix is for interloping daisies. "Pick it. And I'm sure Rio would plug any holes from the outside."

"I'm just saying, the earl is running out of money."

It's like someone stole the air from my lungs. "That's not true. The earl doesn't know about daisies growing in Basil's sitting room."

"Doesn't he?" she asks.

"Basil likes to complain, but only to people who can't do anything to fix it. If he told the earl, the earl would do something."

"Not if he couldn't afford to, he wouldn't," Granny says under her breath.

"He's an earl," I say. "He's got. . .investments."

"You know this for a fact, do you?" Granny pats me on the shoulder as we cross the lawns and head straight through the glass double doors into the long room. "Whatever happens, just remember we'll be fine."

"What does that mean?" I ask.

Before she can answer, we are surrounded by people as we all fill up the long room.

Granny's right, they've put a collection of chairs at the front, and we make our way through the crowd to find Granny a seat at the end of a row, where I can stand behind her.

I bend and whisper into her ear. "What does *we'll be fine* mean?" Did she know something concrete or was she just listening to Basil's silly rumors?

The room falls silent and I look up to see the earl coming through the long room's north entrance, his head bowed, a crumpled piece of paper in his hand. He seems sprightly enough. He's in his seventies, but as far as I know, is in perfect health. He looks just as he always has to me.

He stands in front of the twenty or so chairs at the front, nodding to Granny as he spots her. He clears his throat. "Thank you for coming," he starts. "I wanted as many of you as possible to hear this directly from me."

Anxiety knots in my chest. That doesn't sound good.

"I understand there has been rumor and speculation over the last few years about the future of the Crompton Estate. I'm without an heir and the place, as you all know, takes a lot of upkeep. Well . . ." He takes a deep breath, then lifts his head, a forced smile on his face. "I have good news for you all."

The knot of anxiety dissolves and I squeeze Granny's shoulder in an I-told-you-so gesture.

"I've been very keen to ensure the generations of love and work that have gone into making Crompton what it is will be maintained for generations to come. I can say with confidence that that future is now guaranteed."

I knew this wouldn't be bad news. I could tell. I smile and look around the room, making sure everyone is feeling the same relief.

From their expressions, it doesn't seem like everyone is having the same reaction to the earl's announcement as me. I expect Basil to look dour. Even on his birthday, he looks like someone stole his favorite cap, but why is everyone else looking like the earl is telling us that he's going to burn the place down? He's saying the exact opposite.

I notice someone leaning against the wall on the north side of the ballroom, but he's obscured by some of the younger gardeners. I dip my head to see if I can see between their beefy arms because for a second, I think it's Vincent.

That man is still haunting me, even weeks after our night together.

The earl continues. "I have sold the estate to a very charming fellow who will steward this magnificent home toward a bright future."

The knot of anxiety tumbles back into my chest and explodes. Heat floods my chest and memories circle my mind like ticker tape:

Me making my own lunch because Mum was in bed after a late night.

Me at school after everyone else had left except Miss Jamie, who stayed with me until my mother turned up an hour and a half late.

Me on a pew at my mother's funeral, dressed in a black coat, not knowing how I should feel.

Sold?

Sold Crompton?

That was simply unacceptable.

"No!" I think I'm shouting, but I realize I haven't made a sound. I can't get the word out. It's stuck in my throat like it's painted on in thick strokes.

Granny grabs my hand on her shoulder and pulls my fingers into hers. "It's going to be okay, my girl. This is just a new chapter."

I don't want a new chapter. I want to stay on the current chapter forever. My life is a fairy tale—perfect just how it is. I don't want a different ending or a bend in the road or a new horizon or whatever other pretty words mask the devastation of this announcement. I want to rewind time to ten minutes ago and just get on with my day.

"Good evening, everyone," a familiar voice says.

I look up to see my handsome American one-night-stand at the front of the room.

TEN

Kate

This can't be happening.

Vincent is the new owner of the Crompton Estate. Vincent. The guy with the hard body and nipple obsession. It's impossible he owns Crompton. *Impossible*.

"Thank you all for coming," he says.

My knees fizz and I hold tight to the back of Granny's chair because if I don't, my legs won't hold me upright.

This. Can't. Be. Happening.

I can't look up. I might explode or vomit or explode in a cloud of vomit.

"I want to be as open with you as I can. Today, my team and I will submit plans to convert Crompton into a hotel."

It's like someone has punched a hole through my chest. I'm hollow.

A hotel?

Mumbling fills the air. Somehow I find the strength to lift my head a little to glance around at the people I've known my entire life. They must be feeling as discombobulated as I am. This is such a complete upheaval.

"I want to preserve as much of Crompton's history as I can," Vincent continues. I stare at him, focusing on his mouth and the way it's moving and how it seems to be talking faster than the words are coming out, or maybe my brain just can't process what he's saying at a speed where things look connected. "It's a beautiful estate and I want people to continue to visit. But it has to be profitable and that means things will have to change."

"What kind of hotel?" someone shouts from the back. I think it's Jamie, one of the gardeners.

Good question. What kind of hotel? And does it *have* to be a hotel? Could he not just live in it himself? Replace the earl, but keep things exactly as they are apart from that?

Since I was a little girl, being at Crompton has brought me peace. Happiness. A stillness I didn't have anywhere else. It was the slow swinging of a pendulum I could focus on through the crazy chaos of life with my mother. As a child, before my mother died, no two days were ever the same, unless I was with Granny at Crompton. Sometimes my mother would take me to school, sometimes I'd get a lift. Sometimes I'd just end up staying home because she was sleeping or distracted. Once, I walked. It had taken nearly an hour, and although I knew the way and was very careful crossing the road, I'd gotten Mum into terrible trouble, and she'd made me promise never to walk to school on my own again. After that, I'd just miss school on the days she wasn't out of bed.

Other times, we'd be away. Liverpool seeing her friend because it was three days before her birthday and she needed help organizing her party. Or the time she'd decided on a Sunday afternoon to drive to see Kenilworth Castle.

We hadn't arrived until late and it was long closed. We'd slept in the car that night because she was too tired to drive back.

But Crompton was always the same. I would bask in the unvarying routines of Granny and everyone around her. The way the sun would always rise on one side of the house and set on the other. The way no matter what, Granny had a boiled egg for breakfast at exactly eight each morning. The way when I stayed with her, I always went to bed at the same time every evening, after listening to her sing me the same, soft lullaby. Small things most growing children find dull and confining, I found fascinating and desperately comforting.

Vincent's deep voice cuts through my memories. "It will be a five-star hotel. Crompton is under two hours from London. I want this to be a destination for people from London to come for a weekend or a weekday break. They don't have to travel too far, but they're getting out into the beautiful British countryside. Many people aspire to have a house in the country. But it's expensive and a lot of upkeep. I want Crompton to be their country house—a home away from home—but without the downsides of maintenance and cost."

"What about the flower gardens?" Basil asks. "Will you maintain them?"

For the first time, I look up and right at Vincent. I want to see his expression when he answers. For the longest time, Crompton and I have been inextricably linked. This is where I grew up. Had my first kiss. This is where I've lived since my mother died. I can't bear to see anything happen to them.

Vincent pushes his hands into his pockets and glances down, before looking Basil in the eye. "There are two answers to that question. The grounds of Crompton are and will continue to be very important to the hotel. However. . .the flower gardens currently open to the public will have to be scaled back and reserved for hotel guest use only. They are beautiful, but very costly to maintain. I also intend to put in a leisure complex and an indoor and outdoor pool, which will take up some of the spaces currently occupied by the gardens."

Ringing starts in my ears. *Clang. Clang. Clang.*

It's like I'm not biologically equipped to hear what's being said. My body is at capacity and is overflowing.

I try and swallow, but my throat is swollen with all the tears I refuse to cry in public.

"This is a big change," Vincent says. I feel his gaze burrowing into me, and I glance at him, unable to resist the pull of his attention. "I know many of you have worked here a long time and hold the place in great affection. I respect that. And I want to honor that."

"What does that mean, though, young man?" Granny asks, and I grip her hand. "What about people's jobs and homes and livelihoods?"

Vincent nods. "I am going to have my team hold meetings with you to go through the details. But the short version is, I will offer a job to everyone who currently works on the estate, if they want one. Now, it might mean we have to upskill or retrain people, but I want to keep you if you want to stay. We won't need as many gardeners, because as I said, we're closing the flower gardens, but the hotel will employ many more people than the Crompton Estate currently employs. There will be new roles and responsibilities that need filling and I'm confident we'll be able to find a new role for each and every one of you. I hope that answers your question, ma'am." He looks at Granny.

"Not quite," Granny says. "I live on the estate. As does my granddaughter and others who work here. What happens to us?"

Vincent nods like he was expecting the question. "We're still working on the plans, and my team will reach out as those plans develop, but we will be rehousing any employees who live on the estate. You will have plenty of notice, and it won't happen until we've found you something suitable."

The mumbling in the crowd grows, but Vincent raises his voice. "I've seen some of the housing you're in and it's in dire need of repair, I'm sure you'll agree."

Dire. He's exaggerating of course. It's not dire at all. Yes, there's the odd weed here and there and the occasional leak and of course the central heating isn't entirely reliable, but we live in houses that are hundreds of years old. There are bound to be issues.

The noise dies down and people tune in to what Vincent's staying. "We've identified a builder who's developing the land behind the car park in the village. We hope to be able to offer housing there."

"Thank you, young man," Granny says. "I look forward to hearing more about it."

I frown. That's it? She's just going to let him off the hook like that?

"Any other questions?" Vincent asks.

"Will we be allowed to take pets into the new house?" Sacha asks.

Vincent grins. "We're still working on some of the details." He turns to speak to a shorter man I didn't notice before, standing beside and slightly behind Vincent. "I have a note to make sure we make that clear in the briefings." He mutters something else to his lackey.

Vincent turns back to his audience. "I'll be moving my office into the house."

He's going to be working from the house? Will he be sleeping here too?

"I want you to know I have an open door, if you have any concerns. If I'm in a meeting, my assistant, Michael," Vincent nods to the man next to him, "will help you and make sure I get any messages."

Michael steps forward and gives a small wave. He seems nice, but he's about to ruin my life, so I shouldn't judge a book by its cover.

"My plan is for my team to sit down with you at regular intervals to keep you abreast of developments. As we work out staffing requirements, we will post on a bulletin board in the café." He turns to me. "If that's okay with you, Kate?"

"You own the place," I say, my tone clipped.

His friendly demeanor doesn't change at my almost-rude answer. "We'll put a board up there and if there's anything you think you might be suited for, even if you don't have the experience, let one of my team know. We'll see what can be done."

"So when is this all happening?" I ask. "When are the tea shop closing? The flower gardens?"

Vincent looks at me and for at least three seconds, the rest of the room falls away; it's like we're alone in his hotel room, just like we were a few weeks ago. "Not yet," he says to me and then raises his voice so everyone can hear. "As far as I understand, there are coach bookings to see the gardens through the end of August, so we'll honor those. We don't have firm dates to start work because planning hasn't been granted, but we anticipate construction starting in about a month. As I said, the majority of the landscaping will need to be maintained throughout the refurbishment and after the hotel opening."

But the tea shop will close.

Granny and I will have to move.

My life will change forever.

ELEVEN

Vincent

Michael is chattering about how well the meeting went, but I can't focus on anything but the look of devastation on Kate's face. It was like I'd ruined her life.

It's not a good feeling.

I really want to talk to her one-on-one, but I have no idea where she might be. In her cottage maybe. But it's not like I can knock on her front door. I'm her boss now. It would be too much of an invasion of privacy. Perhaps I can catch her in the tea shop tomorrow.

I scroll through Instagram, and I notice Kate takes a similar shot at different times of the day. It's at the bottom of the estate by the lake, overlooking the water to the wooded area.

"Is that okay, Vincent?" Michael asks.

"I'm going to get some air," I say, ignoring his question because I didn't hear what he was asking. I stalk out. I need air or to clear my head ... or something. Even if Kate's not there by the lake, maybe it will help me find a solution to her obvious disappointment. I know what it's like to have to leave a home you feel a connection to. It's been a while, but the memory never fades. I may have turned adversity into motivation, but the hurt is still there like a flickering ember, firing my drive and ambition.

"You have that meeting with the US office," Michael calls after me.

"I'll be late," I say as I take the grand, oak-carved staircase down to what will be the lobby of the hotel.

The double doors at the entrance to the house are impressive. If it's possible to restore them, we should. I pull out my phone and voice-note Michael so I don't forget to mention it later.

In the doorway, I turn to look back at the lobby. I take in the chandelier and the staircase, the wooden paneling, the artwork I negotiated as part of the sale. If I could have a conversation with me as a ten-year-old, I'd tell myself not to worry and that it would all work out. I'd even tell the kid who applied to medical school, so he could be just like his cousins, that everything would be okay. That he wouldn't be like them, but that was okay too.

I exit the house and look up.

I own a fucking estate.

Who would have thought it. I'm not going to live here, but I could if I wanted. I could be an earl in all but name.

I shake my head, almost incredulous, and cross the driveway into the dusk.

Kate's exactly where I thought she might be.

As I approach her, I almost want to take a picture. It would be like all her others, except better, because she would be in it.

"Kate," I call as I approach. I don't want to frighten her.

She turns and stands. "What are you doing here?" She looks confused and frustrated.

"I was just wandering and saw you."

She sighs. "Am I trespassing?"

I tilt my head. "Kate. Come on."

"Kate what? You own the place now. The earl never minded us using the grounds. Maybe you do." She crosses her arms like she's putting up a shield between us, except I'm not here to attack her. "Not that we'll be here long if you have your way."

"The house was always going to get sold, Kate. The earl couldn't afford to keep it. You must know that. You're smart. You can tell things haven't been maintained as they should have been."

"An estate like this requires constant upkeep."

"Exactly," I say. "It's expensive. And the earl doesn't have the cash. Most estates like this have either been sold or turned into safari parks or museums. There isn't much of the British aristocracy left."

"You could restore the house and open it to visitors. Like an extension of the garden tours." She looks up at me pleadingly, and I hate that she's so obviously in pain. The woman I first met was fun and carefree and full of wonder. And now she's looking at me like I erased all of that.

I shake my head. "It doesn't make sense. The house is too far gone. Restoration would take millions—"

"So will turning it into a hotel. So why not choose the path of least resistance? That way the gardens can stay as they are and we can keep our homes." Her voice hitches on the last word. It's like someone's plunged a dagger into my gut.

I swallow, hoping it will clear a path for my words. "I get it, Kate. Believe me, I know what it's like to be uprooted from your home, I really do, but the accommodation we're going to find for you all is going to be so much better than what you're in at the moment. It will have triple glazing and central heating that works—"

"But I don't want to move. Neither does anyone else. I want to stay at Crompton."

Her words awaken something in me. I remember saying the exact same thing to my mom after my dad left, and she brought home ten cardboard boxes. Our new apartment was much smaller, so we had to squeeze as much as we could into those boxes. We took trash bag after trash bag of our possessions to Goodwill, including toys I'd grown out of but still wasn't ready to part with. I realize now that those days marked the end of my childhood. Once we moved into the new place with blindingly white walls—with memories of a happy childhood and my father, both of which were gone—I vowed I'd never get attached to anything again. Not a home, not a possession, and not a person.

"The new place will be bigger," I say. "You'll still be working at Crompton. There are plenty of jobs I can see you excelling in—"

She turns away from me to face the lake. "I don't want another job. I like the job I have now."

I take a deep breath. Maybe I shouldn't have come after her. She needs time to process what she's heard. It's obviously come as a complete shock to her—but not for everyone. From a number of expressions on the staff members' faces, they knew what was coming, or at least expected a significant change. After all, the earl isn't getting any younger and it's not like he had children to pass Crompton down to. Maybe it was because of our physical connection, but Kate's reaction seemed to be the most dramatic of everyone's.

"I never thought it would come to this," she says. "The flower gardens are so beautiful."

"They really are," I agree.

She spins to face me again. "Then keep them. Keep them open to the public. Keep the tea shop. You could keep the staff cottages as they are. You don't have to change everything."

She needs time to adjust. I need to get her excited about the change. Or at least accepting of it.

"I'd like to show you the plans I've had drawn up. I can show you the spa, images of the bedrooms and some of the common areas. I'm planning to show everyone at a later date, but why don't you come and see tomorrow? It will help you get a feel for how incredible the hotel is going to be."

She swallows, her expression pained. I fight the urge to reach for her and pull her close to me. I know how well she fits against this body and I want to provide her some comfort. But the last person she wants touching her right now is me. "If I look at the plans, will you look at my plans?"

I frown. "What plans?"

"If I was to draw up plans. Like viability plans for the gardens staying open, will you look at them?"

I push my hands into my pockets. "I'm not going to lie to you, Kate. The flower gardens are too close to the house. I don't want hotel guests to feel like they're being gawked at by coach parties. And the swimming pool area is right over the red and blue borders."

"What if we relocated the tea shop?" she asks. "You could put the pool there."

"Come and see the plans." She'd see for herself things were organized a certain way because it made the most sense.

"I'll come and see the plans if *you* promise to look at any proposals I give you with an objective mindset."

She was nothing if not tenacious. I couldn't help but be drawn to that.

"I'll look at whatever proposals you provide."

She started to smile, and I had to look away so it didn't break my train of thought.

"I'm not saying I'll change anything. I have a team of people who have thought all this through and things have already been submitted to planning. So it's very unlikely anything will shift."

"But you'll look?" She searches my eyes like she wants to see the promise in them. I'm many things, but I'm not a liar.

"Yes, I'll look."

Our eyes lock for one second, two, then three. It's me who looks away first. I glance over to the lake. "You like it here," I say.

"Who wouldn't."

She's right. It's beautiful. A far cry away from Pittsburgh, where I grew up.

"Can I walk you back?"

"Don't ruin it," she whispers.

Despite the woman in front of me being a near-stranger, a thud of responsibility lands in my gut and I shake my head. "I won't."

TWELVE

Kate

The turnout for my meeting is better than I'd hoped for. Granny couldn't make it, but she wished me luck. I need it, too, because going through the figures for the tea shop, which I was privy to, and flower gardens, which I'd obtained under duress, it was clear the earl was operating at a considerable loss. But luck is back on my side because there are nearly fifty people here, squeezed into the Golden Hare. It goes to prove people aren't happy with Vincent's plans. He's going to have a fight on his hands.

George isn't happy with me taking over the place for the next hour. I offered to work the rest of my shift for free, but I really sold him on the idea because he'd have a captive audience of customers, ready to put down their money as soon as our meeting finished, which I'd timed to coincide with the pub opening and the start of my shift.

I lift myself up onto the bar, grab a wineglass and tap it with the knife I use to cut lemons, trying to get everyone's attention.

"Thank you all for coming," I say as all eyes face me. "I thought we needed a meeting to discuss Vincent Cove's plans for Crompton House." I ignore the murmurs coming from the crowd. "As you know, he's submitted his plans but permission hasn't been granted yet. The deadline for objections is this Friday. That doesn't give us long to make a plan."

"What are you thinking?" asks Basil.

"Well, I thought we should all repeat a similar argument. That way the local authority are more likely to take us seriously. If we take a scattergun approach, we're easier to ignore. We need to be joined up. First, I think we need to talk about the loss of jobs."

"But he's going to keep some gardeners on, and everyone else can apply for positions in the hotel," Rupe says.

"Exactly," I reply. "Horticulture isn't some kind of unskilled work. It's a passion. A calling. It takes training and heart and—"

"Honestly, I don't mind a change," Amarjit says. "If he wants to pull me off gardening and have me unloading luggage and ferrying it about, I'm happy as Larry. I heard you can make good money from tips on top of your salary."

"Okay, but that's just you," I say with a little more bite in my tone than I intend. "We don't all feel like that."

"He told me I'm likely to be kept on if I'm prepared to do some training on the new air-conditioning system," Rio says, so enthusiastic, you'd think he'd won the lottery.

"The way I see it," Rio continues, "with the earl, you never knew whether you were going to get paid at the end of the week. He was either going to cark it or run out of money." There's a collective intake of breath at the mention of the earl's death. "The place is a shit show. My missus went in the house a few months ago to give him a pie she'd baked and said the place was empty inside. Like he'd moved out already. I reckon he sold all the furniture trying to keep this place running. This way, at least we all know we're going to get paid at the end of the month. This guy Vincent's a millionaire by all accounts."

"I heard he was America's first trillionaire," Mindy shouted out.

"There's no such thing," Rio says, and everyone starts talking over each other.

I try to get control of the meeting again, but no one is listening to me clinking on the wineglass.

"Hey, everyone, let's calm down," I shout. "This meeting is important. People are going to lose their jobs and the roofs over their heads."

"I can't bloody wait," Chris, my neighbor, says. "Hopefully any new place will have central heating that bloody works."

"And will allow pets," Sacha says. "It makes no sense that I have ivy growing through my kitchen window, but they won't let me have a sausage dog."

"It's the poo, Sacha," I say. "The earl never wanted it in his gardens."

"Well, the earl is gone now," Rio says.

Tears gather at the back of my throat. How can they be so flippant? And they all seem focused on their own needs rather than the bigger picture. Crompton represents hundreds of years of history. It needs to be saved.

"Kate, why don't you tell us what your idea is if Vincent doesn't get planning," Basil asks.

"Thanks, I'm glad you asked. Well, like you said, Mindy, Vincent's very, very rich. He has family . . ." Where did he say his aunt and uncle were from? "Locally. I think we convince him to renovate the property and keep it as a country retreat for himself."

"But he bought it as a business," someone says, though I can't make out who it was. "He's not going to keep it. Especially if he thinks the entire village is against him."

"We're not against him," I say. "We're against Crompton being ruined. About it being turned into a hotel."

"Better than a safari park," Amarjit says.

"Or a museum. The place needs life," Basil says.

I'm starting to think I'm the only person opposed to Vincent's plans.

"Let's have a show of hands. Who here is in *favor* of Vincent Cove's hotel plans?"

Hands shoot up everywhere. My heart thuds through my chest with such vigor I think my t-shirt must be moving.

"Remember, if you have your hand up right now, it means you're *in favor* of everyone in staff accommodation being evicted—"

"And rehoused," shouts a voice.

"And people losing their jobs," I say.

"And being retrained to do other jobs," Rio says.

Hands remain in the air. It's clear most people are in favor of what Vincent is trying to do. But I want to know who is on my team. "Hands up if you're against Vincent trying to destroy Crompton." I raise my hand and see Sandra raise *her* hand. I glance around and it's clear we're the only two people who aren't taken in by Vincent's charms. "Come on, people, did he bribe you all or something?"

"We're just being realistic, sweetie," Mindy says. "There's no alternative. Better to go along with things and make the best of it."

My heart falls in my chest and clangs against my rib

cage on the way down. This is it? Everyone is just giving up? The last twenty years of stability will be gone in the blink of an eye?

"Make the best of it?" Rio says. "This is an opportunity. We're all being given a fresh lease on life alongside Crompton House."

My gaze settles on the floor. I just can't bear to hear this.

"You'll probably end up the manager," Rio says. "You're a bright woman, Kate. Could have gone to university."

"I don't want to be a hotel manager," I say.

"Why not?" asks Meghan. "You're more than capable of doing. . .more." She's leaning on the bar and says it quietly. Most of the room won't have heard, but it still feels like a betrayal.

"Or maybe the restaurant manager," Basil says. "If you want less responsibility."

Why are people so focused on me? I'm concerned about Crompton. About keeping things the same. "I don't want to be restaurant manager," I say. I like things as they are.

"You can't imagine it?" Amarjit says. "Vincent says it's going to be a five-star hotel. I bet staff lunches will be brilliant."

"I'm perfectly happy with a slice of Sandra's Bakewell tart," I say.

"But this could be better," Amarjit says.

"I don't want better."

"But we do," Basil says. "I'm sick of the weeds crawling through my walls and the lack of central heating. And like Rio says, the uncertainty of not knowing if our jobs are safe or what's going to happen next. It won't be like that anymore. Kate, we all love this place, but it can't stay as it is. Every year has gotten progressively worse—no pay rises, less money for plants and feed and equipment, the houses falling further and further into disrepair."

Tears sting my eyes. The way Basil describes life at Crompton is so different to the way I see it. It's such a happy place for me.

"We'll still all be here, Kate," Basil says. "It's not like he's getting rid of us. And you're just as much a part of this place as any of us. You won't be going anywhere either."

He makes it sound so simple. So obvious. They don't understand my life outside Crompton was nothing but misery. Before my mother's death and even those few months away at university—nothing outside of Crompton worked. At least, not for me.

"Right, time's up," George bellows from behind me. "Get out or order a drink. No moping around."

People start to murmur, obviously deciding whether to stay for a drink, and I slide off the bar, defeated.

Meghan comes over. "I know this is hard. Crompton is your whole life, but this could be good for you," she says.

I shake my head. "Not for me, but for everyone else maybe. That's what I've got to focus on—that it's going to make everyone important to me happy."

Meghan and I move out of the way so people can get to the bar. I head to the till and find my apron. "You want me to do your shift?" she asks.

I shake my head. I want this bit—the time before my life is upended—to last as long as possible. I don't want to skip shifts.

"Hey, doll," Sandra says as she slips her hand around my waist and squeezes. "This is going to be okay. I promise."

There's no way she can promise that.

"I've known you since you were a little girl, and you've always been bright and happy and full of confidence."

Sandra didn't know me before I came to live with Granny. She's only known me at Crompton. And at Crompton, I *am* bright and happy and full of confidence. But that's not the same me who existed outside these grounds.

"This could be such a great opportunity for you. Basil's right. You're bright and could do anything you want."

"It seems like people think it's going to be a great opportunity for them," I say.

"You can't blame them," Sandra says.

"People have been worried for years now. You know they have," Meghan says. "Now people's minds are at ease. They know they're not going to lose their jobs or be thrown out of their homes."

"People don't know what will happen. This hotel could be a disaster."

Sandra sighs. "Maybe. But this Vincent seems like a good man. And he's very rich. He's more likely than the earl to make a success of the place."

Even Sandra is convinced.

"And I promise, I'll make you a Bakewell tart every month for the rest of my days. You don't have to miss out on that, I can assure you."

I smile and squeeze her back before glancing over the people still left in the pub. They're laughing and joking, and even I can't ignore the buzz of excitement in the room. Without question, people are on board Vincent's hotel train.

Unless Vincent doesn't get planning permission or there's some other huge obstacle to the hotel opening, people will get the change they so clearly want.

And me? I'll end up in some rented starter flat, which won't be next door to my grandmother. She'll probably be shunted off into a home. It will be the first time I haven't lived with her or next door to her since I was seven years old.

For the last twenty years, I've basked in simplicity and stability. I know a good life means the world, *my* world, staying the same. Thanks to Vincent, everything is about to change.

I'm not ready.

I never will be.

THIRTEEN

Vincent

I didn't expect the pub to be so full of people. Have I missed something?

As I walk in, I see Kate, the other waitress, and the older woman from the tea shop huddled together by the till. Kate looks gorgeous—her hair in a bun on top of her head, jeans and a t-shirt that shows off all her curves. Not that I should be noticing them.

As the door behind me closes, everyone turns to look at me and the place falls silent.

Aha.

I have a feeling I've walked in on a community discussion about me—or my plans for Crompton.

Kate ties her apron and pulls back her shoulders.

"Hi, boss," Sacha says as she bounces over to see me. "I know you're off the clock and everything, but do you mind if I ask you a question?"

"Go ahead." I make my way to the table I sat at the first night I ate here—the night I walked in and caught Kate before she hit the floor. I figure if I'm in the wrong seat, she'll tell me. She's not shy.

"I really want a dog," Sacha says. "A sausage dog. I should say Dachshund. The earl never allowed them in the staff cottages. None of us were allowed pets. I know I asked about this at the meeting, but any word on whether or not we'll be allowed pets in the new housing?" she asks.

"I don't know, Sacha. But let's make sure we find somewhere sausage-dog friendly."

Sacha breaks into a smile. "Thanks, boss. I knew you were alright."

I nod in gratitude at the compliment and Sacha heads off.

Basil, one of the more senior gardeners, is the next visitor at my table. This evening isn't turning out how I expected. Yes, Kate's here, as I hoped. But I wanted a tequila and a steak and thirty minutes to myself. That's not going to happen, but I can't shake the feeling that it's fortuitous I arrived when I did. Kate might have whisked everyone up into a frenzy in my absence, although given her forlorn expression, maybe things didn't go her way.

"How are you?" I ask, leaning back onto the bench where I'm sitting, stretching my arm along the back.

"We're all fine. Nothing for you to worry about, by the way. You're not going to face a mutiny or anything." He winks at me and I nod in gratitude. Again.

"Thanks, Basil," I say. I don't tell him I wasn't worried. What could Kate have done? Yes, she could have made life a little more difficult, but people have short memories and practicality would have won out for most of them. I'm not here to burn Crompton down. I'm going to create jobs, bring business to the area. What I'm going to do will benefit the entire community. Most of them understand that already, and those who don't will eventually.

I watch as Kate comes over, menu in hand, studiously ignoring my gaze.

"Menu," she says as she approaches the table. "Would you like a drink?" She takes out her pad and pen from her apron pocket and stands poised and ready for the most complicated drink order the pub has ever seen.

"A tequila." Then I add, "Please." I know Brits love a please.

She doesn't say anything. She doesn't note anything down on her pad, just turns on her heel and heads back to the bar. Her ass looks spectacular in her jeans.

Maybe it's the challenge, maybe it's because I genuinely want her to know she doesn't need to worry about what's going to happen with Crompton because I have no desire to destroy it, maybe it's just because she has a great ass, but I want to talk to her. I'd like her to try and understand where I'm coming from.

Most of the Crompton workers leave over the next ten minutes. But there are a couple tables over by the bar where people are huddled around their drinks, talking in hushed voices. Every now and then one of them glances over at me, and every now and then one of them glances at Kate.

I chuckle to myself and focus on the menu.

Kate returns to my table with a tequila and her pad.

"Thanks," I say as she places the drink on the coaster. She still doesn't look at me. "How was your get-together?"

"What can I get you?" she says, ignoring my question.

"I'll have the rib eye. Medium rare. With a side of broccoli."

"That's a lot of protein. Broccoli has more than people

realize." Then she screws up her face and mutters, "Bloody hell," under her breath like she's pissed she spoke to me.

"I didn't know broccoli is a big protein source," I reply, smiling at her.

"Well, you do now." She shrugs, plucks the menu out of my hand and spins back to the bar.

I pull out my phone to check my emails, but before I have a chance to open my inbox, a couple of the junior gardeners wander over to the table. I'm not sure of their names—I think the tall, lanky one is Amarjit, but even if I were a betting man, which I'm not, it's not a bet I would take. "Evening," the one who's definitely *not* Amarjit says.

I pick up my tequila and raise it in his direction.

"Just so you know, most of us think you being here's a good thing," Probably-Amarjit says. "Some people might not want to admit it, but it was time for the earl to sell. I don't think his heart is in it anymore."

"His bank balance definitely wasn't," the other one says. "A hotel will be good. Take a while though. What's going to happen to us in the meantime?"

"It will happen fast for a renovation of this size. I have no patience for anything else. Twelve months from start to finish."

"Twelve months," Amarjit says, obviously surprised. He doesn't realize this is a fraction of the time it would ordinarily take a project like this to be completed.

"That's not such a long time. Much of the landscaping will need to be maintained. Training for new roles will need to take place. And if I have some willing helpers, there will be other interim roles that will need filling."

"I'm up for it," Not-Amarjit says.

"Good," I say.

"Like we said, most people are in favor."

"I'm pleased to hear it."

"I told Kate there was no way you were going to be convinced just to keep it as a country house for you and your family," Amarjit says.

I try not to let my surprise show. Why would she think that was an option? And what family? She must know I'm not married—we slept together. "You're right. There's no convincing me of that."

"Well, whatever you need from us, Vince. Just let us know."

"Not calling me Vince would be a start. Vincent works just fine."

Not-Amarjit laughs. "Absolutely, Vincent."

Amarjit nudges him. "Let's leave the man in peace." He lifts his chin at me and waves. "Enjoy your dinner. And don't let Kate wind you up about the omegas."

I can't help but smile at that comment. Kate clearly has everyone's nutritional requirements in mind.

As if I summoned her, Kate appears with a couple plates of food. She sets everything down without looking at me.

"Mustard?" she asks, still avoiding my gaze.

"That would be lovely."

When she returns with the trio of mustards, I dip to try and meet her gaze.

"You know, you thought I was charming when you first met me," I say, reaching for a jar of the whole grain. She hasn't brought me a spoon, but as I move to stand, she turns and heads back over to the cash register, where additional flatware is stored. She returns with three teaspoons.

"Thanks," I say, beaming up at her.

She puts her hand on her hip. "When I first met you, you weren't my boss. And you weren't evicting me."

I can taste bitterness on my tongue—not fresh, like it was for so long, but dulled around the edges. Almost like the memory of bitterness. "I'm not destroying—"

"And I didn't find you charming," she says. "I had an itch. And you were available to scratch it."

I can't help but chuckle. "Well, I'm very happy to have scratched your itch for you. I don't mind at all that you just used me for my body." I want to add, "Use me again anytime," but I don't. She's upset and she's right—I'm her boss now.

"I was serious when I asked you to come see the plans we've had drawn up for Crompton House. You can see for yourself how things are going to look. There's a mock-up video tour. And you can have a tour of the house as it is now, so you can see the kind of investment we're committing to the property."

"You're trying to win me over," she says, focusing on my left shoulder.

"Yes," I say. Wasn't it obvious? "I don't want you to be unhappy. Just come and look. I see how important you are to the other staff at Crompton. If you take a look at the plans, you can tell them what you think."

She pauses for a moment, shifting her weight from one foot to the other, her eyes focused on the mustard, my steak —anywhere but my eyes. "I suppose I could come and. . .see if what you're telling us is . . ."

"Come and see if I'm telling the truth."

We lock eyes for the first time since I arrived and she pulls in a breath. "Okay."

I can't help but smile. She's beautiful and I can't tear my gaze from her. She's going to see that I'm not trying to make her life worse. This hotel will be a great investment for me and the community where it stands.

"Oh, and take a look at this." I pull the two-page job description I had my VP of employment draw up.

"What is it?" She takes the papers.

"A job description—head of guest relations for the hotel. You'd be a perfect fit."

"I don't have any experience," she says, clearly flustered.

"We're going to retrain you. You're great with people. I've seen how comfortable you make people in the pub and the tea shop, how you notice little details and genuinely care for people. You'd be great. But think about it. I don't need an answer now. Come and see the plans tomorrow and we can talk more."

She doesn't return my smile. "Eat your steak. You're going to need the creatine."

I smile up at her. "Does that mean you're going to give me a workout?" I know I shouldn't be flirting with her, but she's completely irresistible.

She shoots me her meanest look, which I probably shouldn't find quite as sexy as I do, and leaves. Again.

FOURTEEN

Kate

I've brought a notebook and pen with me. I'm sure he'll find that less intrusive than me photographing everything, although if I get the chance, I will snap a few shots. If I find something I think the other Crompton staff won't like, I want evidence. Even if I've had to accept Vincent turning the house into a hotel is something everyone wants, I see it as my job to make sure he stays true to his word. If I find any difference between what he's promised and what he does, I'll be the first to pull him up on it. If the Crompton staff don't want me to lead their opposition to Vincent's plans, I can at least be their advocate and protector. Somewhere along the way, I hope I'll get comfortable with the change ahead of me. I just don't know if it's possible.

I square my shoulders and press the huge Victorian bell that must have been installed long after the house was built, but still a hundred years ago.

I brace myself to come face-to-face with Vincent, who's

very probably the best-looking man I've ever laid eyes on and very definitely the best lover I've ever had.

The double doors swing open, but instead of Vincent, I'm greeted by another man—the one who was by his side during the announcement. I can't remember his name. Michael maybe? He's in his twenties, with brown hair, with a body Granny would call wiry—thin and milky white. She always says wiry people are stronger than they look and fiercely loyal. I don't have the heart to tell her there's scant scientific evidence of a correlation between body type and character.

"Kate, thank you for coming," he says, all smiles. He knows my name. Vincent has briefed him about me. Goodness knows what he said: *Doesn't want the house to turn into a hotel but gives excellent blow jobs.*

Of course Vincent wouldn't be greeting visitors at the front door. Why would he when he can employ someone to do it for him?

I smile tightly. "Thank you for inviting me." I step inside the house. Before the earl's announcement, I hadn't been in here for years and years. Even last week we only got to see the long room.

The entrance hall is exactly how I remember it from when I was a little girl, although it seems slightly smaller now. The sweeping staircase with the almost irresistible banisters I dreamt of sliding down is still there, looking completely magnificent.

"Will he keep the banisters?" I ask. "And the staircase?"

"Yes," a familiar voice from the top of the stairs booms. "It will require some restoration, but there are no major works planned to the staircase." Vincent comes down the stairs, the top buttons of his white shirt undone, showing a hint of brown skin I know feels so good.

I need to focus on the banister. Not his skin. Not *him*.

"Shall I show you around before you see the plans?" Vincent asks as he reaches the foot of the stairs where Michael and I are standing. "You can refamiliarize yourself with the layout and it might be a little easier to envision things."

I shrug, pushing down my excitement at seeing the house again, ignoring the fluttering in my stomach at having Vincent so close.

"You can leave us, Michael," Vincent says and Michael heads back up the stairs.

"Let's start here." Vincent sweeps his arm to the left, guiding me to a room I've never been in before. It's lined from the floor to the very high ceilings with bookshelves filled with books.

"The library," Vincent says. "The plan is to keep this and make it part of the casual dining experience. The hotel will serve light snacks and afternoon tea. That kind of thing."

This is where Sandra wants to work. I wonder if I should mention it. No, I decide. There'll be time for that.

I look up, taking in the rows and rows of books and the light streaming into the room from the windows on the upper levels. It's a stately home, but this room's so cozy and warm.

"This might be my favorite room," Vincent says. "I think it's the stained glass." He lifts his chin at the windows with multicolored glass in them. I'd never noticed them from the outside. "It gives a church-like feel, which is completely appropriate given the importance of books."

I can't help but smile. "You won't get an argument from me on that."

Vincent meets my gaze and there's a softness in his eyes,

almost as if he's proud to have found common ground with me. I look away. I need to focus on this tour and protecting the people of Crompton, not Vincent Cove's dreamy eyes.

"And through here?" I ask, nodding toward an oak-framed arch.

"This leads into the morning room, which is perfect because it will also serve afternoon tea. Michael is a huge afternoon tea man, so no doubt, he'll be all over the details on that. He says afternoon tea is the best thing about being in the UK. Are you a fan?"

For a moment, I think he's asking whether I'm a fan of Michael, but then I realize he's still talking about tea. "I can't say I've ever had a formal afternoon tea. But Sandra makes the best Bakewell tart in the world. Good old-fashioned cake is more my jam—pardon the pun."

Vincent laughs. "You're a lover of history and tradition. I thought you might be into that kind of thing."

I shrug. He doesn't need to know how little I leave the estate. Whenever I mention to anyone how rarely I leave Crompton, it sounds weirder than it actually is.

"Let's go through to the next room. It's another sitting room that leads on to the long room. I know you've been in there recently."

I catch his gaze and he's looking at me as if he wants me to respond.

"Oh yes, after you reappeared as the new owner of the estate. I wasn't expecting to see you again."

"Must have been a huge disappointment," he says as we wander down the long room, along the back of the house.

"A shock more like. It's not like you mentioned to me you were thinking of buying the place."

He laughs. "No. Of course I didn't. Would it have changed anything if I had told you?"

"You mean, would I still have slept with you?" I ask as he looks at me, waiting for an answer that I'm not going to give him. "Before or after my panic attack about losing everything good about my life?" I try and say it in a calm, light, only-joking kind of way, but it doesn't come out like that.

Vincent stops and I can't help but mirror him. "Kate," he says. "I'm not here to make your life miserable. Really, I'm not."

I turn and start to walk. "I know you haven't come here with the *intention* to make me miserable." He's doing his job. On a logical level, I understand. Now that I know everyone else welcomes his arrival, I see it even more clearly —how it works for them. Maybe it's selfish, but I just can't get past how drastically this is going to change *my* life, when there's nothing about my life I want to change.

"Why do you feel so differently than the rest of the staff?" he asks.

How does he know how the other staff feel? I suppose he's seen them in the pub. When he was there after the meeting, I saw Basil and Sacha and Amarjit talking to him. I suppose people have been telling him they're in favor. And I get it. Pay raises and job security are important. Those who live on the estate get to move into brand-new homes with updated amenities. By all accounts, everyone wins.

Everyone but me.

"I've just always loved this place," I reply. "And I know you're not bulldozing it and I can see what you're doing through other people's eyes ... I get that from their perspective it makes sense, but ..."

"This isn't about Crompton," he says, and I snap my head around.

"It's absolutely about Crompton," I reply.

He winces, but doesn't say anything more and I'm grateful. I don't want to feel the need to explain or excuse why I feel like I do. Vincent Cove doesn't need to understand how utterly devastating the thought of moving off the estate is for me. He can't know the fear that swirls in me about what life has in store if I'm not next door to Granny, living my life as I've lived it for the last twenty years.

Vincent and I make our way to the other side of the long room to a rabbit warren of rooms that look like they might need to be demolished. There are no rugs on the floors, just stained floorboards, ripped wallpaper, and damaged architraves. It looks like some kind of deserted haunted house. Vincent doesn't use the state of these rooms as more reason why what he's doing is a positive thing, and I'm grateful. "You'll see on the plans this area will be knocked into one and used as a formal dining room, which will lead out into the extension."

"Extension?" I say and instantly wish I hadn't given away my shock.

"Yes, a two-story extension will house most of the bedrooms."

"More bedrooms are being added?"

"At the moment, there's only space for some of the suites and a couple of specialty rooms within the original house. The bulk of the bedrooms will be located in the extension."

I want to see these plans right away. Already my mind is spinning with images of a vast, sprawling, modern monstrosity tacked to the back of the house. "Can we finish the tour after I've seen the plans?" I ask. I want to see what he's talking about. Vincent has been very clear about his desire to restore Crompton. Now the truth comes out: He's willing to bolt an ugly extension onto a beautiful, historic building for the sake of profit. Surely the local planners aren't going to let a stately home like this be ruined?

"Absolutely," Vincent says, like butter wouldn't melt in his mouth.

Vincent leads the way up the winding stairs. I follow him, trailing my hand up the smooth, weathered oak, definitely not looking at Vincent's bottom.

"We've set up our office in here," Vincent says, opening a door straight ahead of the stairs.

The room is flooded with light and my eyes have to adjust. I glance around and see Michael behind one desk at the far end and a young blonde girl, who looks like she's in her early twenties, sitting behind one of the other two modern desks at either end of the room. In the middle is a large table, covered in papers.

"The earl didn't leave any furniture?" I ask, glancing around. Surely they could have found office furniture a little more in keeping.

"Most of the rooms were empty when I first toured the place," Vincent answers. "The earl took some things. He left a few pieces for downstairs that will be used in the hotel, much of the art. And the books in the library, of course."

What did he mean the rooms weren't furnished? They must have been. This was where the earl lived, after all. Then I remembered someone at the pub said the same thing. Had times been so tough for the Earl that he sold furniture to keep the place afloat?

"Let's show you the video of what the place will look like when it's finished," Vincent says. "Molly has it up on her screen." Vincent pulls two chairs over to the blonde's desk and she adjusts her large screen so we can all see it.

The video opens with a sweeping aerial shot of the

grounds that looks like it must have been taken from a drone. But the blooming gardens have disappeared, and in their place is what I can only assume is the extension—a beautiful, red-bricked building that looks as natural as the main house itself. There's a large conservatory and, even if I hate myself for thinking it, a rather appealing pool.

It looks beautiful. Most of the landscaping is exactly as it is now. But it's still not the place I know and love. The changes might be visually appealing, but they still make my insides seize into a tight ball of anxiety.

"This is how it will look when all the renovations have taken place."

"It's not just renovations though, is it? It's extensions and removal of the flower gardens."

"You're right," Vincent says, to my surprise. "'Renovations' doesn't encompass enough. What would be a better word?"

"Renewal," Molly says, and I try not to crack my teeth as I clench my jaw.

"Let's just call it *works*." I try and keep my voice steady.

"Okay, let's go with that," Vincent says. "After all the works take place, this is how it will look. Obviously the brickwork on the house will all be cleaned. Experts tell us that hasn't happened since the property was built in the seventeen thirties—"

"Seventeen twenty-eight," I correct him.

"Yes, it hasn't been cleaned since then. We've been told it's amazing how well preserved it is, considering the lack of investment."

Does brickwork need investment?

"All the paintwork will be refreshed. The windows will need to be restored. Many of them are rotting and letting in leaks, so we plan to commission new windows that are handmade with triple glazing to ensure it feels like a luxury hotel, but it's also energy efficient."

It *sounds* good, and Rio has mentioned a few times how the windows need work. "Will the windows look the same?"

"Just as it shows on the video. You won't really be able to tell the difference."

Our gazes meet and the angry fire I've been trying to stoke in my belly fizzles out. I don't know if it's because he's giving me so much time or because he really does sound like he cares. Either way, I can feel myself melting.

The camera sweeps through the front doors—which I can't help but notice are the original front doors, brought back to life—and into the entrance hall, converted into a hotel lobby. Not a detail has been missed in this video: fresh flowers adorn a large circular table at the bottom of the stairs, and a man and woman in matching navy blazers stand behind the reception desk.

The camera sweeps left into the library and focuses on the stained-glass windows Vincent pointed out earlier.

"The stained glass will be restored, as well as books and shelving. The floors will likely need to be replaced, although further due diligence is needed on that. We're trying to keep as many original features as possible."

The library is set up for afternoon tea with small duck-egg-blue sofas and chairs gathered around tables set with crisp white linen and glinting cutlery.

The books lining the shelves look warm and inviting. There is no doubt about it—the place looks beautiful. Granny, Sandra, Basil, Meghan—everyone from the estate will love it if this is how it turns out.

The newly restored staircase seems to gleam, as if proud of the fresh, moss-green stair carpet and bright portraits hanging on the walls.

Part of me hoped it was going to be a disaster—that Vincent would insist everything be whitewashed and modern, but the feel of the new place is traditional and familiar.

And lovely.

It's still a hotel. It's still not the Crompton you know, I remind myself. The warning has lost a bit of its edge in the face of this incredibly thoughtful presentation. What hasn't lost any of its strength is the fear gripping my heart that this is more change than I will ever be able to cope with.

As the video continues, I actually feel myself willing the next frame to be better and, more often than not, it is. The spa looks incredible—like things I've seen on Instagram. The two pools are astonishing—simple and understated, but inviting and very luxurious. The indoor pool's roof—which looks like a conservatory from the outside—makes it seem like a palace. The ballroom looks like something out of *Bridgerton*, and even the smallest bedroom looks fit for an earl.

The place looks revived.

Recovered.

Loved.

I close my eyes, willing myself not to cry. Not to panic.

"Kate?" Vincent asks, his voice soft.

I take a breath and open my eyes. He's watching me. He looks at me wordlessly for a beat too long and then glances to Michael and Molly. "Leave us, please."

For a moment I think he must be chucking me out, until Michael and Molly stand and file out of the door.

He didn't shout. He wasn't harsh when asking them to go. His voice was low and controlled and completely authoritative. And it was a whole lotta hot.

I mentally chastise myself for still finding this man

attractive. So he has a great body and a nice smile. So he smells like rain-soaked pine and can silence a room just by entering it. So he can make me orgasm more in one night than all men had in the previous decade. So what?

He's making me homeless-ish, throwing me back to my life before I knew how to be happy. There is no way I can allow myself to fancy him. My hormones better get a hold of themselves.

"How can I help?" he asks.

I shake my head because there's nothing he can do. "It looks lovely." I manage to croak out the words, twisting and turning my fingers in my lap. "Really."

He smooths his hand over my arm. "Tell me how I can fix this—whatever this is."

If he was planning to bulldoze the place and turn it into a theme park, it would be easier. I could hate him then. I could pin my misery on him.

But I don't hate him.

Not even a little bit.

FIFTEEN

Kate

I transfer the tin of muesli onto my left hip, knock on Granny's door and open the latch.

"Morning," I call out. "I brought you some more muesli."

Granny sounds like she's upstairs, but I can still make out her moaning. She's not a big fan of my muesli.

"It's good for you. Fiber. Phosphorus. Plus the omegas and protein from the nuts and seeds." I set the tin down, pull out two bowls from the cupboard and flick the switch on the kettle.

"I'll be there in a minute."

A pang of sadness hits me in the chest. How many weeks have I got left of having breakfast with Granny? To distract myself, I set about pouring out our breakfast and making us each a cup of tea. Granny takes hers like watery builders' tea and I'm drinking green, which I hope to convert Granny to at some stage.

"I hope you haven't given me any of that green rubbish,"

she says as she comes into the kitchen in full gardening getup. "I want a normal cup of tea."

"Tea is made. And your bowl of muesli is just there too. Do you want milk or Greek yogurt with it? You know the yogurt is better for the gut bacteria."

She sighs. "I'll take the yogurt if you give me a break from trying to control what I put into my body."

"Not control. Inform. I'm trying to help. You need to look after yourself." I grab a yogurt from the fridge and a spoon from the drawer and slide them across the table.

Granny takes a seat. "If I dared to say such a thing to you, I'd be interfering."

"You absolutely would not. Have you read something? I read something yesterday that coffee is now good for you." I like reading about the latest research on the healing and preventative benefits of certain foods and lifestyle choices. One of the reasons Granny's so healthy at her age is all the gardening. People offer her seats wherever she goes, but usually she's the least likely to need one. She's an inspiration. I'm just trying to help her help herself even more.

"How was yesterday?" she asks.

I decide to pretend I didn't hear the question. "I've added even more good stuff in this latest muesli. You'll never guess what the secret ingredient is."

"I'm not sure I want to know."

"Mushroom powder."

Granny freezes, her spoon hovering midair. "Psychedelic mushrooms?"

"No, lion's mane mushrooms. You wouldn't believe all the amazing things it can do—everything from reducing inflammation to protecting against dementia. It really is an all-purpose fungus."

She puts her spoon down without sampling my new

recipe. "Mushrooms in muesli doesn't seem right to me. And you didn't answer my question. How was yesterday? What did the plans look like?"

I sigh, partly because I'm disappointed she won't try the new muesli but more because of the disastrous meeting. "You can't even taste the mushroom." The muesli is delicious and I take a spoonful to prove it.

"I'll have a taste if you tell me about the plans for the hotel," she says. I nod, then wait as she tastes the muesli. As predicted, she shrugs. "You're right, I can't taste anything."

Hopefully, that means she'll be eating it every day.

"I'm waiting," Granny says. "Do you like this Vincent Cove?"

"It doesn't matter if I like Vincent or not," I say. Granny doesn't know I slept with him. She doesn't need to know. And it's not like it's any big deal, but I just don't want her or anyone else to think I have something against him personally when quite the opposite is true. I'd like to have something extremely personal—namely *me*—against Vincent. Or at least I would have done if he hadn't bought Crompton. Then again, if he hadn't bought Crompton, he wouldn't be here to feed my daydreams of seeing him naked again—which I'm definitely not doing.

"Okay, so what are the plans like?"

"They're...impressive. Obviously the flower gardens have gone. There are vast extensions, but if I'm honest, it looks really wonderful."

I glance up to find Granny beaming at me.

"This could be a new chapter for you," she says. "You could meet new people if you were to move. You might even find yourself a boyfriend."

"I don't want a boyfriend. I'm happy with the way things are."

She slides her hand over mine. "Things have been the same for a very long time now."

"But if it's not broken, why fix it?"

Granny rubs her thumb over mine in the same way she's been doing for twenty-seven years. "Darling, it *is* broken." I'm not sure what she's referring to: me or Crompton. Her voice is gentle when she continues. "The earl should have sold the place years ago. He couldn't afford to keep it up. I suppose he was holding onto something almost as tightly as you are."

"Why wouldn't I hold on tightly? I'm happy here. Isn't it normal for people to want to be happy?"

Granny nods. "Of course. But there's not just one way to be happy. Standing still isn't always the best way."

I pull out the papers Vincent gave me yesterday and drop them on the table. "He's already offered me a job heading up the guest relations team in the hotel."

I dismissed the idea when he mentioned it, but after my shift, I read through the description. There's no doubt the role is a promotion. And it involves many of the things I like about my current job: lots of interaction with people, improving people's days. But because of the transient nature of hotels, it's unlikely I'd really get to know anyone, like I've gotten to know the regulars at the tea shop. I had one couple who comes every day of July and August and has been doing that for the last six years. They feel like part of the furniture now. There would be nothing like that at the hotel.

"That's wonderful, my darling," Granny says. "When do you start?"

"I haven't accepted it."

Granny shoots me a look of disappointment.

"I'm sorry," I say. "You're disappointed in me."

"Oh gosh, not in you, my darling. *For you.* Are you not the teeniest bit excited at the thought of being the head of a guest relations team at a five-star hotel? I would have thought a job like that was right up your alley. You'd be fantastic at it. You love the estate so much, you can talk about it with real, genuine affection, and you've lived in the area most of your life. There's no one better to help guests enjoy Crompton and the surrounding villages."

"He's only offering me the job to get me on his side."

"I doubt that's true and even if it is, who cares? You've got to grab these opportunities when they come up in life. You'd be good at the job and he clearly knows it. Frankly, it fills me with confidence that the man knows what he's doing if he can see *your* potential."

On the outside looking in, the guest relations job is a good opportunity for me. But it's not a future I ever envisaged for myself. "I don't know. I'm still hoping that—"

Before I have a chance to finish my sentence, Sacha comes crashing through Granny's front door. "There's things about the housing stuff in the library." She looks from me to Granny. "So are we going or what?"

"Going where?" I ask.

"To the library. In the house. They've set up some... information or something. Apparently there's a man answering questions."

"What sort of questions?" Granny asks.

"I have no idea." Sascha is practically vibrating with excitement. "But I might be getting my sausage dog."

I'M STILL GETTING USED to the new open-door policy at the house. When the earl was in residence, it was understandably off-limits. Now the door stands open every time I pass by. I suppose it's no longer a home—just an office. A business. A place people come to work, not build a life.

We step through the doors into the lobby. Things look as drab and empty as they did when Vincent gave the tour.

"Gosh, I haven't been through these doors in a long time," Granny says. "It looks in dire need of some tender loving care."

"At least he's keeping the staircase," I mutter.

"Of course," Granny says. "The place is listed. They won't let him get away with anything that destroys the history of the place."

I try not to roll my eyes.

"In here," Sacha says, practically tugging at Granny's shirt.

Voices drift into the hall from the library, and the door swings open as we approach. Our trio comes face-to-face with Vincent.

My disloyal heart flutters at the sight of him. It must be his height. And those perfect forearms on display beneath rolled shirtsleeves. It's like he's trying to torture me.

"Welcome," he says, his tone full of charm and warmth. The soporific sensation I get when he's near returns. "News travels fast. Come in, come in, and let me introduce you to Beck. He's the developer on the site behind the parking lot in the village, and lucky for me, I met him about ten years ago, halfway up a mountain. We've stayed in touch."

Why is he so bloody affable? Why can't he be more villainous? I could hate him then.

A beautiful blonde woman comes toward us in a tight red skirt and matching red lipstick and in an instant, I feel like a frumpy country bumpkin in my wellies and hand-knitted jumper Grandpa made me before he died. No doubt, Vincent's used to being surrounded by women like this and, despite myself, I can't deny that a sliver of jealousy lodges in my heart.

"Hi," she says, grinning at the three of us. "I'm Stella, and I'm going to be working with Vincent and his team on the design of the hotel. I'm moonlighting today, helping my husband Beck, who's building the houses in the village. He's trying to make a good impression, so clearly needs my help."

Granny chuckles and even I can't help but smile. She's being so nice. Plus she's married to someone who isn't Vincent. My jealousy fades.

"So you're just going to buy these houses behind the carpark?" I ask Vincent.

"Well, not all of them," Vincent replies. "Eleven of them. To house the people in the eleven staff houses."

Is it really that easy for him to buy eleven houses? "Do you have that kind of cash hanging around?"

He lets out a half-chuckle. "It's an investment. You're going to be paying me rent."

"Is it a good investment?" I ask. "Are you going to be making a lot of money from us?"

"Not according to my finance director."

"So, why are you doing it?"

"Because I don't go around making people homeless. I'm not that guy." He looks at me as if it's just the two of us in the room. I swear if it was, I might be tempted to kiss him.

"Of course you're not," Granny says. "Now, what have you got to show us?"

Vincent takes Granny's arm and leads her to a chair by a desk that's been set up with various bits of literature.

"What's your vision for the interior of the house?" I ask Stella. "I've seen the video."

Her eyes sparkle with excitement and she clasps her hands together. "I can't wait to get started. I do a lot of modern interiors in London, because Beck builds and refurbs a lot of new projects and that's what people want. But Crompton House will be different. I really want to use Vincent as my muse." She laughs. "I bet a lot of women have said that before me. But seriously, I want to create the feeling of an English country home. So it should be exactly what an American would imagine an English country home should be—more luxurious than the real thing, but completely classic and in keeping with Georgian architecture. I'm going to really press Vincent to restore the moldings and architraves that are either damaged or rotten. I can use those elements to anchor the rest of the design."

She pauses and I smile at her. She's telling me everything I want to hear.

"Have you worked with Vincent before?" I ask.

She shakes her head. "No, I work with Beck mainly. It's how we met." She narrows her eyes. "Sort of. It's a long story." Her smile is so wide as she talks about her husband, I glance over at him.

"Do you have children?" I ask.

"Yes, a daughter. She's three. We'll get around to number two soon. It's just a lot—work is so busy. And we have a busy social life. Probably not as busy as Vincent's."

A dull ache wraps around my heart and I can't quite understand why. Is it the mention of children, Vincent, or the busy social life?

"You're Kate, right?" she asks.

I'm a little taken aback she knows my name. "Yes," I say.

"Vincent's trying to impress you," she says conspiratorially. "He wants people to know he's not here to destroy anything. He's going to honor the house because people are invested in it being brought back to its former glory."

"What makes you think he's trying to impress me?"

She smiles. "Just the way your name comes up when we're discussing things." She pauses. "Are you single?"

"Happily so," I reply. What does she mean, my name comes up? I want to ask her more but I don't.

"I guess Vincent's the same way. I've tried to introduce him to a couple of my friends but he doesn't seem interested."

I give out an attractive snort-laugh combination. "Really?" Vincent seems like a consummate seducer...or at least he was with me. Wasn't he? "You think he's trustworthy?" I ask. "I mean...he's offered me a job. In the hotel. When it's done. You think I should work with him?"

Am I really considering his job offer? With the rest of the villagers on Team Vincent, what other choice do I have?

"My husband doesn't work with people who aren't trustworthy," she says. "He's a good guy. And it's not like Vincent's going to stick around and be the hotel manager, is it? Your direct contact will only go so far."

The dull ache in my heart deepens and I shift my weight from foot to foot. "I guess not."

"You know the thing he's not good at?" she says.

My body stiffens, almost in loyalty to him. "What?"

"Detail. It's very hard to get him to make decisions about the design of things. He just wants me to get on with it, but it's hard without a little direction. I try and use Michael as a go-between, but he's so busy. I just hope it doesn't hold things up."

"What do you mean?" I ask.

"Vincent is focused on the things he—and the project

manager—see as a priority. Right now, that means the planning permission, appointing the main contractor, getting housing sorted out for the staff who live on the estate. I get it, I really do. But I need him to tell me I can commission the rugs for the library and morning room because they'll take about ten months to fabricate. Same goes for the material for all the drapes across the house and extension. With the quantity we need, lead times are horrendous."

Before I can ask more questions, Vincent approaches. "Kate, can I get Beck to show you the floor plans for the new houses?" he asks. "Or even better, we can do a site visit. I just mentioned it to Sacha, but she's tied up, and so is your granny. Do you have time?"

"Visit the new houses?" I've not had any time to think about leaving the estate. I'm not in the slightest bit prepared.

Beck joins us. "It's a bit muddy down there, but we have one fully built, so you'd be able to see the space, rather than just look at a plan. Foundations have been laid in some of the others."

Maybe I'll feel better if I see the new houses. Better yet, maybe I'll still be able to see Crompton from the new housing development. If I could look out my window and see the estate, I might not feel so...unmoored.

"It will be fun," Stella says. "And you've got your wellies on already."

I glance down at my feet and then back up to Vincent. "Are you going?" I ask.

He shrugs. "Absolutely."

It's no big deal. Just a few minutes in a car. It's not like I've never been to the village before. Except I can't quite remember the last time I went into the village. Ever since

Meghan's cousin started a grocery delivery service, I haven't had to leave the estate on a consistent basis. Try as I might, I can't recall *why* I last left, let alone when.

Soon, I'll be coming in and out of the Crompton gates every day. Getting in a practice run today can only help.

SIXTEEN

Vincent

It's the fake smile that tips me off about Kate's anxiety. I haven't known her long, but from what I've seen, she doesn't fake anything. Usually. But now, as we head down to Beck's construction site, she's smiling as if the corners of her mouth are pulled apart by some invisible vise. She's totally faking it.

"You okay?" I ask.

She's been gripping the edges of the seat like she's expecting the car to take off into the air at any second since we drove through Crompton's gates. "Fine," she says, her smile still firmly in place.

"I thought you said it was behind the car park," she says as I get to the stop lights in the village. Her voice sounds thinner than usual. Strained.

"It is," I reply.

"Well we just passed the car park."

"I'm just turning left here and then the entrance to the site is a little farther down."

"How much farther?" she asks.

The light turns green and I turn left, my peripheral vision completely consumed by Kate and her obvious discomfort. Although I could be blind and still feel her anxiety. Is it the thought of moving, or me? Maybe she doesn't like cars.

"We're nearly there," I say. The entrance to the site is about three hundred yards from the lights. I slow down, getting ready to turn.

"It's farther than I thought." She turns to see behind her. "I thought it would be directly behind the car park."

"There's a row of houses there already," I say, then I wish I hadn't because she must know there's a line of buildings there. She's lived in this place her entire life.

"There is?" she asks. "Oh yes. The vet and the dry cleaner are there."

I don't remember the stores in that strip of buildings. All I know is Beck's development starts behind it.

"Here we are," I say, pulling up in front of the site office.

She dips her head, trying to get a good view of outside rather than just getting out. "I'm not sure I'll be able to see the estate from here."

I don't think she's talking to me. It's like she's having a conversation with herself.

"Let's go out and see."

We get out of the car and she takes a few steps back toward where we've come from. "I don't think I can see it," she says again, an edge of panic in her voice. "Can you see it?" She whips her head around and looks at me, waiting for my answer.

"It's beyond the trees," I say. You can't quite see any part of the estate apart from the wooded area toward the bottom of Crompton's land. "I think some of those trees mark the edge of the estate."

"Where?" She scurries across to me as if I'm carrying binoculars she wants to use.

I point. "Over there."

"You think that's the estate?"

Why's she so concerned with seeing the estate? She knows it's not far away. We were on the grounds less than five minutes ago.

"It's too far to walk," she says. "Is there a pathway so we don't have to follow the road? Perhaps you could build one. Or get a shuttle bus between the estate and these houses. People don't drive. I don't drive. We need to be able to reach Crompton easily."

Her speech picks up pace with each word she speaks, like she knows she's running out of words and has to get them all out as quickly as she can.

I reach for her arm—it's an instinct, like rocking a crying baby or patting a friendly dog. My instinct says she's panicking and needs soothing. Or distraction. "Why don't we tour the finished house?"

She nods a little frantically and begins to twist and pull at her fingers. What happened to the confident, ballsy woman I first met at the tea shop? It's like she's totally disappeared.

The site manager comes out of the office as we approach.

"Hi, I'm Ziad. Kate and Vincent, I assume?"

A chill runs down my spine at the way he says our names together, like we're linked or something.

"I've brought one of our valued staff members to look at one of the houses," I say. "Beck said you've got one complete."

"We absolutely do. It's not furnished or anything, but we just put the kitchen in last week and yesterday we did a mist coat on the walls. Let me show you."

He heads off up a slight incline and I turn to Kate. "Ready?"

She glances between me, the car, the trees up in the distance and then nods.

As we follow Ziad, Kate falls behind. At one point she lifts her hand to her face and might be wiping tears away with the sleeve of her sweater.

"You okay?" I ask. It's a stupid question because she's clearly not okay, but I want to know what's wrong and I want to fix it.

"Fine. How many houses are there on the development?" she calls after Ziad.

Ziad stops and turns. "Twenty-eight. It's a mixture of one-bed maisonettes, and two- and three-bedroom houses." He points his thumb over his shoulder. "This is a two-bedroom house. We have eleven of these. Let's go in."

It's a big step up to the first house and Ziad goes in first, then turns and takes Kate's hand to help her up.

We go through the hallway to the living room at the back of the house.

It's actually nicer than I expected inside. It's not a standard new build. There are details that give it an edge.

"Don't know if you've seen the site plans, but the twenty-eight houses have been designed together to look like a large stables from the outside. That's why you've got the black ironmongery everywhere and the stable doors on the kitchen and back door. It's a quirky house, not a bog-standard box. Beck wanted thatched roofs on some of them, but the council said no. Fire hazard."

I focus on Kate. Does she like it? Hate it? She heads

straight to the window. "I definitely can't see the estate from here," she says. "The windows don't face the right way. Do I get to choose which house I want?"

"Absolutely," I say without hesitation. I want to do anything I can to try and relieve some of the devastation she clearly feels about having to move out of staff accommodation.

"Is there one with views up the hill?" she asks.

I look to Ziad.

"I'd have to have a think," he says. "Probably." He squints. "I'm not quite sure. Do you want me to go and get the site plan?"

Kate has started pacing from one side of the living room to the other.

"Yeah, that would be great. Maybe give us a few minutes to look around as well."

Ziad nods and heads out.

"Why don't we take a look upstairs," I suggest.

She nods but doesn't speak. I let her lead us both upstairs. It doesn't take long to look at the two bedrooms and bathroom, then Kate goes to the back bedroom and presses her hands to the glass. "There's no view. I can't see anything."

I follow her gaze. It's just farmland I can see, with trees out in the distance. There's plenty of view, but not the view she wants. She can't see Crompton.

"We can take a look at the site plan when Ziad brings it back."

"It's so far away." Kate puts her hand on her chest. "I can't catch my breath." She bends over, her hands on her knees. "I can't breathe, Vincent."

She's hyperventilating. I glance around to see if there's any kind of bag she can blow into, but there's nothing.

I stalk toward her and she straightens, panic in her eyes. "I think I'm going to faint." Her voice is higher than normal, wobbling on each word.

"I'm here," I say. "You're not going to faint. Let's sit."

She looks horrified. Probably because the floor is filthy, but better that than fall down.

I take her hands in mine and guide her to the floor so we're sitting opposite each other, knees touching. "Look at me," I say.

"I can't breathe," she says again.

"Just stay focused on me," I say, keeping a tight hold on her hands. I don't know what I'm doing, I'm just trying to get her to stop thinking about whatever it is that's causing her to spiral.

"See how our hands are joined," I say. "I've got you."

She looks at our linked hands and then back up to me, shaking her head.

"I want you to take a deep breath in."

She sucks in a staccato breath, but it's a start.

"Longer this time. Watch me."

She looks up and I start to inhale. She mirrors me.

"Then out."

She copies me, and we fall into a rhythm, breathing together in and out. In and out. Her body starts to relax. Her shoulders drop, her arms grow heavy in mine and her breaths get longer and deeper.

"I'm sorry," she says. "I just don't leave the estate very often. And when I do, I never feel like myself."

I'd already figured she didn't spend much time off the estate—she lives and works there after all. But a panic attack after moving just a few miles down the road? I have to wonder how often she actually steps foot off the grounds.

"Don't be sorry," I say.

When she calms down, I want to talk to her. She's right about a shuttle: we need to arrange transport between the staff cottages and the estate. Kate sees details Michael and I don't—not only because she's familiar with the estate, but because she's an essential part of the community that's grown around it and because of it.

If she's willing, I'd like to employ her to help Michael. He needs someone like her—someone with a different perspective, whose attention to detail won't get steamrolled by more pressing responsibilities. And it might help Kate, too. If she's on the inside, helping shape things and push the project forward, she might start to look forward to the future.

Good things can happen after your world crumbles. I'm a testament to that.

SEVENTEEN

Kate

I'm sitting at Granny's kitchen table, scrolling through Crompton's Instagram page, when I say, "I got another job offer last night." I put down my phone. Granny's knitting. I'm not quite sure what it will be when she's finished, but it will definitely be colorful.

"Another one?" The clack of the needles doesn't falter. It's a comforting, rhythmic soundtrack to many of our conversations, and it's just what I need right now. So much is changing or about to change. At least Granny's knitting is always the same.

"An interim one. From Vincent...Cove." I add his surname because he's not just "Vincent" to everyone. He's still Vincent Cove to everyone else. I wonder if I would have slept with him if I'd have known what he was at Crompton to do. Probably not, unless I could have foreseen how good it was going to be. It shouldn't have been, because we were strangers, but it was so...I don't know a word to describe it other than *intimate*. We seemed to know what each other was thinking, what we needed, what we wanted. It was as if we'd known each other a lifetime. Or maybe just that on some molecular level, I knew I was always going to know him. Or I was waiting for him. Or something.

It was the same yesterday during my anxiety attack— something Granny definitely doesn't need to know about. She worries about me too much as it is. Vincent seemed to know exactly how to calm and soothe me. Like he was a Kate whisperer or something. The visit to the new houses yesterday was overwhelming. It didn't help that the development is a little farther out of the village than I thought it would be. I'm surprised at how calm Vincent was. He talked me down. Made me feel safe.

"Oh yes, has it got something to do with the guest relations job?" Granny asks.

I haven't accepted that job either. Yet. "He wants me to assist his assistant, Michael. He reckons I've got good attention to detail and think about things in a different way because I'm a local. He says I'll be an asset to his team. I made a suggestion about having a shuttle from the village to the estate. He says my ideas are good and he doesn't want important details missed because it's such a big project."

"Wow," Granny says. "That sounds like a very responsible position. Did you accept?"

"I was more focused on the new houses. You should go and look at the site too. He says you can pick the one you want."

Granny sighs and sets down her knitting. "Actually, I've been meaning to talk to you about that."

My heart begins to thud in my ears. This sounds ominous. "About what?"

"I don't think I'll be moving into the houses that nice man Beck is building."

My pulse is racing and I have to fight the urge to stand. Leaving the estate will be bad enough. But is Granny talking about moving us out of the village entirely? "Then where will we go?"

"I think one of those houses will suit you perfectly. But I think I need something else. I don't manage the stairs as well as I used to. I'd like to be all on one floor."

"What about the maisonette?"

"Too small."

"We could ask Beck about possibly building you a bungalow."

Granny laughs. "He's not going to do that. And anyway, I don't want the hassle of my own garden and—"

"I'll do your gardening. You won't have any hassle at all."

"I've made an appointment to look at some flats being built in Wayton."

My stomach drops like someone's punched a hole through the world and attached an anvil to it. "Wayton? That's four miles away."

"They look very nice. And I can afford one with my savings and the lump sum Mr. Cove has kindly offered me."

"Lump sum? What lump sum?"

"I spoke to him this afternoon. Told him I wasn't interested in the properties Mr. Wilde was showing. I explained about Wayton and that's when he said he'd give me a lump sum toward the purchase of one. He doesn't want to buy a flat, which is completely understandable."

Anxiety knots in my throat and my breathing turns shallow. It's happening again. I take a deep breath and try to focus on what Granny's saying. "When were you going to tell me about this?"

"I'm telling you now. Anyway, no decisions have been

made yet. I'm still to see the place. But I know a couple of people who have already paid deposits—"

"People from the staff cottages?"

"No, no," she says. "Friends I have in other villages. The world is bigger than Crompton, my darling. It would be nice to be closer to them."

"You won't miss your friends from the Crompton Estate? You won't miss living next door to me?"

"Well, I do hope you'll visit." Her grin's mischievous. Until now, her smile has always made me feel safe, like we're a team with an inside joke—us against the world. But now all I can do is wonder whether I'll get to see that smile as often.

"It's four miles away. Is there even a bus that goes to Wayton?"

"You used to have a driving license. You could get a car," Granny says.

Whenever she's suggested this before, I've always assured her there's absolutely no need for me to have a car. I never go anywhere beyond walking distance. There's never any need. But now? Granny would be a car ride away. And she's getting older.

"Visiting isn't the same as living next door."

"You're quite correct. It isn't the same. It's different. It *might* be better. This is just a different chapter, my darling. I know it's frightening. But have you thought that it might be time? Crompton has helped you heal. It's kept you safe. Maybe now's the time for a little adventure. And perhaps a new job is the start of that new adventure. Two new jobs." She laughs.

"Change is supposed to happen incrementally," I say. "I'm not supposed to lose my home, my job and my granny all together."

She reaches across the table and squeezes my hand. "You're not losing me. I'm just going to be a few miles away. And there's a new invention called the telephone. I hear it's terribly easy to use."

I rarely need to telephone Granny. But if she lives four miles away, it's not like I'll be able to pop round, just to let her know I'm home.

"And you're going to come to Crompton three times a week to supervise the gardeners?"

She pauses and glances at me. "Maybe. But I'm sixty-eight. I might also take the opportunity to retire."

The blood pounding in my ears falls silent like it's frozen in shock. "Retire?"

"Onto my next chapter. You might think of this as your opportunity to turn the page and start a new chapter of your own."

"But I like the one I'm in right now."

"But it's drawing to a close, my darling. Sometimes it's our choice to turn the page. Sometimes life chooses for us. Neither way does it mean the next chapter won't be better. More exciting."

"I've done exciting," I mumble. Granny retiring? Everything's just falling apart.

"You've done *chaos*. And you may have a similar chapter in your future. There are no guarantees. But at the moment, what I see are incredible opportunities lining up for you. If you don't grab one of them, or at least figure out what you want next, you'll be left with whatever other people don't want. No decision is still a decision. You can howl at the moon for the next few weeks while everyone else makes plans and comes to terms with the change at Crompton, or you can grieve that this part of your life is over and start planning for the next. Decide what you want. Work toward something better."

Everything begins to blur together. The idea that Granny won't be next door or working within shouting distance. The fact I won't be surrounded by people that have known me my entire life. Singing along to musicals with Sandra won't be a thing anymore. Neither will I get to see the wisteria bloom every spring.

It just feels so terribly sad. When I closed the last chapter of my life, it had been a relief to be over with it and I gladly moved on. But moving on when you don't want to? When you never thought you'd have to? When you thought you'd found your happy place and want to stay in it forever? It's far harder than anything I've ever done.

"I know things didn't work out at university. But that was a long time ago now, and this will be different. *You're* different."

I don't want to think about the last and only time I left Crompton since I came here full-time at seven. The memories just prove what I already know to be true: I belong here, at Crompton.

And if Crompton is where I belong, then I have to take the opportunities Vincent is giving me—the chance to make sure it all happens on time and according to plan. Maybe I'll even get to influence the way things are done in this new version of my world. Though fear still grips my heart like a vise, a small voice inside is getting harder and harder to ignore. It's the one whispering that if I can be brave, I might be able to stay connected to Crompton—and make sure it remains the safe haven it's always been for me.

EIGHTEEN

Vincent

Although I have a desk in the bedroom where Michael and Molly work, I spend most of the day in the makeshift boardroom—another bedroom—which is adjacent to my bedroom. All I need is a laptop and most importantly, my phone.

My phone buzzes and someone knocks on the boardroom door at the same time.

"Come in," I say, simultaneously accepting the call.

"Hello." It's Brad from the New York office on the line. As soon as he replies, Kate walks through the door.

She quite literally takes the breath from my lungs. Her hair is scooped up into a ponytail and she's wearing makeup —just a little blush and some lip gloss, but I haven't seen her in makeup before. She catches me off-guard. Not her visit— I've been expecting that. But just the way I'm so glad she's here.

She forces a smile.

"I'll call you back." Without waiting for a response, I cancel the call and stand. "Come in. Take a seat."

She's wearing a blue blazer, white t-shirt and jeans, and for some reason I picture her on a balcony in the South of France, laughing with sunglasses on, the warm breeze lifting her hair. Me taking pictures of her. I feel a deep sense of peace.

I need to get a grip.

"Do you have a minute?" she asks.

"For you?" I say. "Always."

She smiles again and it's a little less forced this time, although I know she thinks I'm bullshitting. But I'm not. I really would give her a minute at just about any time of day. Whenever I see her, she makes me smile and not just because I remember our connection in bed—although that's hard to forget. But her loyalty, her humor, the way she speaks to me like I'm just Vincent. Not her boss, not a billionaire, not someone whose worth is determined by how many checks he can sign.

She takes a seat around the table, in the chair opposite mine. "Is this from the dining room?" She glances around the table, which looks like it could have been in this house all along. It's highly polished mahogany and seats about thirty-five people. I probably should have a coaster under my bottle of water.

I don't take my eyes off her. "I have no idea. Michael set it up."

"At least you're honest," she says.

"I'm always honest." I want her to know that and feel comforted by it.

"Were you serious about the job you talked about yesterday?" she asks.

"Absolutely. You'd be perfectly suited." I'm not lying but I definitely have an ulterior motive. The last thing I want to do is make someone—anyone, but especially Kate—

feel like I'm taking away their home. She clearly loves Crompton and I want her to love the new Crompton Hotel even more. If she joins the team, hopefully, she'll grow to love what we're doing. She'll own it and love it just as she does the current place.

She narrows her eyes. "You know I don't have any real qualifications to do anything. I dropped out of university and nothing I learned at A Level is going to help me...assist anyone."

"You know the estate, you're great with people, you care about detail. And I know you work hard. Those are the qualifications this role requires. It also helps you're one of the few people in this world who doesn't care that I'm..." I falter, unsure how to finish my sentence. "You speak to me like I'm normal."

"Aren't you normal?" she asks, then tilts her head as if considering the question. If I'm not mistaken, there may be a hint of a smile at the edges of her mouth.

"Maybe *normal* isn't the right word. But you're not afraid to tell me what's on your mind and you don't mind being honest with me about...well, anything."

"And that's unusual?"

I fix my gaze on the sharp peaks of her Cupid's bow, which contrast against the pillowy softness of her lips.

"Vincent?" she pulls me out of the trance she caught me in.

I clear my throat. "Yes. I've attained a certain amount of wealth and power, and with that comes a pedestal where people try and keep things from you—either because they're embarrassed or don't want to bother you or are afraid of offending you."

"But Michael—"

"Michael...he's more forthcoming than some, but there's

still an element of gilt he paints the lily with. Anyway, he's drowning. He needs the help."

"I want to keep shifts in the tea shop and the pub."

"How you fit it in is up to you," I say.

"But my job is to assist Michael, so it's not just up to me, is it? Is he happy with help just twenty hours a week?"

"He will be," I say. Twenty hours of her time will be better than nothing from Michael's point of view.

"And I'm not doing it for the same salary as the tea shop. Apart from anything else, it's just a short-term thing and I don't get to sing show tunes during my shift—"

"On the contrary, I *insist* you sing show tunes while in the office."

A small smile curls around her mouth. "I want a monthly amount equivalent to fifty thousand a year, prorated for twenty hours a week," she blurts. "I know it's a lot, but you need me on this project—you said it yourself. And fifty thousand isn't so much if you look at how much you're investing in—"

"Done," I say.

She covers her mouth with her hand like she's afraid if she says anything else, I might change my mind. But I won't. I would have paid more.

I stand. "Let me show you to your desk."

"My desk?" she asks.

"It's right next to mine." I had Michael and Molly set it up yesterday after I offered Kate the job. I knew she'd accept eventually.

"Am I still in the running for the guest relations job when the hotel opens?" she asks from behind me as I head out of the boardroom and back into the office.

"Yes. That job is yours if you want it, so long as you're prepared to do the training."

"I am," she says.

I don't know what changed her mind, and mostly I don't care. I'm just pleased she's here now, a smile on her face rather than the scowl I'd gotten a little too accustomed to seeing lately.

"Michael, Molly, Kate's joining the team as Michael's assistant. Kate, this is your desk."

"You have the desk ready?" she asks. "Just in case...what?"

"In case...this," I say. She turns to look at me and I can't place her expression but I feel it deep in my gut. It's part gratitude, part incredulity, and I have to fight the instinct to circle my arms around her waist and pull her to me.

She heads to the desk, circling it, like it might bite her if she gets too close. "So no one else sits here?" she asks.

"We set it up for you," Michael says. "Vincent said you'd be joining us."

She presses her finger down on the hole punch and flips open the laptop. "The laptop. Is that mine?"

"Yes," Michael says. "It's networked to ours so we can easily share files."

She nods. "And I'll come into work here. Every day."

"So long as you do your job, I don't mind what hours you keep," I say. "Bear in mind, you might have to have meetings in London with Stella or the project manager."

She freezes. "I'd prefer to stay on-site."

"You don't like London?" Maybe yesterday wasn't a one-off. Maybe she isn't able to leave Crompton because of her anxiety.

She clears her throat. "I think it's better to have me here. The house is my focus. This is where I should be."

She's not wrong, but there's more to her answer than that.

"Make it work," I say.

"I will," she replies, and I believe her. With her passion for Crompton, her clarity and focus on the details as well as ability to communicate with me so ...well, so clearly, it's the perfect recipe for getting the Crompton renovation completed on time.

"Is someone working on a website?" she asks. "And social media?"

"Website? For the hotel already?" Michael asks.

"I know we're ten months away, but we need to be building interest in the place. I noticed on the project plan, there's no PR and marketing stream due to go live until six months before. It can't hurt to get a head start, can it?"

I have to bite back a smile. She's absolutely right.

NINETEEN

Vincent

Maybe it's just me, but the atmosphere of the office has changed with Kate working here. Over the last few weeks, there's been more drive. More energy. It's more than I could have ever wished for. What has this woman been doing working in a coffee shop?

Her presence has also meant I've spent more time working in the boardroom. The more time I spend with Kate, the more distracting I find her. She needs to do her job and I need to do mine, so I avoid her.

I like her, and it makes me uncomfortable.

I've just finished up a call from a contact of mine about a potential opportunity in Arizona when there's a soft knock at the door, which I now recognize as Kate's knock. I don't respond, because I don't need to. True to form, without waiting for a response, Kate opens the door.

"Hi, I need to go through some things with you." She's wearing a soft pink sweater and jeans and she looks...*alluring* is the only way I can describe her. But there's barely a day when she doesn't look alluring. When I don't want to pull her against me and feel her hands in my hair. And there isn't a day when I don't find her completely fascinating.

The way she tilts her head up slightly when she's thinking has me totally mesmerized. The way she goes completely still when she feels a little out of her depth. The way I can tell whether she's worked a shift in the pub the previous night because of the sweep of gray under her eyes. It's just a hint, but one I goddamn congratulate myself for picking up on. It's like she's a thousand-piece puzzle and I'm the only one who knows how to solve her.

How to read her.

How to unlock her.

It makes me feel special—like I've been chosen. And it's infuriating. Because I don't know if it's something in this British air I'm breathing, but I've never felt this before.

About anyone.

Fuck. What did she do to me that night over the pub? It's like she planted something in my brain that has me fixated on her exclusively.

"I'm just about to get on a call with New York," I explain. "I'll come into the office when I'm done." I feel safer in the office, where there are other people—people whose presence hinders my instinct to reach for her. When it's just the two of us, the air thickens and I swear I can hear her heart beating. Her perfume seems to fill my head with the scent of roses and vanilla and I can't fucking think straight.

"I'll wait," she says and takes a seat. She's not sullen or frustrated. She's just matter-of-fact and steadfast. She's not going to move until she gets what she wants. And that's for me to make some decisions.

I fucking love it.

I love her determination and the way she doesn't give up. I love her quiet intensity. When I hired her, I totally expected her to come in and bang her fist on the desk and demand what she needed from me and that would have been just fine—what I thought I wanted. She sure was vocal enough when it came to all the things she didn't agree with when she found out I bought Crompton. That's why I suggested her for this job in the first place. But she's surprised me. She's like a quiet, determined bulldozer; she doesn't scream for people to get out of her way, but if they don't, they're going to get flattened.

There's no point in trying to get her to change her mind and come back later when I've finished my call. "What do you need?"

She smiles in victory and I look down at my laptop to distract myself from the way her hair is falling on her neck. "Planting plans. Are you happy with those now?"

"Did they do what I asked with the golf course?"

"They did," she says.

"Then I'm fine with the planting plans."

"Great." She slides a piece of paper toward me. "Just sign on the dotted line."

"What am I signing?" I ask.

"That you're fine with the planting plans."

"I just told you I'm fine. Why do you need me to sign something?" Is she kidding? "Do you think I'm going to change my mind and say I didn't agree with them or something?" I had one assistant who wanted to record everything I said so she had an "accurate record" of our every interaction. She didn't last long. I don't work like that. People on my team either trust me or...they're not on my team.

She shakes her head. "No. You'd never do that."

Her statement strikes me deep in the gut. Is it relief? I'm not sure, but it feels like a revelation: she knows me. "Exactly, I'd never do that. So why are you asking me?"

"Because people don't necessarily always accept my authority."

"But Stella—"

"Not Stella."

"The PM?"

She glances into her lap. "I think our project manager sees it as a slight because I can get answers from you he can't."

"Ridiculous," I reply, my tone sharp.

She tilts her head and smiles like I'm being incorrigible, and I have to stop myself from smiling back at her, from holding out my hand, guiding her around the table and pulling her onto my lap.

"You told me yourself that you're a powerful man and people aren't entirely at ease with you."

"But you are," I say. We make eye contact. We pause and wait and stare and I wonder if I should say something, but neither of us does. She looks away first.

"I'm different." She straightens the corner of the paper she just placed on the table.

"You certainly are."

She's not looking at me but there's an extra beat before she speaks again, like I've ever so slightly confused her.

"To them, you are their boss, a billionaire, someone who could stop them from ever getting another job again."

I've never asked for validation from anyone in my life, but something in me wants to ask, *and what am I to you?* But I don't.

"I know." I take the piece of paper and sign it.

"Thank you," she says. "And I've found someone you might want to think about for hotel manager."

I squint at her. "You've what?"

"I know you've left that to the search firm, but they haven't come up with anyone you like so far, have they? I just started looking through industry articles and LinkedIn and I came across someone I think you'll like."

"Who is it? You?"

She tips her head back and laughs. I can't help but smile because it's the most joyous thing that's happened to me all week. I can't imagine Kate is an easy person to make laugh, and the fact I've managed to imbues me with a certain amount of pride. "No, silly," she says.

Has anyone ever called me *silly* before?

"She's been working in Asia for the last decade, but she trained at the Four Seasons in the US."

"Talk to the recruitment agency. I'm sure they must have considered her."

"I don't think so. She has no managerial experience."

I widen my eyes. "Kate, come on. I need someone *very* experienced."

She shakes her head. "You are one hotel in rural England. You're not going to attract someone on their way up at one of the big chains."

"I don't see—"

She puts her hand up, palm facing me to stop me from talking. I go silent from shock more than anything. I don't think anyone has ever done that to me in my life. "I've tracked her career. She's excellent. More than capable. And she's in her early forties. She wants to come back to the UK. She was born here, and her kids are eight and six; she wants them to finish their schooling in the UK."

I sigh. "You've spoken to her? This wasn't part of the

brief. We have plenty of time to find a manager. We need to build the hotel before we staff it."

She shrugs. "As soon as we have the planning permission, we'll have an open date. Staff need to be trained. They need to be recruited. We have no one to run and organize all those workstreams. You need someone with loads of energy. Someone hungry for success."

"I'd prefer someone experienced. Someone with a track record of success."

"I don't think that's who you need."

I don't even bother answering because what she's saying is ridiculous.

"What's the incentive for someone with a track record of success in the luxury hotel industry to come and work here? You have no established brand that will look good on someone's LinkedIn profile and there's little opportunity for promotion. You need someone looking for a long-term role as much as a next step."

I sit silently, taking in what she says. No one had said this before. Recruiters just nodded their heads when I told them I needed an experienced, successful manager. Maybe Kate is right and I've been thinking about this all wrong.

"Who's your suggestion?"

She slides out her tablet and passes it to me. "Olga's very experienced—just not at the top job. But she's managed people and she's worked very closely with upper-level managers."

"So, why hasn't she had a top job? There must be something missing."

Kate sighed. "She's a woman. Plus she has kids. She doesn't fit the mold."

"You're telling me she hasn't had a top job because the hotel world is sexist?"

"Probably. Or maybe she didn't want it until now. You can ask her when you interview her. Tomorrow at ten. I checked your diary with Michael."

Kate stands and reaches for her iPad.

"You're incredible," I say. "You've done everything I thought you would and more."

Our eyes lock and a frisson of electricity passes between us.

She swallows and then says, "Thank you for trusting me with this job."

"Thank you for doing it so well."

She leaves and it takes me twenty minutes to refocus—to think about something, anything, that isn't her.

* * *

BECK and I are having lunch at the pub and we're sitting at what I now consider my regular table. Kate isn't on shift, though she's still here a few nights a week despite the salary increase she negotiated from me.

"It's good to be working with you. Would you have thought it would happen when I met you up a mountain, all those years ago?" he asks.

"Working with you isn't surprising. Buying two- and three-bedroom new-builds in Cambridgeshire from you just isn't how I thought it would happen."

He chuckles and looks at the menu. "Yeah, me neither."

"So have you abandoned Mayfair, the place where you made your name?"

"Not at all. This high-volume residential stuff is a bit of a hedge in case the London market tanks. I've got to see how it goes, but I've been thinking about setting up another division. High-quality housing on the outskirts of large villages. Small developments. No one else is doing it."

"Makes sense to diversify."

"Which is what you seem to be doing. Life in the English countryside suits you. You don't miss New York?"

Honestly, I haven't missed New York at all. "New York is still there," I say.

Our waitress comes over and I'm slightly disappointed when she doesn't make a menu recommendation, complete with nutritional insights.

"I'll get a ginger beer," I say. "And the Cobb salad."

"Sounds good. I'll have the same," Beck says to our waitress.

"So you think you'll settle here?" he asks. "You clearly like being in the UK."

I laugh. "I don't think I'll settle anywhere. Here is good for now. I'm closer to my extended family, although I haven't seen them as much as I wanted to. I'm going up in a couple of weeks though. I guess at some point, I'll go back to New York. Or maybe I'll spend some time in London. It depends on the next opportunity. Do you ever consider investing and developing in countries other than the UK?"

"Now we have kids—or a kid—I don't want to be traveling. I want to see her grow up. I want to hang out with Stella when I'm not working. If we travel, I want us to travel as a family. I have a good life and I want to enjoy it. I wouldn't rule it out in future, but I'm not looking for anything outside of the UK. Why? Did you have something in mind?"

I laugh. "It wasn't a leading question, I just thought you must get opportunities farther afield, yet I know you're firmly based in the UK."

"Yeah, I dabbled in Dubai for a couple of years, but

Stella hated it and didn't want to travel with me. I don't want to be anywhere she's not."

"Stella's great."

"She is. And has plenty of single friends if you want a set-up. She actually told me to tell you that. I don't usually play matchmaker."

"Thanks, man. I'm...I haven't really been dating since I got here."

"Doesn't sound like you."

"I mean, I haven't taken a vow of celibacy or anything. I've just been..." I can't say I've never gone this long without sex, but it's difficult to remember a more celibate time in my life. "I'm actually working with someone who—"

"I have to stop you. I don't know if you know this about Stella, but if I don't tell her everything about my friends' romantic lives, she'll chop my balls off. So just imagine you're talking to us both."

I chuckle. "Nothing I'm going to say has to be kept from Stella. I actually wasn't going to say much at all, other than I've never noticed how...attractive someone doing a good job is." I wince. That can't be right. "I don't know if I'm being an idiot. I work with competent people all the time, it's just—"

"You're talking about Kate?" he asks.

I look up and meet his eye. "How'd you know?"

"Because she's very good at what she does. And...she's attractive. There's an energy between you two."

"An energy?" I ask, intrigued.

"Almost like you're communicating without speaking. I've only seen you together a couple of times, but there's a connection there."

"We had sex. Maybe that's what you're seeing. Before I bid on Crompton. When I first came to have a look around."

"But not since?"

I shake my head. "She works for me now."

"My wife works for—nah, who am I trying to kid? My wife and I work together. Makes sex better I think."

"Did you always work together? I can't remember how you guys met." Beck was single when I met him, but it wasn't long before he met Stella.

"She blackmailed me for a job." He grins at the memory.

"Really?"

"Sort of. I needed something from her. It was payment. But agreeing to her terms was the best deal I ever made."

"I never really saw you settling down."

"It's a cliché, but I'd never met anyone before Stella who I wanted to settle down with. I'm sure it will happen to you."

"I'm sure it won't. I don't really commit to anything."

"Well that's just bullshit. You commit to all sorts of things—buildings, investments, your family. You just haven't found a woman you want to commit to. That's all."

Is it as simple as that? I never graduated college, never lived in an apartment for longer than eighteen months— maybe even a year. Beck isn't like me. I'm hardwired to move on. "Maybe."

"But you like Kate?" he asks.

"Yeah," I say. "Working together makes it complicated. There's the entire abuse of power thing, so..."

"Yeah. It makes it more complicated. But you're not going to be her direct boss forever. And she's an adult. She's over twenty-five and her prefrontal cortex is fully developed."

I chuckle. "Yup. All that is true." Beck is right. There's an energy between us I've never had with anyone at the office. Maybe that's because I haven't slept with anyone I've worked with before. Or maybe Kate is different. Maybe I want her more than I've ever wanted anyone before.

"But one thing I'd say," Beck says. "Don't waste an opportunity because you're afraid."

"Afraid?"

"It's easy to become excellent at the things we're already good at. You got good at making money early, right? You earned millions before you finished university. And you became excellent at it. And you're excellent at spotting investment opportunities." He shrugs. "You get what I'm saying. I'm sure you can pick up women, no problem. But maybe you could be good at other stuff, stuff you're not good at yet, if you practiced."

"You mean like surfing?" I ask.

He laughs. "Maybe surfing. Maybe taking a woman out to dinner and talking to her about stuff and not just flirting long enough to get her in bed. Maybe exploring a connection that clearly pushes you out of your comfort zone." He pauses, giving me time to make sense of what he's saying. I guess the look on my face reveals his advice isn't exactly landing. "Ask her out to dinner, mate. That's all I'm saying."

TWENTY

Vincent

Dinner. Dinner. Dinner. It's all I can think about since talking to Beck last night. He made it sound like I could just ask Kate out, that she'd say yes and that it would be no big deal. If that were true, why wasn't I able to find a single moment to actually ask her today?

I'm a pussy. That's the reason.

I glance at my watch and realize she's probably left for the day. With that in mind, I pick up my laptop and head back to the office from the boardroom. Michael always has the most up-to-date version of the project plan pinned to the wall in there, and I liked to check over it in hard copy every now and then to make sure nothing has fallen through the cracks.

I open the door, slide my laptop on my desk and nearly jump ten feet in the air when Kate says, "Hey."

I snap my head around. She's at her desk.

"I didn't know you wore glasses," I say. The black

frames suit her, emphasizing her small nose and high cheekbones.

"They're new," she says. "I'm not used to staring at screens so much. I guess it took its toll quickly."

This is my opportunity. We're technically off the clock, so I'm not actually her boss at this moment in time. I can ask her now. "You're not working in the pub tonight?"

She shakes her head. "Tomorrow night. Tonight I'm trying to solve a problem here."

I take the couple of steps to her desk. "Anything I can help with?"

"I'll come to you when I'm ready for you to make the decision."

I sit down on the corner of her desk. "Ask me now."

She pauses what she's doing and takes her glasses off. "Okay." There's an edge to her voice like she's expecting a fight. Maybe she'll get one. I probably should hold off the dinner invitation until we're on neutral territory, or at least until we're not in the office. I could go into the pub tomorrow night when I know she's working.

"It's about the moldings in the ballroom." She seems reluctant to continue.

"Okay."

"You know if I don't get the answer I want, I'm going to hound you until I get my way." Her expression is blank. She's not joking.

"I do know that," I reply, wearing the same serious expression.

"Stella wants to completely replace the moldings in the ballroom. There was a flood in there and it's quite damaged, particularly in the northwest corner. I think we should have a bespoke mold made of the surrounding moldings and only replace the sections we need to replace."

"Presumably the sticking point is cost."

"And time," she says. "I think we can jiggle the timetable to accommodate things. But it is more expensive. And the moldings won't look as crisp as they would do if they were all new."

"But you want to preserve what's there."

She nods. "The history."

"I agree," I say, and stand.

"You agree?" She sounds shocked, but she shouldn't be. I almost always agree with her. Sometimes it just takes me a while.

"As long as you can find the cost savings somewhere else, which shouldn't be difficult given the budget for goddamn drapes." I step away to go over the project plan pinned to the wall behind Michael's desk.

"Exactly." Her voice is animated, and I have to look away to stop myself grinning at her like an idiot. Her pleasure is completely infectious. "I think we just switch out the fabric in the study and we'll cover costs." She pauses and wrinkles her nose. "And maybe we change the rug choices in there too."

"You'll figure it out," I say.

She's silent and then I feel her stand next to me. She's not touching me, but she's about as close as it's possible to be without touching.

"Thank you," she says.

"You don't need to thank me for giving you a job you're great at. And anyway, you already thanked me." I glance at her but her gaze is fixed on the project plan.

"Not for that," she says, her voice soft, just above a whisper.

"Then what?"

She pauses for one beat, then two. "For always being the man you say you are."

My heart hitches in my chest and for once in my life, I'm stunned into silence.

She turns to face me and I keep staring at the wall, concerned that if I look at her, I won't be able to hold myself back from telling her all the things about her I just can't get enough of.

"Vincent Cove, will you look at me please?"

Here goes nothing. I take a deep breath and turn.

She places her palm on my chest and its heat burns through my shirt. I want to rip open the fabric and press her skin against mine.

"Vincent. I've been as patient as I'm prepared to be."

I frown in confusion.

"Will you kiss me already?"

A grin tugs at the corners of my mouth. "Kiss you? That doesn't seem very...professional."

Her gaze falls from mine, as if she's accepting defeat.

I shouldn't have said that. This is no time to tease, no time to pretend I haven't been desperate to kiss her since I met her and every moment since.

"But it's all I think about," I say and slide my hand on top of hers to keep her touching me. "The first thing I wonder about in the morning and the last thing that circles my brain at night."

She glances back up. "Kissing me?"

I nod slowly.

"Then why haven't you? I see you every day."

"But for now, I'm your boss and...things are complicated." I don't elaborate. I don't tell her I can't offer her anything more than here and now. That I'm not the kind of man who makes promises about the future. Or even considers a future outside of my work. She's not asking those questions.

"Don't overthink this."

I chuckle, because that's exactly what I've been doing. "I've been wanting to ask you to dinner."

"Like a date?" she asks, beaming up at me.

"Yeah. I have a friend in Cambridge who opened his own restaurant. It got its first Michelin star this year."

Her smile withers, her gaze hits my chest and she freezes.

What changed so suddenly?

"Could we have dinner closer to home?" she mumbles.

"What?" I laugh. "At the Golden Hare?"

She looks up, pain in her eyes. She was serious. And I'm an insensitive asshole.

"If that's where you want to go, that's where I want to take you."

"You know I'm not myself when I go too far away from home."

How could I have forgotten? "Leave it to me," I say. "I'll make sure our first date is on the grounds."

She relaxes again and the smile creeps back. I thread my fingers into her hair, bend, and sweep my lips over hers. Her hands slide over my shoulders and I take a deep breath, savoring the moment, committing it to memory. I circle my other hand around her waist and pull her against me. I've been thinking about this for so long and now it's here. She's here. She's in my arms, right where I've wanted her for weeks now. The feel of her hands on me and the way my skin warms under her touch, the way she fits against my body... It just feels right.

She lifts up onto her toes and takes over the kiss. At first it's small and chaste and perfect. Then she opens her mouth and I can't help but groan at the invitation to more.

How did I get so lucky?

Our tongues press and breaths mix, our bodies so close but not close enough. Her skin is so smooth, so soft, so delicate, and as my stubble grazes it, I have a primal desire to leave a mark so she never forgets how good this feels.

Her hands roam my body, up my back, across my shoulders and then down my waist to my belt. Her fingers hook onto the leather as if trying to find a way in.

I break our kiss and step away.

She freezes and looks at me like I just punched her. "What?" she asks.

Why did I stop things? I want her. She clearly wants me. Why am I holding back?

"I want to take you to dinner," I say.

"Great," she says like I just asked her to print off a copy of the rug quote. "Can we get naked already?"

"Here?" I ask and glance up and around.

"Are you shy?" She glances up at the dramatic chandelier above us. "Or romantic? You prefer candlelight and Bach playing softly in the background?"

"I don't think I've ever been accused of being romantic." I don't add the silent "but" echoing in my head.

"Your bedroom?" she suggests.

What's been building between us hasn't moved for so long and now it's going too fast. I want to slow it all down and figure things out. She steps forward and burrows her finger between the buttons of my shirt, finding my skin and adding fuel to the fuse of my desire for her.

"Kate," I growl.

She tilts her head. "Or here?" She takes a step back and slides onto her desk.

If I fuck her here, I'll never be able to concentrate in the office again.

But I have to fuck her.

Right now.

I grab her hand and pull her off the desk and out of the office.

My bedroom it is.

TWENTY-ONE

Kate

It's like my body disconnects from my brain whenever he's around. I've tried so hard to stay professional. To *not* want him. Given I'm in his bedroom, his hands on my bottom, my skin buzzing from being so close to him, I'd say I've officially lost the fight.

"I've tried so hard to stay away from you," he says, hitching up my skirt, pressing me into the door behind me. "I don't know what's wrong with me."

"I know," I say, my fingers fumbling with the buttons on his shirt. "We just need to get it out of our systems." At least I hope that's what this is—just some kind of chemical misfire that will right itself after an orgasm. Or maybe two.

His skin is hot and tight and my stomach swoops at the feel of him and the thought that we're minutes away from being pressed against each other.

He dips and presses kisses to my neck. The scrape of his five o'clock shadow is like the scrape of a match against the strip, igniting my lust. Why have we wasted so much time trying to avoid each other when we could have been doing this all along?

I press my hands flat against his chest, and he tips his head back and sucks in a breath like just the touch of my hand has the potential to send him over the edge if he doesn't steady himself.

What is it with this man?

Is it him? Or us together that seems to be so explosive?

"You need to be naked," he barks and brushes my hands away. He fiddles with the buttons on my blouse and then growls before simply ripping the fabric apart, then pulling off by bra.

I've seen it happen in movies, but no man I've ever been with has been so desperate to get me naked that he's *ripped* my clothing. It's even hotter in real life—maybe because I can see the tendons in his neck tighten with effort, and the heat in his eyes. He wants me. Badly. It all notches up my desire and when his hands cup my breasts, I can do nothing but whimper.

It's as if the noise pours a bucket of cold water over him and unexpectedly he takes a step back.

"What?" I ask as if yanked from a deep sleep.

He shrugs off his shirt. "Not like this," he says, discarding his shirt behind him and pushing his hands through his hair. "I want to take my time. I want to be fully conscious. I want you to know exactly what I'm doing."

"I'm conscious," I say. Is he stopping this? Because I'm going to be *extremely* pissed off if I'm orgasm-free when I leave this room.

He puts his hands on my hips and it's relief I feel at his touch. He turns me around and for a moment, I think I'm about to feel him between my thighs, when he unzips my skirt and pushes it to the ground.

"I want to see all of you. I don't want to fuck like animals—even though that's exactly what my body is telling me I need right now. If we're doing this, then it's not some quick fuck. It's going to be the best sex you've ever had—that *I've* ever had."

I turn around and stroke my hand down his face. "It already is." He closes his eyes and presses a kiss to the inside of my wrist. "I'm not sure if I should have given you formal feedback after the first time—happy to fill in an online questionnaire this time—but for the record, you touching me is better than anything I've ever felt before. Your kisses, the way you understand my body, everything. It's all better than anything I've ever experienced."

His gaze flits from my eyes to my mouth, down my body and back up again, almost as if he's looking for the right words. "You're...incredible."

I can't help but smile. It's almost like this confident, unshakeable American is...kind of awkward.

He takes a half-step forward, pinning me against the door, cupping my face and kissing me like he wants to prove me right. Like he wants me to be assured his kisses are the best I've ever tasted, the most passionate, shudder-inducing kisses I'll ever experience.

The passion rachets up between us and I press my hand on his chest.

He doesn't want it to be frantic and frenzied. He wants things a different way. So that's what he'll get.

I shimmy out of my knickers before hooking my fingers into his waistband and crouching so I can take off his trousers and boxers.

"You're beautiful," he says as I stand. He presses a kiss to my lips. His expression is almost pained and part of me wants to delve deeper—understand what's behind it.

"Is it better now we're both naked?" I ask, taking his hand in mine.

He nods and leads us over to his bed. "I just needed to find some self-control."

The bed's high and I sit on the edge, pulling him between my legs. "I want you to be exactly yourself with me. If you don't feel like you can resist me, that's okay." I smile up at him.

He chuckles. "You can joke, but it's a problem."

"For me too," I confess.

It's lighthearted between us, but we're only telling the truth. My mind skips to thoughts of the future. How will I feel when he leaves? What will happen to Crompton?

"You okay?" he asks.

I nod. I can't think about anything apart from Vincent and me and enjoying this moment between us right now.

He reaches between my legs and instantly I'm liquid. What is it about the way he touches me?

His erection stretches flat against his stomach in front of me and I sweep my fingers up his length. He growls, half desire, half disapproval, and steps back. Again.

"Vincent," I say as he turns his back. But he's not teasing or torturing me. He's obviously looking for condoms.

"This bed," he says. "I've imagined you in it from the first night I slept in it."

He finds what he's been looking for and retakes his position between my legs.

"Wish granted." I smile up at him.

He shakes his head, the corner of his mouth turning up slightly. "You've been occupying far too much of my brain."

Expertly, he opens the condom and stretches it over his erection.

"You mean, the brain in your..." I point at his penis as he grips the base.

"My...?" he asks as he smooths the head down my folds. I sigh, relieved this is finally happening. "You should really be able to name it given I'm about to fuck you."

My stomach flips over at his raw words. I can't wait.

"Maybe I'll be able to after you fuck me," I say, and my entire body throbs. I'm not sure if it's because he's teasing me or because I'm looking forward to what's next or I'm about to come.

He holds my gaze and drives into me. It's not harsh or sharp, just determined and unrelenting. When he finally stops, I gasp, exhaling with short, sharp breaths.

"Oh, baby, we're only just getting started and you need to catch your breath already."

Did he talk to me like this the first time? Maybe it feels more intense because I know him now. Because tomorrow he's going to look at me with the same eyes he's staring at me with now, only from behind a desk.

I steady my breathing and just as I feel settled, he starts to piston his hips, pushing in and drawing out, filling me to the brink and then leaving me bereft with every press and pull. I curl my fingers around his shoulders, gripping as if my life depended on it, trying to resist the inevitable for just a few moments longer. It's futile. My orgasm has been pacing up and down, waiting for the feel of him for weeks. Now he's here, between my thighs, leading a marching band to my climax.

"Vincent!" My voice is breathless and desperate. I'm so close and if he doesn't stop, I'm only going to last a few more seconds.

"I'm here, Kate. Let go."

I don't know if it's his permission that sends my orgasm

shooting up my spine or whether it was what came before it: *I'm here, Kate.* The words tumble about in my brain as I press my fingers into his skin. He smooths his hands up my back and pulls me close and I realize my entire body is convulsing.

What did he do to me?

He slows but doesn't stop, pushing into me, through my orgasm, keeping us together, linked, bound.

I cup his cheeks and pull his face to mine, pressing my lips against his, stealing wet kisses as we both fall back onto the bed.

"This feels too good," he says. His jaw clenches as we shift, the new angle causing pleasure bombs to detonate inside me.

"So good," I say.

His eyes grow dark and the crease between his eyebrows deepens as he builds his pace. It's like he's studying me, watching for micro-reactions he then responds to with changes in speed or pressure or position.

He's always thinking about me. About us. This man could have anything, anyone he wants, and he's choosing me. Choosing to kiss me, make me happy, make me come. The thought is intoxicating.

I bend my legs either side of him and then wrap them around his waist. He groans as he continues to push into me.

"I need more of you," he says, and he lifts one leg higher, pushing deeper, faster, harder. I'm gone, spiraling, another orgasm making my blood spin in my veins. I can't see or hear or feel anything but him.

"Fuuuck," he says as he pushes in again, and I feel the deep, steady throb of his climax.

I don't know if it's the sound of his heart beating or

mine, but for a few seconds or minutes or even hours, that's all I can hear.

Until finally, he says, "What are you doing to me?"

My entire body is still pulsing, but from somewhere I get the energy to move. We shift. He takes off his condom and I sit astride him.

"I'm greedy for you, Kate. I'm not sure I've *ever* been greedy for anything in my life before."

My heart inches higher in my chest. I press my hands onto hard abs.

"I'm here," I say, repeating his words back to him. He closes his eyes in a long, lazy blink.

"Then here is the only place I want to be."

And just like I've been saying for weeks now: everything would be perfect if we could stay exactly *here* forever.

TWENTY-TWO

Kate

Granny's going to hear it eventually, and frankly, it won't be *that* eventually, since the news will reach her within five minutes of me sitting down with Vincent. Better to tell her myself, rather than have Sandra or Basil break the news.

"Vincent Cove asked me to dinner," I say as I scroll through my phone, sitting at Granny's kitchen table.

This time, the click of her needles does falter, but she covers it well and gets back on track. "What did you say?"

"I said Vincent Cove asked me to dinner." Granny's hearing is normally sharp as a bat's.

"I mean what did you say to Vincent," Granny says.

"Oh, I see. I said yes." I reply like it's no big deal. As far as Granny is concerned, I don't date. She doesn't need to know about the casual hook-up with the Australian barman who worked behind the bar a couple of summers ago, or the occasional stranger who comes onto me at the pub. They were nothing serious—certainly not worth mentioning to Granny.

Vincent is different. Vincent, she'd hear about.

She stops knitting and puts her needles on the table. "I'm delighted for you."

"It's not a big deal," I assure her.

"It doesn't have to be," she replies.

"And it's not like he's going to be my direct boss forever."

"No. And who cares if he is? You only live once, my darling."

"And it's not like it's going to turn into anything serious. Don't start wedding planning. I'll probably hate him after spending a nonstop two hours in his company." That is unlikely to be true. The more I get to know Vincent, the more time I spend with him, the more I like him. Yes, I am attracted to him—the guy is hot, there's no denying it. But I like his mind, the way his brain works. He's focused on the bottom line, on profits and his investment. But he's also a man who stays true to his word and has a sense of responsibility to Crompton and the people here. I can't help but like him more for seeing that side of him.

"Just enjoy yourself. Are you going into Cambridge?" she asks.

I scoff. "We're going to the Golden Hare." That's what Vincent said, wasn't it? He knows I don't want to leave the estate.

Granny visibly deflates.

"What? I know the menu and I'll have all my nutritional requirements satisfied."

Granny raises an eyebrow. "Is that what they're calling it now?"

Did I mishear her? "What did you say?"

"Nothing. But why not venture into Cambridge?"

"Why would we? It's nearly half an hour to get there. I

don't know the restaurants there and I'm not sure if I'll like it."

"It would be a nice change."

"But it might not be. It might be an awful change."

"If it is, it will only last two hours."

"You keep telling me life is short. Why would I waste two hours—no, three hours, when you factor in travel—on the off chance something is nice, when I can get guaranteed nice when I'm at the pub?"

Granny looks down with an expression of disappointment.

"You don't ever believe I'm happy at Crompton. I don't need to leave. Everything I want and need is here."

She shakes her head. I thought she'd be delighted I'm going on a date, which hasn't happened in forever. "What did Vincent say when you said you wanted to go to the Golden Hare?"

"He was fine with it. Of course."

"And if there's a second date?" she asks. "You going to go to the tea shop?"

I roll my eyes. Of course we wouldn't go to the tea shop. But I'm not sure where we would go and the idea needles me in my chest. "Marangon's," I say, talking about the Italian place in Watley.

"It closed two years ago," Granny says.

"It did?"

She doesn't answer, but picks up her knitting and starts again. "Basil was telling me all about a course he's doing online. It's live, in a virtual classroom."

Thank goodness for the change in subject. "On Zoom?" I ask.

"Teams," she says. "I think some of the schools did it like that during lockdown."

"Yes, I think they did." I resume scrolling through my phone.

"Means you don't have to go anywhere, really."

Something tells me we've not changed subject at all.

"And I was talking to Sacha, whose friend's daughter, Aurora, did therapy online. Got to see one of the top psychologists and never left her sitting room. Apparently it was marvelous. She'd had a problem getting over an old flame. Therapy helped her tremendously."

"Good for Aurora. Despite the fact she's a perfect stranger to me, I'm happy for her. I really am." My tone is sharp and defensive. I instantly regret it.

Granny's needles continue to *click clack* in the silence between us.

"I'm sorry, Granny. I shouldn't have spoken to you like that."

"It's okay. I know it's a prickly subject."

"It's not really prickly. I just don't need therapy."

"Well if you say you don't need it, that's that. But it's an option if you decide the world outside Crompton is one you want to get to know."

"You're acting like I never leave the grounds! I still have four shifts at the pub every week."

Her expression is of pity, but she's misunderstood me. I'm happy. I don't need her pity.

"And soon I'll be moving behind the car park in the village. I'll be at least three miles away from Crompton."

"If you say so, darling. But if money is an issue, I'd be happy to pay for you to have a chat with someone. You had a lot to cope with as a child and no one can judge you for the choices you made."

"I chose to make myself happy," I say simply. We don't often talk about or even allude to life before my mother died. Or if we do, we focus on the happy times when I was at Crompton. But life outside the estate with my mother wasn't often happy. It was stressful and tense. I remember coming to Crompton and being relieved to find it was the exact opposite. I used to leave notes under my pillow to the fairies, asking them to let me stay forever.

And then my mum died and I *did* stay.

Adult-me knows I didn't cause my mum's death, but for a long time I carried the guilt of thinking that by wanting to stay with Granny so much, I willed Mum dead. I know better than to wish for a life different from the one I have now—one where everything and everyone in my orbit is familiar. Or it was.

Until Vincent.

Now I want him. But he won't stay. I have to push thoughts away of any other scenario, because he *will* leave.

And I will stay.

I can't wish him here.

I won't.

But one of the things I can take comfort from is, whether or not Vincent is here, the leaves on the trees of the estate—none of which Vincent is cutting down—will turn yellow, then orange and red in the autumn before falling. They'll bud and grow again next spring. I might not be working at the tea shop. I might not be living on the estate, but I will be here, every day, welcoming people to Crompton and watching the trees change as the seasons pass.

My grandmother stands and moves toward the kettle. "Would you like a cup of tea?"

The question is a perfect palate cleanser. "Yes, please. I bought some green and popped it in your cupboard. The studies are saying the antioxidant benefits are incredible, plus it can protect the brain against Alzheimer's."

"Really?" Granny says. "I'll give it a try. Maybe I can swap out at least one cup of my builders with green."

Joy blooms in my heart and I stand. "That's great. I'm so happy you'll try it. Let me make it."

"We can do it together, and you can tell me all about how you ended up saying yes to dinner with Vincent Cove." She wraps her arm around my waist. "I'm sorry if I skipped over that bit."

"It's okay, Granny. And I want to assure you, you don't have anything to worry about. You gave me such a wonderful childhood in this magical place. I just love it."

"I know you do. But you can love more than one place. Just like I don't have to give up my normal tea, just because I'm trying green tea. I'm open to the idea that I might like green tea even better."

I get what she's saying. Maybe it would be nice if we went to dinner somewhere other than the pub. Somewhere a little more private, where absolutely everyone didn't know everything about me, even if it does require a car ride to get there. One evening can't hurt, can it? The problem is, it's easier said than done. Logically she's right. The problem is, logic doesn't override fear.

Granny tugs me around the waist and gives me a kiss on my temple. "And what about Vincent? Does he think Crompton's magic?"

I laugh. "He thinks it's a good business opportunity. But you never know, I might convince him of the magic at some point."

"Has he ever been married?"

I shake my head. "I don't think so, but we haven't discussed it." We've spent a lot of time in each other's presence. And we've had sex. But we haven't shared much about our pasts. In some ways, it's a relief. "I suppose that's what dinner is about. Getting to know each other. It's nothing serious, though, don't worry. I'm not about to get my heart broken."

"Oh I don't worry about that," she replies. "In fact, it might do you good. You're stronger than you think, you know."

What Granny doesn't realize is that I don't want to be strong. Being strong is overrated. "No danger of that. But it's nice to be asked out to dinner by...a man like that."

"And he's from New York. I heard he has family over here."

"Yes. An aunt, uncle and five cousins. They're split between London and Norfolk."

"And Crompton is the halfway point between them all. Imagine being so rich you could choose to buy a stately home because it's halfway between two places you want to be."

"I get the impression Vincent is rich enough to get just about everything he wants."

"I can only hope," Granny says, and I don't quite know what she means, but I understand her tone well enough not to ask.

TWENTY-THREE

Vincent

I'm not sure why, but I have a jittering in my stomach that, in theory, I associate with nerves.

But I don't get nervous.

It's just dinner, but I showered after work. And changed into a clean shirt and pants. It's probably too smart for what I've got planned, but I don't want to make Kate uncomfortable if she's dressed up. Plus, I want her to know that an evening with her is worth dressing up for, no matter where we're going.

I start down the stairs of Crompton House.

"You're leaving?" Michael says from the bottom.

"It's nearly seven," I say. "Can this wait until tomorrow?"

"Sure," he replies as I pass him and head to the front door. "Have a good time on your date."

I don't look back but raise a hand in thanks. I didn't expect we'd keep it a secret. After all, we're having dinner in front of the entire village. I'm just not quite sure how Michael knows.

As I close the doors of the house behind me, Basil is tending to the plant that grows up the front of the house. I don't want to tell him I want it cut down completely. The first impression of the house must be clean and crisp and welcoming.

"Good evening, Basil," I say as I pass.

"Good evening, Mr. Cove." He won't call me Vincent, despite me trying to convince him. "Enjoy dinner with Kate."

Clearly it's safe to say every person who works on the Crompton Estate knows I'm taking Kate out to dinner. "Will do."

The staff cottages are just a few minutes' walk to the side of the house, and I can see them as soon as I turn left. The jittering ramps up as Kate's cottage comes into view.

Could I actually be nervous about taking a woman to dinner?

Surely that's impossible.

I get to her front door but Kate opens it before I have a chance to knock. I can't stop the huge smile sweeping over my face. This is my favorite side of Kate: straightforward, unabashedly herself. There are no games, no keeping me waiting, no pretending she wasn't watching for me.

"You look so handsome," she says and my heart lunges toward her like a puppy enjoying her attention.

I finally break eye contact and glance down at her. She's wearing a white sundress with pink flat shoes, her hair is loose and the sun-kissed ends curl up as if trying to find the last of the day's rays.

She looks like an angel.

"You're gorgeous." Without thinking, I take her hand and press my lips to her knuckles, like I'm the earl of Crompton eight generations ago.

She laughs at the gesture, and I can't help but laugh too. What are we doing? I feel like a kid. All the jittering in my stomach has been pushed out by joy and warmth and happiness.

"To dinner," I say, reaching out a hand. She slides her palm against mine and I feel something. I can't quite put a name to it, but it's an easy, light comfort. That's how it's always been with Kate, even when I first saw her singing show tunes and introduced her to my family.

"I bet you really wanted to go somewhere other than the Golden Hare," she says. "You've eaten in the pub a lot recently."

"We're not going to the pub." Before she has the chance to panic, I add, "But we are staying on the grounds of the estate." I guide her down toward the back of the house.

"Where are we going?" she asks.

"I thought a picnic would be nice," I say.

She squeezes my hand. "Really? That sounds wonderful. I know the perfect spot."

"I've set up a couple of things. I think you'll like the view."

We round the corner of the house and the lake comes into view, along with the temporary gazebo I've had erected. Only three sides are open, with the side facing the house covered—my modest attempt at privacy. Little good it will do, since the entire world seems to know about our date.

"What's this?" she says. She tries to catch my eye, but if I look at her and see her smiling as wide as I think she is, my heart might fucking combust. So I keep my gaze focused forward.

"I thought you might enjoy dinner down by the lake."

"That's a wonderful idea." As we get closer, she sees the flowers decorating the roof of the gazebo. "Are they from the garden?"

I shake my head. "No, but I managed to track down the same types of flowers. Or Molly did. My idea. She executed."

"Vincent Cove, you're quite the romantic."

Under the gazebo is a table set for two. The table decoration is an elaborate floral display among the glass and china.

"This is...beautiful. I should say, even more beautiful. The lake—this view—it's my favorite place in Crompton."

"I thought it might be. The Crompton Instagram page gives you away." I pull out her chair and she sits.

"I suppose it does. But I'm not sorry." She sweeps her hand across the table, taking in the gazebo and the lake. "This is perfect."

I take a seat opposite her. "Is that why you don't like to leave? Because it's so beautiful?"

She looks a little embarrassed, and I wish I hadn't said anything. I just want to know everything about her. "You're probably used to much more glamorous places, right? Which one is your favorite?"

I don't know if she's *deliberately* trying to change the subject, but I'm not going to press her. "I like getting to know a new place. I like figuring out the coffee shops, which parks are the best to run through, when a place gets started for the day. Like in DC, it's insanely early. New York is a little later. Arizona, much later. In each city, the air always smells slightly different and the sun sets in a different way. I guess I just like all the sensory inputs."

"Is it New York that has your heart?" she asks.

"Wherever I lay my hat..." I say.

"So nowhere feels like home to you? What about your aunt and uncle's house?"

The hairs on the back of my neck bristle. "Well they've moved since I first stayed with them as a kid, but I like hanging out with them, for sure."

"But it's not your safe space?"

The word *safe* echoes in my head. I turn it over and silently repeat it to myself.

"Vincent?"

"Sorry, um, no. I don't think I have a safe space. I don't really get attached to places."

"Oh," she says. "So you move around a lot?"

"Wherever work takes me." It had occurred to me to give up having any kind of home base entirely. I could just live out of hotel rooms. It's what I do most of the time anyway.

"Were you an army brat or something?"

It's not the first time someone has mistaken me for an army brat. If only the explanation was that simple.

"Or something," I say.

"You moved around a lot?"

Lucky for me, our conversation is interrupted as the waiter brings two tequilas and two glasses of champagne. Just to cover all bases.

"But you always sit at the same table at the Golden Hare," she says, smiling at me. "Maybe that's how you make yourself feel at home—you create routines and patterns in ways people normally wouldn't. When *normally* people would go home to the same city, the same flat, the same people."

I laugh. "I hadn't thought about it like that. Does that

mean you don't like routine and patterns—if you've always lived in the same place, around the same people?"

"Maybe. I've never thought about it, but actually I don't think so. I have lots of routines and patterns. I find them reassuring. Crompton was my place of calm and certainty growing up when there was little about my life that was calm and certain."

I narrow my eyes, wanting to hear more.

We raise our glasses. "To a lovely evening," Kate says.

"It's already my fav—" I start to say, then interrupt myself. "*Second* favorite evening since I came to Crompton."

A delicate blush brushes over Kate's cheeks. "Mine too."

The tequila melts down my throat and I stretch out my legs, brushing against Kate's and resting there—connecting us. The silence between us is so comfortable, it's as if we've known each other for years.

"You were talking about your mom when you said things for you weren't calm and certain?" I want to hear more.

She pauses before she says, "My mum was a...she said she had gypsy blood. That seemed to be a catch-all for her being a disorganized mess."

"She grew up on Crompton?"

"No, although my grandparents moved here before I was born. My mum moved out from living with them into her boyfriend's house as soon as she could. And then onto a friend's sofa and in with another boyfriend, and then into a house share with ten other people. Her life was always like that. She thrived on chaos. On not knowing what was next."

"And that didn't change when she had you?"

"Maybe it got worse. I think having a child, someone tied

to her, made her crave her freedom more. I just remember my life being very different to the lives of my friends. I would miss school, turn up late to parties, change schools, miss gymnastics. My life lacked...structure." She moves the salt and pepper shakers like they're pieces on a chess board—forward, back, left and right. Her fingers are delicate but deliberate.

"So you like that everything stays the same at Crompton." Things are starting to slot into place.

She looks up and smiles and it's all light and brightness. "Well it did until you got here. Although I'm not comparing you to my mum."

I offer a half-smile in return. "I don't think I thrive on chaos." I've never really given it any consideration before, but then I've never been compared to someone else like that before. "Like you say, I have patterns and routines in the world I'm in."

"And you're not irresponsible," she says. I'm not sure if it's a question.

"Like how?"

"I mean, you're responsible. You're the exact opposite of my mum. You're never late to work or unavailable if Michael or I need you. It's not like you'd miss an important hospital appointment or something. You do what you say you're going to do. And that's...nice." She smiles but it's smaller this time, full of warmth and stacked with relief and reassurance. It isn't the smile that greeted me at the tea shop or the Golden Hare—it's more intimate than that. A smile reserved for only a fortunate few. Somehow, I inherently understand how lucky I am.

That smile is a hook that catches on my insides.

"Change doesn't have to be chaos," I say.

She pulls in a breath and nods. "I know. And I'm still

going to work at the estate and the village is just five minutes away and...it's going to be fine."

"It could be better than fine," I say.

"So I keep being told."

I don't want to lecture her. It isn't my place. As much as she doesn't like change, I can't stay in one place too long—we are the opposite sides of the same coin. I'm in no position to be throwing stones in my very glass house. "It explains...a lot about you."

She laughs, and I love the way her eyes shift from serious to sparkly. "I'm trying to think about it in a different way. I love Crompton. I think it's the most beautiful place in the world and when it's a hotel, lots more people will come and get to see why I choose to be here."

I nod. "You'll get to show them how to enjoy what you've enjoyed for so long. The only thing is, when they meet you, they might never want to leave."

Our eyes lock and for a moment I can't imagine being anywhere but here for the rest of my life—because why would I go anywhere when being here, with her, is so damn great?

"Vincent Cove, do people know how sweet you are?"

"Sweet? Not sure I've been called that before." *Asshole* is the way the last woman I was sleeping with referred to me, just before I left New York.

"Then I can only think most people aren't as lucky as me and don't get to see that side of you."

My insides tug again and I want to say something just as complimentary that tells her I feel the same, but our waitress comes over with our first course.

"Oh this is different. It looks...incredible," she says, staring at the plate. "When you said picnic, I thought we'd be having M&S sandwiches and a bit of Sandra's Bakewell tart."

"Not quite," I say. "The friend I told you about, with the place in Cambridge? Well, I borrowed his chef for the night."

Her eyes widen. "Gosh, I suppose it pays to know people."

"Unfortunately it means you don't get input on my nutritional needs tonight."

She laughs. "Phew. I get a night off. What a blessing."

"What's that about?" I ask her. "The food stuff? You harbor some desire to be a nutritionist or something?"

"No, I never thought about that actually." She pauses. "I just like people to take care of themselves. And I like it when I can help."

Of course she's not being bossy or provocative, like a stranger to her commentary might think. She's trying to help people make the best choices for themselves.

"Do people know how sweet you are, Kate?"

"Tell that to a woman who came in a couple of months ago, who ordered the chicken on my recommendation but failed to tell me she was allergic to peanuts. She had to get stretchered out of the pub."

"Jesus."

"Good intentions don't matter if you kill someone."

"She died?" I ask, trying to disguise my shock.

"No, she was fine. Turns out it was just a mild attack. She thought she'd grown out of her peanut allergy and she used the Golden Hare to test out her theory."

"Wow. Maybe 'nice' isn't the word I'd use for you anymore. More...potential murderess."

She laughs. "I can add that to my LinkedIn profile. What about you? Ever tried to murder anyone? I bet you're so rich, you could have someone killed if you wanted to."

Is that the kind of man she thinks I am? "I've never found a price list, but maybe I am. I can honestly say I've never tried to murder anyone or have anyone murdered on my behalf. I'm not sure I've ever even been in a fight before."

"What about enemies? You must have made plenty in your time."

"You think? Because I'm an asshole?" I'm getting whiplash from this girl.

"No, silly," she says, and like a chump, the pull inside me grows stronger. "Because you're powerful and rich and stuff. Don't people like you make enemies?"

People like me? The question takes me by surprise. She sees herself as someone inherently different from me, but I'm sitting here thinking how similar we are. "Maybe?" I say. "But it's never been my aim to make money at other people's expense. I might be naïve, but..." I trail off. I'm not sure what she's trying to get at. "I can be an asshole," I confess. "I'm sure I've pissed people off. But I don't deliberately try to hurt people or take something unwillingly given."

She starts to speak but stops herself, then reaches for my hand across the table. "I feel bad," she says. "I wasn't trying to say you're an asshole. I wouldn't be having dinner with you if I thought that."

I shake my head. "That's okay. I'm sure people have thought worse of me."

"One of the disadvantages of spending all my time at Crompton is that I tend to assume the world out there is worse than it is. I feel safe when I'm in this bubble. Nothing can go wrong—"

I pull my hand from hers and scratch the back of my head. "Until I arrived. Right?" This evening was going south quickly.

She looks me in the eyes, her expression serious. "This is terrible. I'm saying the wrong things all the time. I'm the arsehole, and if I'm not careful, we're going to be enemies by the end of the night." She stands, and I think she's about to run out when she says, "We're going to start again."

"Okay?" I'm confused, but she's right—tonight took a wrong turn and I'd like to get back on track.

She rolls her shoulders back, shakes out her hands and takes a deep breath before sitting down opposite me again. "I'm Kate Saunders. I'm twenty-seven and I think you're completely attractive."

I can't help but laugh. She smiles and I feel like a teenager, like I did earlier in the evening—like I always do when I'm around her.

I start to speak but she leans in and places her index fingers across my lips. "And not just because you've got a pretty face and an amazing bod. I like that you're a man of your word. That you care about the people of Crompton. You're buying up properties to rent out to those of us displaced by the renovations; you're investing in retraining people. You're a good man, Vincent Cove, and I do know that, despite practically accusing you of having mafia connections or whatever I was going on about."

Her words erase all the discomfort and irritation. It feels good to have her tell me what she thinks in such crystal-clear terms. She starts to lean back but I catch her hand and thread my fingers through hers.

"I think you've got a pretty face and amazing bod too."

"So poetic," she teases.

"They're your words!"

She frowns like she's taking absolutely no responsibility for them and I shake my head, trying not to laugh.

"I like how you handled that bump in the road back there."

"Yeah, anyone would think I'm a pro at this dating thing," she says.

"You're not?"

"Well, if we don't count Basil, then no."

I close my eyes and scrunch up my face. "Please unsay that."

"He's an amazing lover. Wears his cap in bed."

"Stop." I rub my hands over my face. "You're the worst."

"I'm kidding about Basil. But not the stuff I said about you." She looks at me, her gaze soft but purposeful. "I'm sorry. Did I fuck this up?"

I shake my head. "Never."

Our waitress comes over with our food and wine.

"Speaking of Basil, it seems like it's impossible to keep a secret around here," I say. "Michael and Basil knew we were having dinner tonight."

"And tomorrow morning, people might put two and two together."

"Does that bother you?" I ask. I'm not sure how I'd feel if everyone around me knew everything about my life.

"I mean, we're not doing anything illegal. These people care about me and want me to be happy, so no, but I could imagine there might come a time when it might."

"When I'm with my cousins, it's similar. Everyone's in everyone's business and it doesn't come from a bad place. And it's nice, because you feel part of something, but I have the luxury of disappearing if it gets overwhelming." I sit back in my chair. "Huh. I never actually thought about that. I've always felt like I'm on the periphery when I visit them."

The prickling on the back of my neck has returned. "They're very welcoming and I definitely feel like part of the family, but obviously, I'm not their brother or their son—I'm always slightly removed. But maybe I put myself there. It's always felt...*I've* always felt like a bit of an outsider. I guess that's why I ended up at medical school."

Kate's eyes widen. "Wait, you're a doctor?"

"No, I dropped out. I was making investments, even back then, and struck lucky a couple of times. I realized medicine wasn't for me."

"Wow," she says.

"I've always loved my cousins. I wanted to live with them in the UK—I'd spend summers here and hated going back to the States. I wanted to be just like them, and they're all doctors. Well, two of my cousins aren't anymore. But I saw studying medicine as a membership card."

"If it makes you feel any better, you didn't seem like an outsider when I saw you all in the tea shop."

"They're great. They would never deliberately treat me differently. But I'm their cousin. Their nephew. That's just a fact. I'm actually going up there in a couple of weeks. You should come with me."

"Where?" She looks like I just told her JFK walked into the Golden Hare with Marilyn.

"To Norfolk. My aunt and uncle are celebrating their wedding anniversary. They're having a family celebration. I'm going up to see them." Suddenly, I realize why she's shocked—not because I'm asking her to go away with me, but because I'm asking her to leave Crompton.

"Think about it," I say, trying to soften the invitation.

She nods. "I will."

"It's not a big deal if you don't want to leave Crompton."

"With you," she says.

"With me."

"I don't know if I can," she says. Her voice a whisper. "But I don't think I've ever wanted to more."

My heart crashes against my ribs. I want to gather her up in my arms and promise to keep her safe. It's not a sensation I'm used to, but there are lots of things about Kate and Crompton that are extraordinary.

TWENTY-FOUR

Kate

It's not like I don't see the long stares or hear the open-ended questions. I just don't respond to any of it the morning after my date with Vincent.

It's nice to have people care. But no one needs a front-row seat for what's happening between us. Because it's casual and fun and he'll be leaving soon.

Except...being with him feels better than I've ever felt with someone before. And I don't want to admit that to anyone. Not even myself.

I scoop up my laptop and notepad and stand. "Is Vincent in the boardroom?" I ask Michael.

"I think so," he says.

I've not seen him this morning—well, not since I left his bed anyway—but that's not unusual. And it's better in a way. Because if he was in the office, sitting at the desk opposite me, I'm not sure I would be able to concentrate. It's bad enough as it is. I can still feel him all over me from last night. His teeth on my neck, the press of his hand on my bottom, the drag of him between my thighs. At least with him in the next room, there's half a chance I'll get something done today. But first, I need to get his decision on something.

"Thanks," I say and close the door behind me.

I knock on the boardroom door and just like normal, I don't wait for a reply before I enter.

What's not normal is Vincent's grin as I step inside.

"Hey," he says.

"Good morning," I reply, trying to inject a bit of formality into the room.

He stands and rounds the table.

Before I can step back or tell him to keep away from me, he has me pinned up against the wall, pressing kisses into my neck.

"This isn't very professional." I can feel myself turning liquid under his touch. Even though I came in here with a real, important purpose, I can't imagine a scenario in which I would ever ask him to stop touching me.

I can't move my arms because I'm holding a laptop, so I'm helpless as he trails his tongue from my neck to my collarbone and down my chest.

"Vincent," I say. I sound breathless and squeeze my thighs together, trying to maintain a modicum of control. "We need boundaries. Rules. We can't do this here and now."

He pulls his mouth away and sweeps his hands up my sides. "I know, but I can't—it's been hours since I touched you like this."

"Vincent," I say, but it's not an admonishment. More a cry for help.

He pauses, pressing his forehead against mine. "Tell me what the rules are."

My heart is pounding against my sternum, trying to get out and make out with Vincent all by itself. "Not in here. Not during working hours. I'll meet you by the lake tonight. We can go for a walk."

He pulls in a breath like he's trying to summon all his will and then steps back. "You're right." He pushes his hands into his pockets like he doesn't trust them to be free and heads back to his chair. "Jesus. I want to drink you down like a cold glass of water."

"I'm not sure if that's a compliment." I slide my laptop onto the table and take a seat. "Although it's good to stay hydrated." I flip open my computer. "I want to talk to you about the flower gardens."

"Haven't we had this conversation? Did you think about coming to Norfolk with me?"

My eyes widen. "Rules. Not here. Not now."

"I'm asking you a question, not trying to remove your panties."

I shift a little in my seat, acutely aware of the lace around the edge of my underwear. This guy is more than distracting. "Let's just keep the personal stuff for after work." If I start thinking about Norfolk and how I'm going to tell him I can't go, I'm going to veer off course.

"If you insist," he says.

"I do. As I said, I want to talk to you about the flower gardens. I've come up with something I think you'll...tolerate." I pull out the presentation pack from under my laptop and slide it across to him. "Please turn to page one." I know Vincent's not going to accept something that doesn't make financial sense—not even if I'm a cold glass of water. Hopefully, I've found a compromise. "This is a plan of two-point-five hectares of land on the edge of the Crompton Estate. The gardens currently open to the public are ten hectares, so this would be about twenty-five percent of the size."

I'm grateful he doesn't interrupt me. He'd be in his rights to throw me out. He's heard me go on about these gardens for weeks and weeks now, and he's been consistent in his refusals. Kind, but consistent.

"At present this area is open field, so it would require complete redevelopment. The advantage of this plot— outlined in red on the slide—is that it abuts a small B-road."

I'm proposing to develop the area into a series of small gardens that honor those that have been at the house for hundreds of years.

"Please turn the page to slide two." I glance up from my computer to see if Vincent is taking this in. He's diligently turning the page and studying the slide, and my heart inches higher in my chest. "I propose to fund the ongoing maintenance of the gardens through volunteers and ticket sales. The current gardeners at Crompton are all prepared to volunteer their spare time to create and maintain the garden. In fact we think there will be more volunteers than we actually need. Because you are concerned with the privacy and exclusivity of the estate for hotel guests, we propose to not allow visitors through the Crompton Estate, but to allow them access from the B-road just three days a week. Four days a week, the gardens will be reserved for the exclusive use of hotel guests."

"Is the house visible from the gardens?" Vincent asks.

I'm prepared for the question. "The house is visible from a portion of the site. A row of high hedges or a decorative wall will maintain complete privacy for hotel guests."

"But presumably if the guests are on the golf course or simply walking the grounds, visitors to the gardens would be able to see them."

"In some areas, yes," I admit.

"Unless we could do some more screening."

"Hedges would be the most effective. We could screen off the entire area. But it would cost more money than I've budgeted." How many people does he really think are going to have their golf game disrupted by people looking at a flower garden? I don't say anything, but I think it as loudly as I can.

"Okay," Vincent says. "And what about the initial cost to establish the new garden?" He flips another page in the presentation packet. "There's a pond here, hard landscaping, lots of planting obviously."

"Fundraising. We won't be able to do everything at once, but we think we could get there." The fundraising part will be difficult. But where there's a will, there's a way. "I also thought it would be a nice idea to take cuttings and seeds from the plants in the current gardens, to replant in the new site. A heritage garden will mirror what you're doing with the house—taking something old and reworking it into something that works for the present day."

He doesn't respond, which I take as a good sign—it isn't like he's scoffing at my ideas or dismissing them before I have a chance to finish. So I continue my presentation and take him through the plans for the garden in detail. I go through the financials in terms of how much it will cost in upkeep and worst-case scenarios in terms of visitor numbers.

"One final thing on the last page."

I wait for him to flip over.

"These Airstream trailers can be converted into a tea shop of sorts."

He laughs and shakes his head. "You thought of everything."

"Do you have any questions?" I ask.

He looks me straight in the eye and all of a sudden, I feel his mouth on my neck, his thigh between my legs, his hands everywhere.

I pull in a breath and look away.

He chuckles, and I'm more than certain he knows exactly what's going on in my brain.

"Speak to Michael and get him to put you in touch with my CFO in New York. I want to see if there's a way of creating a charity we can donate that piece of land to. That will make the financials look healthier."

"You'd donate that land?"

He grins. "Don't think I'm going soft on you—it might be good for me. Planning approval will probably come easier if there's an additional nod toward historical preservation of a sort. It also might mean more write-offs for the hotel. Speak to him and come back to me."

"I will."

"I'm not promising anything," he warns.

I gather up my laptop and stand. "I know. But thank you for hearing me out." He didn't have to sit through this and take me seriously. He could have been irritated I refused to drop it. He has other things to focus on. But Vincent Cove is a good man. And I'm finally starting to understand how lucky I am to know him.

TWENTY-FIVE

Kate

I'd agreed to meet Vincent for an evening walk, and I know he's going to ask me about Norfolk. I wish I had an answer for him—or rather, I wish I had the answer he wants.

I knock on Granny's door and walk in. She's sitting at her kitchen table, knitting.

"Hi, how was work?" she asks, smiling up at me.

"Shall I put the kettle on?"

"Sounds great."

"How was dinner last night?" she asks as I turn on the cold tap.

"We had five courses," I reply.

"Not quite what I was getting at."

I pull in a breath, turn off the tap and then place the kettle in its holder and switch it on. "It was nice. I like him, but..."

Granny doesn't ask me to elaborate. I pull two mugs from the cupboard and the green tea from the counter and set about making our drinks.

"He wants me to go with him to visit his family in Norfolk."

She nods. She knows she can't say, "How lovely, darling. When do you leave?"

"It's nice of him to ask me," I say.

"Very nice," she agrees.

"But...it's been a long time since I've gone that far away."

"It has," Granny says.

I know I'm a twenty-seven-year-old woman and traveling a couple of hours in a car is no big deal to most people my age, but it is to me.

"Part of me wants to go." I like Vincent and I think it would be fun to spend more time with him. It would be nice to see him with his family again. "I just don't think I can."

"How long is he suggesting you go for?" Granny asks.

"The weekend." He didn't actually tell me the exact number of nights we'd be away. But "the weekend" definitely implies a multiday trip.

"And then you'd come back," she says.

I nod and pour the hot water from the kettle and bring both mugs over to the table. "I made green tea and didn't ask you. I'm sorry."

"This is lovely. And good for me. Thank you."

I lean back on the chair and take a sip of the tea. It's still too hot, and I wince a little at the burn.

"How do you think you'd feel if you did go?" she asks.

"If I went and it was okay, I'd feel...relief."

"In what way could it not be okay?"

I sigh and set down my mug. "Well, that's the problem. I don't know. If I stay here at Crompton for the weekend, I know exactly how it will be. I know it will be lovely." I will iron my bedsheets and maybe steal a rose from the side of

Granny's house for the bud vase that sits on my kitchen windowsill. I might have a drink with Meghan and wander down to the lake, see if I can spot any frogs. Every moment of every day wouldn't be set in stone, but what I do will be set within certain parameters. No surprises. No emergencies or disasters.

"In what way do you think a weekend in Norfolk could be wonderful?" Granny asks.

I close my eyes and a movie plays in my head. I imagine walking down the beach holding Vincent's hand. I imagine his family gathered around the fire, playing charades and eating a roast dinner on Sunday before we're forced to say goodbye. I've only had a chance to see that kind of thing in a film. But Vincent's offering the chance for me to be there, to experience it myself. "There are lots of ways it could be wonderful. I think...I'd like to try."

Granny sets down her knitting and takes both of my hands in hers. Her eyes are glassy and her voice cracks when she speaks. "That's wonderful, my darling."

"Do you think I can? I want to."

She closes her eyes and takes in a deep breath before opening her eyes and smiling at me. "Wanting to is a start. *Wanting to* is a *great* start."

"And I get to come back," I say.

"In just a few days," Granny says.

"Why do you think that Mum was like she was?" I ask. "Do you think she didn't like to be tied down with a child, so she ended up overcompensating?"

"She loved you," Granny says. "I know she did. But I don't think she understood how to be anyone other than the person she was. Even as a small child, she got bored easily, hated going to bed, going to school, doing anything she had to repeat over and over. Trying to get her to clean her teeth or even bathe regularly was a battle. Most kids can avoid things they don't like, but it wasn't that she didn't *want* to brush her teeth, it was more she didn't want to be tied down to anything. Not even taking care of herself."

"You're not like that. Grandpa wasn't like that. Where did it come from?"

Granny shook her head. "I don't know, my darling. Some people are just born a certain way."

"Is that why she didn't like to go to the hospital appointments?"

"I think so. It was easier to manage when she was a child, because I would force her to do some things, but as an adult...there was little hope she would manage her condition on her own."

"You knew that?"

"Your grandpa would keep track of the appointments and beg her to get to them. He was devastated when she died—we both were obviously—but I think he thought he should have done more. I don't know why I accepted it more easily. Maybe I felt it in my womb or something, but I just saw it happening as soon as we got the diagnosis. I had a long time to grieve my daughter before she died."

My mom's epilepsy shouldn't have been fatal. If she'd just taken care of herself, she could have lived a long and happy life. If she'd made her hospital appointments, taken her medication regularly...she could have lived. A small voice in the back of my head adds *for me. She could have lived for me.*

I try and steady my breathing to stop myself from crying —not for my mother, since my grief for her has long passed, but for my grandparents. They saved me, yet it doesn't make up for the suffering they endured because of my mother's choices.

"I always worried more about you after her death," Granny continues. "I still do."

I know why she worries. Even though we don't talk about it much, it's always there, buried slightly under the surface. It's not until now that I've even considered anything changing. Guilt catches in my throat at the thought of worrying Granny all these years.

I swallow. "But what if I say yes to Norfolk and then I can't do it? What if I get there and something happens or I just can't handle it and I need to come home?"

"Then you come home," she says.

"Vincent's going to think I'm a lunatic."

"If he does, his opinion doesn't matter. You should talk to him, though. Tell him how you feel. Tell him what you're struggling with."

I'm not sure about that. I confided bits and pieces to him about the importance of Crompton to me and why I'm so attached to it. I haven't been quite as clear about the extent of my attachment. Namely, how I don't like to leave. Ever.

"Trust him," she urges. "If he's half the man I think he is, he'll be sympathetic."

I know he's a good man, but what I have to tell him will surely change how he sees me. He could be sympathetic, but want to rescind his invitation when he hears what I have to say. But since I can't leave Crompton without talking through the variables in Norfolk, and since Vincent is the only one who can set my mind at ease...it looks like I'm in for a difficult conversation.

TWENTY-SIX

Vincent

She's sitting on a blanket by the lake, facing the water. I can't wait to hear what she's thinking about. I don't know if it's because I don't have all the distractions of London or New York, but a woman has never taken up so much of my brain as Kate does. We saw each other last night and it didn't occur to me not to see her tonight. I've probably not spent as much time with any woman in such a short space of time as I have with her. And all I want is more.

She hears me coming and turns, giving me a huge, welcoming smile I can feel in my bones.

I bend and kiss her on the cheek.

"I brought a picnic," she says. "It's a lot less...amazing than last night, but I hope you haven't eaten."

I shake my head. "No, I finished a call, changed and came straight out. This is great." I peer into the bag she's brought and sit next to her.

"How are you?" I cup the back of her neck and lean over to kiss her again.

She smiles around the kiss like it makes her happy. I'm happy I'm making her happy.

When did I get so soppy?

We break our kiss and she looks around, presumably to check no one saw.

"First, ginger beer!" She holds up two glass bottles and a bottle opener. "You're in charge of that."

I take the bottles and pop off the tops while she unpacks the food. "It's just some cheese and crackers and fruit."

"Thank you," I say. "It's perfect. And sitting here...the view. You. Life is good."

She smiles and pulls in a breath. "I want to talk about Norfolk."

I hand her the bottle of ginger beer and her gaze sticks firmly to the bottle. "Okay."

My mind starts to flood with possible things she wants to talk about and I push them all out and listen to her.

"I've told you a little about my mum. Well, even before she died, Crompton was my safe haven. Afterwards, it became a sort of life raft. It felt that so long as I was here, I'd be safe. Happy. I built my life around that. Around not leaving the place where I was happy."

"That makes sense," I say, smoothing my hand up her arm.

"I took it to an extreme. At first I only ventured into the village and that was fine, but about a year after Mum died, we went into Cambridge and Grandpa had his first stroke. Not the one that killed him, but he ended up in hospital. I didn't leave the estate then for a long time."

"I get that."

"I went to school of course. First in the village and then when I was twelve, I moved to the high school about four miles away." She pauses, obviously feeling uncomfortable.

"You don't have to talk about this if you don't want to, but I want to hear everything you've got to say. Take all the time you need."

She slides her fingers inside the cuff of my shirt and looks up at me. "Apart from school, I never went anywhere. When I was in sixth form, I saw a therapist. I wanted to go to university, but I wasn't sure I could move away from Crompton. Still, I applied. I got in. And from somewhere I found the courage to go. And then during my first term, Grandpa had another stroke." She swallows and glances down at the blanket. "That time he didn't make it."

I stroke her face, wishing I could take away her grief.

"Anyway, I dropped out of university and never went back. At that point my brain associated being away from Crompton with...pain. Disaster. Sadness. The wind changed and somewhere in there," she taps her head, "I've convinced myself that if I leave, something bad will happen."

My heart thumps wildly in my chest. She really never leaves this place. It's more than just a preference for home—what she's describing is a goddamn disability. "You don't have to come to Norfolk," I say. Should I be encouraging her to go?

"The thing is, for the first time...in a very long time, I want to go somewhere outside of Crompton. I don't know if it's the prospect of having to move off the estate, the house changing into a hotel or..." She looks at me, the sunlight on her face making her skin luminous. "Or you. But I'd like to come to Norfolk."

I pull her onto my lap, wrap my arms around her waist and bury my face in her neck. I don't know how this works exactly, but I'm grateful she's confided in me, told me as much as she has.

"But..." She presses her hands against my chest and I look up. I grit my teeth to stop myself from kissing her. "I'm not sure I can."

My chest collapses in on itself, pushing the air from my lungs. "I can help you."

"Would you?" she asks.

I want to tell her I'd do anything for her. Thank goodness she starts talking again before the words escape.

"It's just... I might not make it all the way. And if I do get there, I might need to come back early. But I'd love to meet your family again. I'd love to see the sea, feel the sand under my toes. More than all that, I'd really like to spend the weekend with you."

My chest expands and I can breathe again. "If we don't make it all the way, we don't make it all the way. If we need to leave early, we leave early. We'll have a great weekend, whatever happens."

She presses her cheek against mine. "Thank you," she whispers.

I push my fingers into her hair and press a kiss to her mouth. "You taste so good."

"It's the ginger beer," she says.

I chuckle. "It's not the ginger beer. It's you. It's all you. *You're* so good." I can't find the words to describe it, but everything she does makes me like her more, every word she utters makes me want to listen intently. Every time she touches me, she sets me on fire. It's like she was made for me.

"You're so good," she says back and then slides her tongue into my mouth. I groan at her hot, sweet, wet kisses and smooth my hands up her back.

"The downside of living next to the office is, I know

Michael is still working upstairs so we can't go back to the house."

She laughs. "And I live next door to my grandma. Maybe it's not that I want to go to Norfolk at all. Maybe I'm just horny and would like a bit of privacy."

I groan again. "My aunt and uncle will expect us to stay with them." I shake my head. "I'll book a hotel."

"Are you sure? I don't want to offend them."

"Of course I'm sure. It might even be easier for them. All my cousins are going to be there apparently. They're going to have a full house as it is." The prickles at the back of my neck return.

"How long will it take to get there?" Her voice is breezy, but the way her fingers fiddle with the edges of my shirt tells me the question is important.

"Less than thirty minutes," I say, hoping that's the right answer.

"But you said it was outside Blakeney. That must be at least two hours."

"By car it probably is, but we'll take a helicopter."

"A helicopter?" She chokes on the words. "What are you talking about?"

"They'll want us to come up on Friday. I have calls all afternoon. We'll just take a chopper. That's what I normally do from London."

"Sounds expensive," she says, shifting on my lap so her back is against my front. She starts to stack cheese and sliced apple on a cracker, passing it back to me before building another stack for herself.

"Sounds quick. Plus, if you want to leave, we can be back at Crompton in no time."

She reaches up and behind her, stroking the back of my head. "I really want to do it."

"I'm literally going to be holding your hand the entire time."

TWENTY-SEVEN

Vincent

Despite the collection of voices on the video call, the *flick-flack* of helicopter blades cuts through the room and I'm eager to bring this meeting to a close. Everyone's on a high. Planning permission was officially granted a couple of days ago and it's our first meeting to set out the operational plan.

Kate was right about the hotel manager, as she is about most things—not that I'm about to tell her that. Olga hasn't relocated to Crompton yet, but she's been able to join this call. She's taking us through her workstreams on the project plan.

"I have a number of contacts at various five-star hotels in London and I'll be arranging for each of the department heads to shadow their counterparts during training."

It's a great idea. Some of the department heads will have never worked in a five-star hotel. They need to understand how things work in practice, not just theory. That doesn't stop me wondering how Kate, as head of the guest relations team, will deal with a trip to London. Despite

Cambridge being so close to London, she's never mentioned having been there. Maybe our trip to Norfolk will be the start of something. I'd love to take her to Sicily. And Paris. Even New York.

God, what's happening to me? We've only been dating a couple of weeks and I'm already imagining vacations with her.

"Great idea, Olga. I think it makes sense if Michael sits in on your workstream meetings. I don't need to be in on those."

Michael shoots me a look. I haven't discussed it with him yet, but he's ready to move on from being my assistant. I need his brain in the depth of operations.

I check my watch. It's nearly six and I need to get going. "I'm going to leave Michael to chair the rest of this meeting. Enjoy your weekends."

As I knew he would, Michael competently steers the focus of the meeting back on Olga's update and I slip out the door.

Kate is waiting at the bottom of the stairs. "I left my suitcase here. You said leave it by the door and I did and now it's gone." There's a look of panic in her eyes.

"It's fine. I had Molly take it up to the hotel earlier today so she can unpack for us and get us situated."

"We're going for two nights. It will take me less than ten minutes to unpack."

I shrug. "You need a quick shot of tequila?"

"No, I think I'd like to be sober when I meet your family."

I wince. "Not sure that's a great idea, but let's go with it."

The door to the house opens and the pilot appears to lead us out to the chopper.

As soon as the doors are closed, silence envelops us. I lean across and fasten Kate's seat belt.

"It's quiet," she says. "I thought we'd have to put—" She gestures to her ears. "Thingies on our heads."

"No thingies," I say, trying not to smile too hard at how sexy she looks in navy shorts and a white t-shirt.

I interlace our hands as we take off. I probably should have asked her if the helicopter is okay, but knowing Kate, she would have spoken up immediately if the prospect frightened her. This way, at least she's not stuck in a car for hours, worrying about what lies ahead and what she's leaving behind. "Ever joined the mile high club?"

"A couple of times actually," she says, giving a brief shrug like she's uber relaxed. She can't fool me, though—her free hand is gripping the armrest like she's on a roller coaster. "Only when I fly private though. Obviously."

"Obviously," I say, stroking her hand, trying to help her relax. "It's a lot easier this way. Turns a two-and-a-half-hour journey into thirty minutes."

"Is this how you live?" she asks. "Helicopters and people helping you with your luggage? People unpacking for you—that's the craziest thing I've ever heard."

I laugh. "Compared to most people who have a lot, I live quite modestly."

She glances around the cabin of the helicopter and it's clear she's not awed or impressed. She's just observing. "Well, not by my standards."

"You've lived most of your life on the estate of a home that looks more like a castle than a private residence. I don't believe displays of wealth are really that surprising to you."

"It's different. Partly because I don't live like that and it's not like the earl used to invite me up to the house for dinner. And partly because I don't think the earl had much...cash. Although he did have people in helicopters visit him."

"You're right. It is different. How are you feeling?" I ask.

"Surprisingly okay, if I don't look down."

"And about being away?"

She nods as if she's trying to convince herself she's fine. "Granny is going to text me regularly and knows not to ignore it if I text her. And the way I see it. . ." She threads her fingers through mine. "I'm taking a piece of Crompton with me in you." She looks up at me. "You're basically a very large key chain."

I laugh. "I've been called worse. That reminds me. I have something for you." I reach into the inside pocket of my jacket and produce a flat, blue box.

Kate narrows her eyes suspiciously. "A present?"

"You look like you think it might be a bomb," I say.

She laughs. "I'm just surprised. This is my shocked face." Whatever the expression, she's completely beautiful.

She takes the box from me. "Should I open it now?"

I nod and watch as she unties the white ribbon. She lifts the lid and removes the silver frame. It's a triptych: three small frames hinged together that open out into a series of three pictures.

"These are my pictures," she half-whispers.

"I know they're on your Instagram, so you can look at them on your phone, but I thought you might like to put this on your nightstand in the hotel. That way you can take another little bit of Crompton with you while you travel. As well as your oversized key chain."

She smiles and reaches for my face. "That's...'thoughtful' doesn't seem to be a big enough word. It's one of the nicest things anyone has ever done for me."

Warmth burrows into my stomach and I press a kiss to

her temple. "I want you to enjoy this weekend. But if you don't, I need you to promise me, you'll tell me. We can leave at any time. You're not going to offend anyone. These people are family."

She leans over and presses a kiss to my cheek. "Tell me about them. You must love them very much if you wanted to come to the UK to study and...buy a stately home to be closer to them."

"I do," I say. "They're more of a family to me than my own parents in many ways." I don't admit that—even to myself—very often.

"Tell me how?" she asks.

"My father was a gambler. I don't remember it being a problem before I turned eight. He always took me to soccer practice on a Saturday and we'd have family movie nights on a Friday night—he'd make popcorn and the three of us would sit under a blanket on the couch watching Disney movies. Both my parents worked, but both of them were around a lot." My most vivid memories of my dad were in my backyard. The sprinkler being on, chasing me around the yard with a water pistol, playing soccer and frisbee. He'd seemed so happy. My mom too.

"Sounds nice," she whispers, bringing me back to the moment.

"It was. And then on my eighth birthday, my mom answered a knock on the door and life was never the same again. I still remember the feeling of panic I had back then when I heard her arguing with the guy at the door. We were up early and she was cooking me pancakes, and because it was my birthday, they were going to be chocolate chip. She'd left them in the pan while she answered the door and...I can't remember what the man said, or I guess I didn't understand it. But my mother never yelled and she was half-shouting, half-sobbing. I'd never seen her like that. I went into the kitchen and turned off the stove and my dad came barreling down the stairs, yelling at the guy at the door. Then Mom started beating her fists on Dad's chest."

My throat tightens and I take a breath. It's been a very long time since I've thought about that day. Kate releases the armrest and sweeps her hand over my chest. "I'm so sorry. I didn't mean to upset you."

I've come to terms with what had happened that day. And all's well that ends well, right? I have a great life and it's probably as good as it is *because* of that day. "I'm not upset. I want to tell you." I don't know what it is about Kate, but I want to share this with her. I want to share everything with her.

"My dad had gambled the house away," I say.

Kate presses her mouth to my shoulder and it gives me comfort in a way I didn't realize I needed.

"We left that day. I stayed at a neighbor's house that night. They had kids my age. My mom didn't stay. I don't know where she went." I rub my brow with my thumb and forefinger. "We went back the next day and he was gone. Then we packed up and moved. I never saw my dad again."

"Oh, Vincent," Kate says. "I'm so, so sorry. I can't imagine what that must have felt like. Your entire life changed in an instant."

"I think you *can* imagine, actually. You must have felt the same way when your mom died?"

I wonder if that's why I gravitated to Kate. We both had our worlds rocked at about the same age.

"I've never said this to anyone, but I didn't feel the grief that most people would expect a kid to feel when their mum dies. I feel terrible for saying this and even worse for feeling it, but it was more relief I felt than anything else. I got to live with my granny and grandpa at Crompton. I knew exactly how my day was going to go. I knew I was going to have Weetabix for breakfast, get taken to school on time, get picked up at exactly three-thirty. I knew I was going to have my dinner at five sharp. It was the same every day, and I loved it. Life got better for me after she died."

I laugh, but it's not a laugh filled with joy. More irony and frustration. "It was the exact opposite for me. After we moved out of my home, we flew to the UK and came to stay with my aunt and uncle and cousins. It was the greatest summer ever. I missed my dad, but I accepted he wasn't with us because we weren't at home. It wasn't until we flew back to America, moved into a cramped two-bedroom apartment—without my dad—and I started a new school, that I realized life would never be the same again."

"I'm so sorry."

"I can't be angry, though, can I? I live a great life. I'm happy. I'm successful."

"Of course you can be angry. And sad and...everything in between."

I squeeze her hand, grateful she's here, next to me, listening to me, traveling with me.

"Maybe that's what drives you? You don't want to be in a cramped two-bed flat."

"Maybe," I reply. "I think that's why I don't get attached to places. I've never lived anywhere as an adult for longer than a year."

"Wow," she whispers. Is she wondering how long I'm going to stick around Crompton?

Because I am.

I don't want to say it out loud. But...maybe this time it will be different.

"What about your mum?" she asks, breaking the silence. "You never talk about her."

"We're not close. She remarried. Lives on the same street we moved out of when I was eight. Won't take any money from me."

Our conversation is interrupted by an announcement from the pilot. "Just coming in to land now."

"That's the house." I point to the jumble of buildings up ahead and laugh. "My uncle will be swearing about the noise and the dog will be going wild."

A smile blooms across her face and I'm not sure if it's because I'm laughing or because of the situation I'm describing. Maybe both.

"Remember, if you're freaking out, just let me know. We should have a private code or signal or something."

"Like what? I should wink at you?"

"I might not see it. What about telling me you got a message from your granny?"

"But that might be true and not an emergency. I could do a chicken dance? Start barking like a dog? Start singing show tunes? Or—wait for it, this is radical—maybe I should ask you for a private word?"

I chuckle. "Yeah, that just might be crazy enough to work. Although, you have a very pretty singing voice. You can sing to me anytime you like."

TWENTY-EIGHT

Kate

I remember Carole as soon as I see her. She has a kind face and hair that stands on end from the blades of the helicopter. She's wearing an apron covered in pictures of a man's face, and she's smiling ear-to-ear like the sight of me and Vincent is like spotting a double rainbow after a storm. I glance at Vincent as we cross the grass to greet them and he squeezes my hand. "I'm right here. Remember that."

"Vincent and Kate!" She grabs my hand from Vincent. "I remember you, my dear, from the tea shop. Jacob, it's Kate. Kate, this is Jacob, my oldest son. His fiancée has just popped to the loo. She's spending a lot of time in—anyway, we're so pleased to have you here."

I smile, despite not being sure if I might throw up from the surge of adrenaline or nerves or something. "Hi, Carole. Lovely to see you again."

She envelops me in a hug. "Let's go inside."

"Bloody helicopter," a man's voice booms as we enter

through the small door to a large dining hall with red terra-cotta tiles on the floor and white walls.

"John, say hello to Kate," Carole says.

"Not with this one, are you?" the man says, nodding at Vincent in the doorway.

I'm not quite sure how to react. Does he not like Vincent?

"Yes, Kate *is* with Vincent as you well know and we're delighted she could join us, aren't we?" Carole says.

"What's another mouth to feed?" John says.

"I have something you might like," Vincent says. Then, in a stage whisper, he says to me, "The thing about John is, he likes his wine."

Vincent turns and speaks to someone behind him. Maybe the pilot?

"I've got plenty of the malbec left," John calls to him.

When Vincent turns back, he's holding a wooden crate. "But have you tried the pinot noir?"

John's eyes sparkle mischievously. "You're a naughty, naughty boy, young Vincent, and that's exactly why I love you more than my own sons."

I can't help but laugh.

"Bribery always helps get John in a good mood," Vincent says, grabbing my hand.

"Carole, did we try the pinot noir when we were there?" John asks his wife.

We turn right into a kitchen. Vincent has to duck to fit under the lintel. It's a warm, welcoming room, with a battered pine table and the smell of delicious things on the stove.

"You're turning into quite the wine snob," Carole says to Vincent.

"He's always been a snob and not just about wine,"

Jacob says. "Quick tip for a weekend at the Cove house: ignore everything my dad says, eat everything my mum cooks and don't let the dog out."

"Shit," Carole says. "Where is Dog?"

"Who are we expecting when?" Vincent asks. "Oh and we brought these for you." Vincent hands Carole a bunch of flowers from the Crompton gardens I picked on my lunch break.

"Where did they come from?" I ask. "I thought I'd forgotten them."

"Molly brought them up with her," Vincent replies.

I try not to act shocked. I usually see Vincent in very different circumstances. Yes, he's the boss, and yes, he bought the entire Crompton Estate, so of course I know he's wealthy. I just haven't appreciated *how* wealthy. Not until today with the helicopter, the assistant. He's just so comfortable in all of it.

"Is that the minion you had dropping off the car in the drive?" John asks.

"That's my assistant who helps me with personal things," Vincent says. "For legal reasons, I don't refer to Molly as a minion."

"Shall we get this wine open?" John says.

Jacob had left the room and wanders back in, this time trailed by a pretty woman with long brown hair. Had I seen her at the tea shop? "Kate, this is my fiancée, Sutton."

Sutton and I kiss each other on the cheek. "I remember the first time I came here. It's pretty overwhelming, isn't it?"

I just smile. It's a lot. But it's great. Everyone is treating me like I've been coming here for years. It doesn't feel as alien, as scary and awkward, as I expected.

Out of nowhere, Jacob starts handing out champagne glasses to everyone.

"I thought we were going to try the pinot noir?" John asks. "I don't want bloody champagne."

"Honestly, give it a couple of hours and you'll never want to leave," Sutton continues. "Carole and John are secret witches and I swear there's something in the air here that makes you want to come back as soon as you leave."

"Witches." John tuts. "If we were witches, I'd be conjuring you all out of here. Carole and I would have the place to ourselves. We'd only allow Vincent to come up just so long as he brought some good wine." He turns to me. "Of course you'd be welcome too. I hear you're not a medic either?"

"Were you expecting me to be a doctor?" I ask.

"Absolutely not. Far too many of us under one roof as it is." He shrugs. "Although the number has shrunk recently. My son Zach has packed medicine in and is writing books now." He chuckles. "Can you imagine? He's terribly good at it. What do you do?"

"I work at Crompton, in the tea shop, and now I'm also Vincent's assistant's assistant. I'm hoping that when the hotel opens, I'll work in the guest relations team."

"She's going to *head up* our guest relations team," Vincent clarifies.

"A little toast," Jacob says. "To the calm before the storm."

"What does that mean?" Carole says. "What storm?"

"Just this weekend. It feels like every few months one of us brings a woman up here and expands our crew. This time it's Vincent. Next time maybe it will be Beau."

"Who would have Beau?" John asks. "They'd have to be desperate."

John is less than complimentary about his sons, but I get the feeling it's a bit of an act. They clearly all love him dearly. No wonder Vincent wants to be part of all this. It feels like a community, or a club with very exclusive, if eccentric, membership requirements.

"He's got a pretty face and could sell sand to Arabs," Jacob says. "He'll get someone to marry him."

My stomach roils. Is that what people are thinking? That Vincent and I are on our way to marriage? I don't let myself think about next week when it comes to Vincent, let alone the rest of my life.

"How's that Crompton place coming along?" John asks, interrupting my train of thought. "Is it the money pit I told you it will be?"

"We're breaking ground next week," Vincent replies. "I guess we'll know then."

"Well, Vincent," John says. "You have great taste in wine, women, and investment opportunities."

Vincent shoots me a look of concern. "By women, you mean Kate, right?"

I take a step closer to him and circle my hand over his back. He doesn't need to worry so much. I'm not made of glass. I'm also not blind to how handsome Vincent is and how that, combined with him being richer than any person I've ever known, means he must have his fair share of female admirers. I'm not an idiot. But I also don't want to think about anything but right here and now. I don't want to ruminate on what it means that Vincent brought me to a family occasion. I don't want to speculate on how long he'll stay at Crompton. We're together now and that's all that matters.

John scowls as if Vincent is being an idiot. "Of course I mean Kate. I've never met any of your other women, have I?"

Vincent freezes next to me and I can't help but laugh.

"Relax," I whisper to him. "I'm not freaking out and neither should you."

"Let's take our drinks out into the garden," Carole says. "Zach and Ellie should be here any minute. Jacob, can you get another bottle from the fridge?"

"Done," he says. "I'll bring two glasses. Dax and Beau aren't coming until later."

"Thank goodness," John says as he takes a seat around a huge, round teak table under a gazebo full of jasmine. "Three of you are enough."

We all sit down, Vincent one side of me, Sutton the other.

"What about Nathan and Madison?" Vincent asks.

"They're not here until tomorrow night," John says. "They have a human parasite of their own to deal with now."

Carole's sitting next to John and playfully kicks him. "That's our granddaughter you're talking about. We need to do something about seating. Our family is growing and I want everyone to be able to come together."

"We need to move into a bloody mansion," John says.

"Poor Vincent is having to stay at the Blakely Hotel. I don't like it," Carole says. "Not at all. He should feel there's room enough for him. Because there is."

I glance over at Vincent and a small smile nudges at the corner of his lips.

"That was my fault, Carole," I say. "I do hope I've not offended you. The truth is, I don't leave home very often at all, and I was a bit nervous about coming up here. I've not stayed a night outside of the Crompton Estate since I was at university. Vincent thought I might find it easier in a hotel."

"Oh darling girl," Carole says and my heart seems to bulge with the love she's sending to me. "I'm not offended at all. Thank you for telling me and we're very honored you decided to come and visit. This won't be the last time, I guarantee you'll be back." She glances at Vincent. "I know it. And next time you can stay."

"Where did you go to university?" John asks me.

This is followed by a groan of "Daaaaad" from Jacob, and mutterings from everyone else.

"What?" John asks, his expression affronted. "I only asked the girl where she studied."

There's another chorus of *woman* around the table and I can't help but laugh.

"I dropped out in my first term," I say. "But I was meant to study physics at Cambridge."

"What?" Vincent asks. "I didn't know that."

I shrug. "You don't know everything about me."

He presses a kiss to my cheek, then whispers in my ear, "But I want to."

My insides dissolve. I'm so pleased we're in a hotel tonight.

"Vincent says you lived in London for years. What made you come to Norfolk?" I ask.

"Can we talk about you going to Cambridge?" Vincent asks.

I laugh. "No. There's nothing to say."

"Vincent's bummed he's not the cleverest one in the relationship," Jacob says.

"Vincent's never the cleverest one in the relationship. That's why Cambridge kicked him out."

"Cambridge kicked you out?" I ask. "I didn't know that's where you went."

Vincent reaches for one of the pistachios that have been placed in bowls on the table and launches it at Jacob. "Cambridge didn't kick me out. Just like Harvard didn't kick out Bill Gates. *Really* clever people don't need university."

"This is how they show love," Sutton says to me. "I don't know if it works the same way in your family, but it took me some getting used to. Now I feel a little excluded if they don't insult me at least twice a day."

I smile, taking it all in. It's nice. It's warm and cozy and being here feels so special.

I glance at John, who's chortling away, clearly enjoying his sons and his nephew baiting each other. It's such a glorious, happy family. It reminds me so much of Crompton. Not the banter and the jibes, but the bond, the inextricable link you can't see, can't touch, but can't deny. It's everywhere, surrounding these people like an invisible steel ring.

TWENTY-NINE

Vincent

The stars here in Norfolk are one of my favorite things. I never get to see them in London.

"She's great," Jacob says.

We're sitting around the firepit after the anniversary dinner, toasting marshmallows and drinking wine, just like we've done hundreds of times before. Tonight feels different. Better. I always enjoy coming to Norfolk, but having Kate here has made everything exceptional. Even the wine tastes better.

"Gorgeous," says Dax. "Those legs."

I shoot him a look of disapproval. Although her legs do look fantastic in her shorts.

Kate has gone inside with Sutton and Ellie to try and find some brandy. Or at least I think that's what they said.

"You have my approval," Zach says.

"Oh, the one thing I've always wanted," I say, my tone dripping with sarcasm.

"She's really lovely," Beau says. "Kind but also funny. And a charades champion."

Kate has really thrown herself into the weekend. There haven't been any outward signs she was nervous or felt uncomfortable. The third time I asked her if she was okay, she laughed at me and said she'd tell me if she wasn't. It's like she's known my family for years. And it's like I've known her my entire life. It feels so easy. So right.

"Do you think you'll stay in the UK?" Jacob asks. "You'll have the hotel, and now you've met Kate."

"And us, don't forget us," Beau says.

I laugh and take a sip of my wine, to give myself a couple of beats to think about his question. "I don't stay anywhere for long."

"Maybe you've never had a reason to until now," Jacobs says.

My chest tightens like someone has wrapped a rope around me and is pulling. "I don't get attached to places. Or people."

"That's not true," Jacob says. "You're attached to us. We're your family."

"Attached? More like grudgingly tolerant." It isn't true and they know it. But it feels odd to admit I'm attached to them. The British Coves and the UK were the only light in a very dark time in my life and I can't help being drawn back to that light, to their life force.

"You love us," Jacob says, his voice serious, completely disregarding the banter baton I'd handed him. "We love you. We're family. We've never let you down. We'll never abandon you. You can be sure of us."

It feels like a stone has lodged in my throat. I nod, unable to think of anything to say.

"You've always been more than a cousin," Beau says. "It feels like you're one of us. A brother."

"Fuck, man, lay off will you?" I sit forward in my seat. "You're going to have me bawling in front of the woman I'm trying to impress."

"She's impressed," Sutton says from behind me.

I snap my head around, wondering if Kate is behind me too, but she's not, thank god.

"I love her," Sutton says. "She's so funny. She's completely unimpressed with the billionaire businessman part of who you are. She's exactly who you need. You want me to subtly ask her what kind of rings she likes?"

Heat flashes up through my body and I glance back at the house. I don't want Kate to overhear this. "Absolutely not. We're just hanging out. You know what I'm like. I have a girl in every port."

"Woman!" Sutton says. "And you're supposedly a womanizer, but guess what? I've never met any of these women. I'm not saying they don't exist, I'm just saying, no one has ever been to Norfolk. You've never brought any round to dinner. Kate isn't just any woman. She's *the* woman."

I glance over at Jacob for support. But he's just nodding, which doesn't help at all.

"She's great," I say. "But we're—" What are we doing? We aren't talking about the future. I'm not even thinking about the future. Was I? I mean, I like Kate and I want it to continue, but...I don't stay anywhere for long. "We're just enjoying things as they are."

"We found some!" Ellie calls. We all glance over at the two of them coming from the house.

"The brandy is in the drinks cupboard," Beau says. "What took so long?"

"It wasn't the brandy we couldn't find. It was raisins."

"Raisins?" I ask.

Ellie places a large white lasagna dish on the table behind the firepit and Kate pours brandy into it.

"Come on guys. Or are you too chicken?" Kate asks.

"What are you doing?" Beau asks.

We all gather around the table to see what's going on. Kate hands me a small box of raisins. "Okay, sprinkle them in. They have to be spread out though."

She's grinning from ear to ear, and I can't help but be infected with her enthusiasm.

"Is that an entire bottle of brandy?" Beau asks.

I sprinkle the raisins into the bowl and they bob to the surface.

"Okay, now light it," Kate says to Ellie.

"Are we setting the house on fire?" Zach asks.

Ellie lights the bowl of brandy and the blue flames flicker and lap over the bowl.

"Now you have to pick out a raisin and pop it in your mouth to extinguish it."

"What?" I ask. "Did you learn this at Cambridge?"

Kate shrugs. "My grandma taught me."

"You have to be kidding me," Sutton says. "Those flames are hot."

"Just don't knock the bowl by accident. We don't actually want to cause a fire."

"I'm not putting my hand in that bowl. I've seen burn injuries from doing shit like this," Jacob says.

Kate shrugs. "I'll go first." Without hesitation, she reaches over the bowl and takes a raisin, the flames licking around her hand. She pulls it out quickly and puts it in her mouth. "There."

She looks up at me and grins, and I bend down to press a kiss to her lips. "You are...surprising."

She laughs. "Is that a compliment?"

"Absolutely," I reply. "I love seeing you like this. You're so happy."

"I'm always happy. Or most of the time anyway. Especially if I'm with you."

I can't think of a better compliment. And I feel exactly the same.

Everything feels right. Like Kate fits here. Like I fit here.

"Back at you." I kiss her again, pointedly ignoring the whispered speculation and gossip buzzing from my cousins. All I know is that I'm happier than I've been for as long as I can remember. And that's good. I think.

Happiness can't be a bad thing. It's what people spend their lives chasing.

Except I never have.

THIRTY

Kate

I've tried to persuade Vincent to take off his shoes, but he isn't having any of it. I'm not wasting the opportunity. I've never even seen the sea before, so while I'm here, I want to know what the sand feels like between my toes. It's soft and silky and warm from the sun. I could stay here for hours, sinking my toes under the grains of million-year-old rocks and shells and then lifting them out, watching as my feet appear like a whale breaching the waves. It's like magic.

I glance back. Vincent's leaning against the sea wall, watching me, his sunglasses making him look cooler than usual—which is pretty hard, given Vincent's at the top of the cool tree on a normal day.

"It feels wonderful," I call.

He stands and takes off his glasses, squinting in the sunlight as he gazes more intently at me. Then he pulls off his trainers and socks and stalks toward me.

But he doesn't stop when he gets to me. He scoops up my hand and pulls me out toward the waves.

"You changed your mind," I say.

"You've never walked on a beach before."

It's not a question. We're trading facts.

"We should go paddle," he says.

I can't help but smirk. Vincent Cove doesn't strike me as a paddler.

"You paddle?" I ask. "I can't imagine you doing much that's just for fun."

He raises his eyebrows, giving me a meaningful look. "You know that's not true."

"Well, apart from the sex stuff."

"I'll paddle. Today. For you."

The sand turns colder and wet and hard. It feels like I'm walking through wet cement. "Is this quicksand?" I'm slightly concerned at the way our feet are sinking so quickly with every step we take.

"Just regular sand," he says. He doesn't look worried—like he's definitely not concerned our lives could be endangered at any second. I guess I should trust him. He's spent more time on beaches than I have, not that the bar is especially high.

I pause and glance down at my feet. Shells lie like confetti around us, smooth black rocks jutting out of the sand like they could be sleeping animals, napping on the ridged sand. "It's like someone has drawn this." I drop Vincent's hand, bend and trace the ridges with my fingertip. I stand and turn, looking out to where the sand meets the waves and the water meets the sky. "It's like someone designed this entire landscape to be completely perfect."

I glance back at Vincent, who's looking at me just the same way I'm looking at...everything.

"I think they did," he says.

"Who did? God?"

"The universe. Nature. Time."

To think I almost didn't come here and see all this with my own eyes. It's one thing to see things on a screen, but it's a bargain-bin version of the solid gold reality. The salt breeze, the slippery wet stones, the cry of the gulls overhead, all set to the soundtrack of the waves inhaling and exhaling, constant as time itself. I needed to be here for it all to sink into my soul.

"I'm so lucky to be here." I'm always grateful to be at Crompton. There's not a day goes by that I take my life there for granted, but this...this is wonderful too.

Vincent wraps his arms around me, connecting us from head to toe. We both stare out at the waves. "I'm so lucky to be here." He kisses me on the head and then we head out the few feet to the start of the water. I'm wearing a sundress that comes to my knees, but Vincent has his jeans rolled up to just above his ankle.

"Should we skinny dip?" I ask.

"Ask me again when you feel the frigid temperature."

I laugh. "It might be fun."

"I'll take you to the Med or better, the Cayman Islands. Then we can skinny dip."

My heart spins the same time as my stomach twists. The Med? The Cayman Islands? I've never gotten on a plane before the helicopter trip the other day. I suppose that's Vincent's life, always jetting from one place to another. He's so completely different from me, I'm not sure how we ended up here together. But I can't be sorry for as long as it lasts.

The water doesn't feel too cold at first. We step forward just as it's sweeping away from us, leaving behind a thin sheet of water I tap with my toes before it finally disappears too.

"Watch out." Vincent pulls me back as a large wave approaches. It crashes a couple of meters in front of us, but the water races toward us faster and higher than the last one did. This one comes up to mid-calf and it's chillier than I expected.

"You're going to get wet," I say, smiling giddily at Vincent.

He shrugs. "Worth it to watch you smile like this."

I hold his gaze and feel the water rising up to my knees. Vincent's jeans are wet, but he doesn't seem to care.

"Careful, you'll have me swooning." I'm not going to tell him so, but Vincent makes a semi-regular habit of making me swoon. He's so thoughtful. So kind. So good.

"That's the thing, Kate. There's something about you that makes me want to be anything but careful."

He bends and picks something up from the sand. "Here," he says, handing me a smooth gray stone. "You should have a memento from your first trip to the beach."

I take the stone and glance at my palm. Somehow its dark grey edges have been shaped into a heart and white shards of quartz, like lightning bolts, stretch across it, buried into the stone like it was only meant to stay for a moment but never left. "Did you plant this here?" I ask.

"I just found it, but it's beautiful." He looks at me, and the weight of meaning folds around my shoulders like a cloak.

I turn to him and lift up on my tiptoes. He graciously bends so I can kiss him. The waves push and pull beneath us as we slide our lips and tongues together in a kiss that seems more earnest, more important than everything that's come before. I can taste the sea on his skin, feel the salt in his hair. It's like he and this place are a symbol of the world outside of Crompton, of a life beyond the one I've been so content to live until now.

This man...what brought him into my life? The universe? Nature? Time?

Whatever it was, I'm grateful.

THIRTY-ONE

Vincent

Running at Crompton is a newfound passion. And in the heat of the summer, the only time to run is the mornings. I've settled into a routine of sorts where I get up with Kate when she leaves to go back to her place at around five. At that hour, the air is still cool and fresh, and I get the entire place to myself. No gardeners. No tourists. The flower gardens will close at the end of the summer season in two weeks, and they won't reopen until they're relocated to the edge of the hotel property.

But today is the last morning of my routine. Today I move out because demolition is starting and the foundations for the extensions are being dug. I'm staying over the pub for a few days before a property in the village becomes available. Molly arranged it all. I haven't even seen the new place. I'm heading back to the house, spinning through ideas for where I'll run tomorrow, when I see someone up ahead. As I get closer, I recognize Basil. He's up early.

"Good morning, Basil."

He stands from where he was kneeling on the ground and tips his hat at me. "I heard you wanted the jasmine from the front of the house removed. I thought I'd do it early so I don't disturb people coming and going."

"That's very considerate of you, Basil."

"Oops," he says, spotting a stray leaf. He bends and scoops it from the gravel then straightens, closing his eyes. "The first yellow leaf. Autumn is on its way. It always starts here by the house," he says. "You never need a calendar at Crompton, sir. You just need to pay attention to what the estate tells you." He nods. "But you'll find that out for yourself over the years."

Instinctively, I start to say I won't be here over the years. I stop myself because I don't actually know when I'm leaving. We've had planning permission. We've appointed the main contractor. Michael is working together with the project manager and will be leading the workstream heads. Everything is running on rails.

I'm not needed here.

So what am I doing? Why am I staying?

Everything thing feels so comfortable.

Having my family nearby.

Kate.

It all feels good—too good.

I like it here. I'm getting attached. This is not what was meant to happen. I don't get attached. To anything or anyone. Ever. That's how my life is. That's how I survive.

"I guess so," I reply and then point my thumb at the house. "Gotta take a shower. Catch up with you later."

I take the stairs with thoughts tunneling through my brain.

I'm busy. But I could be busy anywhere.

This is my investment, so I could pretend I'm here just

to make sure everything goes smoothly. But I have investments all over the world.

Fact is, I like it here. I like being here with Kate. Waking up with her, having dinner with her, stealing kisses during the day when no one's looking. Getting her naked at night.

My need for the next thing, the next project, the next challenge has cooled.

I'm getting attached.

To Crompton.

To my life here.

To Kate.

The realization turns my blood to ice and my heart claws to get out of my chest. I can't do this. I can't let myself worry about losing something or someone. I vowed to myself I would *never* let that happen again. Not again.

I get to the top of the stairs and pull out my phone. I make a call.

"It's late," Simon says.

I ignore him. "What's happening about the Arizona thing?"

He sighs. "It might be happening. It might not. Things have stalled."

"But it sounded like a great investment."

"Probably will be if it ever gets off the ground. You're not usually so impatient. Found a passion for real estate development?"

I ignore him again. "Would it help if I came out?"

"Maybe," he says. "I just can't get them to commit."

"I can be there tomorrow."

I hang up the phone and head to the shower. I could wait until Michael and Molly arrive, but I'll lose time. If I need to be in Arizona by tomorrow, I need to leave as soon as possible. I'll just pack a few things, dump them in the car and drive myself to the airport.

It's way past time I moved on to my next project. I can't take the risk of staying. Staying, and waiting for it all to be ripped away. I know this time there will be no all's-well-that-ends-well. This time, it would break me. I need to keep moving.

THIRTY-TWO

Kate

Vincent's message asking me to meet him at the front of the house was weird. I left him an hour ago and it's only just gone six. What's so urgent?

My hair's still wet from the shower, but at least I'm dressed, so I walk up the hill to the main house. Vincent comes out of the front door carrying a suitcase.

Where's he going?

I pick up my pace and meet him at the boot of his car as he tosses his case in the back.

"Hey," I say.

"I have to leave," he says, not looking me in the eye. He closes the boot. "I'm going to Arizona."

"Arizona?" I ask, but he doesn't say anything. Instead he slings an overnight bag onto the back seat and slams the door.

"Is everything okay?" I ask.

He turns and pushes his hands through his hair. "Yeah."

I step toward him and he takes a step back. My heart

begins to thud in my chest. "Vincent? What's the matter? Has something happened? Is your mum okay?"

"She's fine. It's a business opportunity. That's why I'm leaving."

I take a breath but my heart doesn't return to normal. It's like it knows something I don't. "So nothing serious."

He looks me in the eye for the first time. "It's potentially a really good investment."

"Okay," I say. "That sounds...good. When will you be back?"

I've never seen Vincent Cove look uncomfortable, but he practically squirms at my question. He looks over my shoulder, down to the gates of Crompton.

Realization dawns and my heart drops into my stomach. "Oh," I say. "You're not coming back."

"Everything's set up here," he says as if it's a perfectly reasonable expectation.

I knew this would happen. He was always going to leave. This was never a long-term thing, but understanding that it's happening. Right. Now. It's like someone's slowly tearing me in two and I don't know how I'm going to survive. I try and keep my breathing steady.

I lift my hand to my forehead, trying to shade my eyes from the sun rising in the sky behind him. "So you're off," I say, hoping I'm not giving away how wrecked I feel. "Because you never stay anywhere for long."

We stare at each other.

I want him to say something. To tell me I've got it wrong, that he'll be back in a few days and...what? We'll live happily ever after? Because that's what happens at Crompton?

Despite knowing it's futile, I want to ask him to stay. I don't. To do so wouldn't be fair. This is what he does. I've known it from the start. I need to let him go. Because that's what will make him happy. And I want him to be happy, even if it makes me sad.

"Right," he says.

"Right. There we are," I say, my tone hardening, pressing down the sadness that's threatening to overspill.

"It's true, Kate. This isn't personal. This is just my life. I'm never in one place for long. I've stayed at Crompton longer than I usually would. That's probably because of you."

His words make me ache and rage at the same time. "Maybe." But I'm not enough to make him stay. "Maybe you should have left before..." Before I started to look forward to waking up with his arm stretched across me like he can't bear not to be touching me, even in his sleep. Before he made me a picnic down by the lake like he would do anything to make me happy. Before he started to feel like part of my life. My happiness.

He nods. "Maybe."

Maybe if I wasn't so happy, so rooted at Crompton, if I were more open to traveling, things would be different. Perhaps then he could imagine a life with me. But he's right to leave. Better now than in a few months, because I can't imagine what our lives look like together. He doesn't want to stay and I don't want to leave.

Where does that leave us but apart?

"You bought Crompton to be closer to your family," I say. "You won't come back when you visit them?"

He narrows his eyes. "What do you mean?"

"The reason you bought Crompton," I say. "Your family —Carole and John, Jacob, Nathan—"

"Yes, I know who my family are. I don't need an excuse to visit them. I bought Crompton as an investment."

"Maybe," I say, although I don't believe him. Why else would he buy a stately home between London and Norfolk? Then again, why would he need an excuse to visit them? They love him. They don't treat him like a cousin and a nephew. They treat him like a brother and a son.

"Arizona looks like a good investment, but I don't think it will happen unless I'm there."

"And you have no reason to come back." My voice cracks on the last work, but I shrug, pretending I'm just stating facts rather than feeling sorry for myself. I don't want to end things on a bad note. I swallow down my sadness and take a breath. "It's been a blast, Vincent Cove."

He places his hands on my upper arms. "Yes."

Yes. That's all he can manage? I know he's enjoyed our time together because I know Vincent doesn't do anything he doesn't want to, and he's spent every night and all his free time with me. He wanted to do that.

And now he wants to leave.

"Yes," I say to him. "Bon voyage, my handsome stranger." I turn and head back to my house. To the place I've lived for twenty years and loved my whole life. So long as I'm here, nothing can hurt me.

THIRTY-THREE

Kate

I knock on Granny's door, my tears dried and resolve hardened. She's the only person I want to see right now. I go inside and find her at the kitchen table, drinking her tea. The sight of her soothes me, if only just a little.

"Good morning, my darling. I've been waiting to hear all your news."

She thinks I've come to tell her about Norfolk. I know she's beyond proud I actually managed to go.

"I had so much fun." I kiss her on the cheek and head to the kettle. "Can I get you another?" She shakes her head and I set about making myself a cup. "His aunt and uncle are so lovely. And I met all his cousins. They are all very invested in each other's lives. They treat Vincent like a brother. And Norfolk. It's so beautiful, Granny. I saw the sea and even had a little paddle."

Her eyes are glassy and she takes out a tissue from her sleeve and dabs her eyes. "Happy tears, my darling. Happy tears."

"I was a little nervous in the helicopter. It's kinda bumpy. But honestly, once we got there, I didn't really think about anything but how lovely everyone was and what a beautiful place we were in and how thoughtful and attentive Vincent was." I pause and try to steady my breathing. I don't want to lose it. Granny's so happy to see *me* happy. I don't want to ruin it for her. "I thought I'd have some anxiety or trouble sleeping or something, but I was fine. Better than fine. I was happy."

"I'm so proud of you, my darling." She clasps her hands together and we grin at each other. "Are you okay? You seem a little...subdued."

I can't tell her he's gone now. "Just a headache," I manage to get out. I have to figure this out. Find a brave face and slide it on. After all, I knew this was going to happen. He's just the investor. I kept telling everyone he wasn't staying. I knew he couldn't. It's just...he'd been around long enough for me to get used to.

"Tell me more about Norfolk."

I didn't want to talk about the helicopter ride. The firepit. The walk along the beach. I didn't want to remember the way he'd been so concerned with my happiness. So desperate to make me comfortable he'd framed images of Crompton I could put on my bedside table.

My heart swings heavy in my chest, as if gravity just got stronger and it's taking all my energy just to stand upright.

"Are you sure you're okay?" Granny asks.

"Yes, just a bad headache. And I just thought, we need to get some boxes. It's only a month before we move out. I need to start packing." I stand as if I'm going to start immediately.

"Can't you stay and tell me about your weekend?"

I glance at my watch. "I've totally lost track of time. But it was lovely."

"You don't look like you've just had a lovely weekend away. What is it? If you don't tell me, I'm just going to assume the worst."

I have the worst poker face.

She's going to find out anyway.

"Granny, will you promise to keep a secret?"

"Of course, my darling. You know you can tell me anything. Are you pregnant? Headaches can be an early sign."

If it were only that.

"I'm not pregnant, Granny. Vincent's left. Gone to Arizona. He's not coming back. It's just a bit of a shock. That's all."

She sets down her mug. "What? Where's he gone? Did you fall out?"

I shake my head. That would have been easier. If I hated him. If he'd hurt me.

"Then why?"

"Because that's what he does. I've always known he would leave. It's just I kept thinking it would be some time in the future. Not today."

I shouldn't have taken a day with him for granted. I knew he'd never stay. He'd even said it to me: wherever he lay his hat, that was his home. And whatever the reason, he'd put his hat back on his head and decided he was going to make his next home in Arizona—five thousand miles away from me.

"Every time I leave Crompton, something terrible happens," I say. Maybe it would have been better if we'd just stayed right here and not gone to Norfolk. My voice is shaky, but at least I have a solution. I just need to stay here.

Right here. Not change anything. I'd been happy before Norfolk. I'd had perspective about me and Vincent and about the changes happening to the estate.

"Darling, you said you had a wonderful time in Norfolk. Going to Norfolk didn't cause Vincent to disappear. Just like you didn't cause Grandpa's death by going to Cambridge. But I've been telling you that for nearly ten years and I don't think you've ever listened to me."

"But Grandpa worried about me."

"We both did. But he was old and sick, my love. You leaving didn't kill him."

"But if I hadn't left—"

"He was sick. You're a very clever woman. You must know that you leaving didn't kill him. And Vincent hasn't flown to Arizona because you left the estate and went to Norfolk. That's not how life works. You've created your own personal superstition and tricked yourself into believing it."

Is that what I've done? Mixed up all these terrible life experiences and concocted a superstition to lend me a sense of control over uncontrollable events? It makes sense. And I guess I've always known it to some extent, but being at Crompton truly made me happy.

"That superstition doesn't serve you," Granny continued. "Crompton was a comforting, stalwart partner after your mum died. Life before then had been challenging for you and it's totally understandable you needed a life raft in those circumstances. But you're safe now. You reached dry land. The life raft is always going to be here, but you don't need it. It's time to explore. Let go. There's so much to see and do out there. You have one life to live, my darling girl. You need to stretch out your arms and squeeze every ounce out of it."

I take a shuddering breath. Granny is right. On some level, I've always known the truth she has so neatly articulated. Though Crompton will always feel safe to me, venturing farther afield doesn't cause bad things to happen. I know this. I've *known* this. It's time to start living like I believe it.

"Vincent leaving doesn't have anything to do with me going to Norfolk." It sounds so obvious when I say the words out loud, but they release something in me—something that's been locked inside for a long time.

THIRTY-FOUR

Vincent

Ari-fucking-zona.

I stand in my hotel room, looking out at the view of the golf course and pool. The red rocks on the left are smattered with green, a stark contrast to the lush emerald golf course and teal-blue pool. The sun beats down on everything.

It's fresh.

It's new.

It's beautiful.

It feels good to be on the road again. I'm more than ready for new sunsets, new views from my bedroom windows and new opportunities.

I'm due to meet Simon at the restaurant overlooking the golf course at twelve to discuss my investment in a retirement village.

I pick up the phone to room service. Usually my first drink in a new hotel room is a ginger beer, but today I want a change. "Can I get an iced tea?" I ask.

"Certainly, sir. I'll have that brought up to you right away."

I exhale. Yup, this is where I'm meant to be. I feel good. I did my job at Crompton. I didn't need to spend as much time there as I did, but I would have had to go back for John and Carole's anniversary dinner anyway. It made sense to leave after that.

The conversation with Kate had been difficult. But she knew Crompton wasn't my home. She belongs there, not me. I head to the shower, not wanting to dwell on the fact I was an asshole for taking her to Norfolk and then leaving.

I always like a cold drink and a shower to settle into a new place.

The doorbell of my suite rings just as I fix a towel around my waist. I grab a small towel from the rail and rub it over my hair on the way to get the door.

"Good morning, sir. I have your drink." The waiter crosses the room and puts the drink on a coaster on the table by the couch.

As soon as I see the iced tea, I want a ginger beer. Jeez, when did I become such a creature of habit? Kate observed my habits and love of routine, but I guess I've never given it much thought.

"Do you guys do ginger beer?" I ask.

"Your assistant called ahead, Mr. Cove. Your fridge is fully stocked with your favorite brand. Would you like me to pour you a glass?"

"That's fine, I can do it." I tip the guy and let him leave.

Why did I order an iced tea when what I want is a ginger beer?

I pull out my phone again and text Jacob that I had to leave the UK unexpectedly. Kate seemed to get along well with both Sutton and Ellie. Perhaps one of them will call

Kate and check on her. Not that she's going to be devastated about me leaving or anything. It isn't like we were...

I grab the glass of iced tea and take a swig. Nope. I definitely want a ginger beer.

Fuck.

I stride across to the fridge and grab a bottle, opening it with more force than necessary. I gulp the first mouthful straight from the bottle. Yup. That's what I want. A shower and a ginger beer, just like always.

SIMON WAS ALREADY SEATED by the time I got to the restaurant.

"Have you ordered?" I ask.

"Nope. I was waiting for you."

"What's good here?" I scan the menu.

"No idea. Never eaten here."

We order—me a quesadilla and him tacos.

"So, when are we seeing the site?" I ask.

"Well, I didn't expect you to get here so quickly, so I'm still trying to arrange it."

"But it's up for sale. Officially."

"Like I said on the phone, they can't decide the price and apparently one shareholder is stalling. Hopefully we can get in this week at some point."

"So, it's good I'm here. I can see it with you."

"Right," he replies, his tone uncertain. "I want to bring a surveyor with us. Obviously, we'll have to have them do some ground tests. We won't know until then how easy construction will be."

"Great," I say. "And then we'll be able to move really

quickly because I'll have seen it. Did you do the analysis on the hold price compared to the development?"

"I did. I just finished it this morning, which is why I haven't emailed it to you. I can send it now." He pulls out his phone.

"Does it work?"

He shrugs. "It's borderline. And you've got the risk of one of the big players setting up next door. Like I said, it's not clear who's bought that plot. But if it's a major brand, we won't get permits for another operation. We'd have to sell. Or change lanes completely."

"Right," I say. I do remember him telling me about that risk. I must have put it to the back of my mind. "Send me what you have on the owners of the next-door plot, and I'll get my team to do some digging. What do you know about other bidders for the plot we're interested in?"

"Not much," he says. "I've started to find out, but at the same time, I don't want to draw attention to the fact that it's coming to market. We don't want to end up in a bidding war before we even know the price."

"No one likes a bidding war."

"Honestly, Vincent, you could have saved yourself the trip. Until we get that initial site visit, there's nothing we can do. Before then, the most important thing is to figure out who bought next door."

I thought coming over here had been urgent. Or did I just want to believe it was? I didn't want to miss an opportunity, which was all too possible when my head was full of Crompton...and Kate.

"I was passing," I say. It's a lie, but he doesn't need to know I need to rip out some roots that had been burrowing without me noticing. "I'll hang around a couple days, see if I can dig anything up about who owns next door. And I have a couple other things in-state to deal with as well." I have an investment in a semi-conductor plant in Tucson. I could drop by, put in some face time with one of the partners.

"It's always good to kill more than one bird with a stone," he says.

Right. Except there are no birds in Arizona.

I got spooked. And I ran.

I didn't see it until now. Crompton had gotten under my skin, and I pressed the emergency eject button before I could look too closely at why.

I'm an idiot.

I realize the silence has gone on a beat too long. Simon is looking at me like I'm wearing a full face of clown makeup. "And...uh...then there's the golf," I say. Simon chuckles.

As if I'd ever come to Arizona—or go anywhere—to play golf. I'm just trying to save face. I glance at my phone and see Jacob has texted back.

How's Kate?

Just the sight of her name creates a flash of heat in my chest. Leaving was. . .maybe not easy, but familiar. I'm on the road again, and the road is where I feel comfortable. Flying city to city is when I feel most like me. I've been this way for a long time, and it suits me just fine. Or...it did.

When Simon goes to the restroom, I reply to Jacob.

Can you ask Sutton to check in on her? I type out.

I'm such an idiot. I expected to walk away without a scratch. We made no promises to each other. Neither of us expected a happily ever after. So why do I feel so shitty?

I get Instagram up and check out Crompton's page. Kate hasn't posted any more pictures since I left. The last one was a view of the lake. The same view we had when we sat down there together for our first date, and again the day after.

I want to reach out, comment and tell her I miss her, but I don't want to make it worse. I don't want her to think I'm capable of coming back and staying for good.

Because I'm not.

The hot, searing pain in my chest doesn't lessen. It's like my body wants her, even though my mind knows it's impossible.

She deserves to stay at Crompton because that's what will make her happy.

She deserves a man who can promise her forever.

She deserves more than me.

THIRTY-FIVE

Kate

Over the last two days, the Crompton staff have watched with excitement as a gigantic tent was erected on the far side of the house, away from the gardens still open to the public for a little longer. There was much fevered speculation about what it might be, but when flooring and air conditioning, along with conference tables and chairs were ferried over there, it was clear the tent was going to be something official rather than anything fun. It's basically a huge office. When I walked by early this morning, Michael was glued to his laptop. It's the new office now that building works have started on the old house.

Since Vincent changed Michael's role to focus on Crompton, he no longer needs an assistant. Which is good, because training for the guest relations role is about to begin.

Michael's making the decisions. Vincent has gone. I'm back in the tea shop and have taken back some shifts at the Golden Hare.

It's almost like Vincent was never here.

"Are you ready?" I ask Meghan, who's sitting next to me on one of the kitchen chairs we've planted outside my front door so we can watch the to-ings and fro-ings of the builders and the delivery trucks, and a miniature poodle that seems to have come from nowhere.

"The earl wouldn't approve of the dog."

I chuckle. "No, he would not. But it's so cute. It must belong to one of the builders."

"You think Sacha is rebelling and it's hers?"

"I don't. Although I hope she gets one when she moves into her new place."

"I went to the new houses yesterday with some of the others from the cottages." Meghan doesn't live on the estate, but in the village.

It takes me by surprise. "You did? How was it?"

"Good. I'm thinking about renting one."

My heart lifts in my chest. "That would be awesome. We could be neighbors."

"It would get me out of the grotty place I'm in at the moment over the co-op. And if I can manage to get a full-time job at the hotel, I might even give up the pub." She's grinning as she speaks and is clearly excited.

"It's going to be a while until the hotel opens properly," I say. "But they might tell us more at the meeting." I have no idea whether or not things are on schedule.

Last night all the staff got an email from Michael asking us to come to a meeting in the tent to meet the new general manager of the hotel. Most of the current Crompton staff haven't been approached for jobs yet. It's just me and Basil and the other heads of department coming from other places—people who will be moving here in the coming months. The rest of the staff are waiting on the vacancies list and opening dates.

"Shall we go?" she says. "We can get good seats."

We take my kitchen chairs back inside and I lock up my house. I knock on Granny's window as we walk past and give her a wave. Granny's going to volunteer at the new flower gardens, but isn't taking a job in the hotel. I don't have the heart to tell her that Vincent might change his mind about the new gardens, now he's not here. Not that I thought he'd said yes for *me*. But with Crompton out of sight, he might prioritize other projects instead.

"Have you heard from him?" she asks as we walk up the slope to the front of the house.

I hesitate, because I did get a comment on the Instagram picture of the lake. I'm pretty sure it was him. "No," I say eventually. If he had commented, it didn't mean anything. If he wants to communicate with me, he has my number.

He won't use it, of course. His hat is somewhere else now.

I've just got to get used to that.

"I feel fine though." It's only half a lie. I miss him. It's not a feeling I'm used to. Everyone in the world I like, I see all the time. Missing him feels like an icy rock, weighing down my stomach.

I don't think it will ever leave me. I think a part of Vincent Cove will stay with me forever. And despite it being uncomfortable—the missing him—it's better than it not being there. I won't wish it away. Meeting Vincent and spending those weeks together were some of the happiest times of my life. It's painful now, but I'm so pleased I had that time with him.

"You think he'll come back?"

I don't, but I don't want Meghan to think Vincent's lost

interest in Crompton as a business. He knows how to make money without needing to oversee things personally. "I imagine he will."

"Are you nervous about your new job?" she asks.

"I'm excited." It's true. I can't wait to tell guests all about Crompton and get them as enthusiastic about the place as I am.

"I know I don't have a job sorted out yet, but I'm excited too. It feels like this could be something really great."

"I agree." I wave at Sandra, who is coming from the other direction. "And the best of it is, I get to work with fantastic people I know, love, and cherish."

Meghan links her arm through mine and we meet Sandra by the tent.

"We're all early," Sandra says. "I want a seat at the front so I get to tell this general manager I want a job giving out the tea."

"You're going to be the hotel tea teller, are you?"

She rolls her eyes. "Earl Grey, not gossip."

We all shuffle through the door of the tent.

"In my day, if a tent had a zip, you were posh. Now look at this place. It's got lights and everything," Sandra says.

I laugh. "This isn't the kind of tent you spend a week in the summer on a beach with. Although, it's got air conditioning, so it's the only kind of tent I'd want for that kind of trip." I think about Vincent and wonder if he's ever been camping. Maybe before his dad abandoned him. His life would have been completely different before he left— almost the exact opposite of mine before my mum died. I wish we'd had a chance to talk more, share more, heal more —together.

Just as we take our seats in the front row, Michael arrives with Molly and a woman I recognize from her profile picture on LinkedIn. Without thinking, I jump to my feet. "Olga, how lovely to meet you. My name's Kate. I'm looking forward to being your head of guest relations."

Olga gives me a warm smile and shakes my hand. "I've heard so much about you. You're going to be able to teach me so much about this wonderful place."

"I'm looking forward to it. We're all very excited you're here." I introduce her to Sandra and Meghan. As they chat animatedly to Olga, I watch as people who've known me our entire lives file into the tent. There's a palpable sense of excitement in the air and I'm contributing to it.

I'm no longer furious the earl sold the place. He probably should have done it ten years ago. I'm not nervous my world is going to be turned upside down, because that already happened when Vincent came into my life. Though I have a badly bruised heart, there are finger marks around my soul—being with him has changed me at my core.

I'd just been existing before Vincent. He brought me to life.

"Testing, testing," Michael says into the microphone at the front of the tent.

"A bloody microphone as well," Sandra says. "Can you believe it?" Anyone would think an alien spacecraft just landed in front of us.

"Sandra, you're not three hundred years old," I say. "You've seen a microphone before."

"Not in a tent I haven't," she replies.

"Well here's your new experience of the day," I say. "I think there are going to be a lot more coming down the road, so strap in."

Once everyone arrives, Michael talks a little about timings of the hotel opening. He has no doubt they'll open as scheduled, nine months from now. He shows us images of what the interior and exterior of the hotel will look like, which I've seen already, and talks a lot about how the luxury aspect of the hotel starts with appearances but comes to fruition with service. He then introduces Olga, who talks about the jobs that are going to become available. The guest relations team will have six members, including me. Then she talks about training schedules.

"Michael is right that the service the guests receive in our hotel will set it apart from other competing hotels, and will also guarantee the holy grail of hoteliers—repeat customers. If we impress people, they'll come back. If they come back, the hotel will be successful, and success feeds success."

She talks about how the hotel will be a boon to local businesses and surrounding towns. I can feel excitement crackle in the air as people realize we have the chance to do something spectacular at the hotel. Like a stone tossed to the center of a lake, our success could have a ripple effect that reaches far beyond the estate.

"What's key is consistency," Olga continues. "That means the service our guests get from the guest relations team is just as experienced and high-end as they get from our housekeeping staff, from the butlers, the restaurant teams, the gardeners, the maintenance teams. There can be no weak links. We need to provide exceptional service, whatever role we have in the hotel."

She pauses, and part of me thinks she's about to introduce Vincent. He'll talk about all the amazing hotels he's stayed at, maybe share anecdotes about interactions that have stuck in his memory. But just as my heart begins to pick up pace, Olga continues.

"I've talked to you about how the heads of department—some of whom are here today—will shadow people doing

their jobs in other luxury hotels. They'll bring that knowl-
edge back to you, back to us, and we can all benefit. But the
first thing we need to do is *understand* luxury. We need to
see exceptional service and know what it feels like before
we can provide it. For that reason, the heads of department
will go to London next week for an overnight stay at the
Four Seasons on Park Lane."

I stop breathing.

I've never been to London before.

Norfolk is as far from the estate as I've been since I
moved here. And although London is about the same
distance away, this will be a very different experience.

I don't know if I can go.

"The Four Seasons is renowned for exceptional service
throughout the world. And the heads of department will get
to see and experience it for themselves. I want you to learn
from it, get ideas, get excited by it. Then I want you to come
back and share it with your teams."

This is a job requirement—the first of my new role. If I
want to stay at Crompton and be the head of guest relations,
this is what I have to do.

Three months ago, if you'd told me I'd leave Crompton
to go to Norfolk, I'd have said it would have been impossible. Perhaps a trip to London with the other department
heads—most of whom I've known my entire life—isn't so
impossible. Not now. Not since Vincent showed me what
I'm capable of. Not since I discovered how strong I
really am.

THIRTY-SIX

Kate

Over the last week, I've tried to act like everything is fine. But it isn't fine.

Vincent's gone.

He hasn't called to say he's changed his mind. He hasn't turned up in the middle of the night with a bouquet of roses and a thousand apologies. He hasn't acted out any of the other fantasies that scrolled through my mind in quiet moments. My heart still hurts, still feels heavy in my chest. My entire body is weighed down with sadness that such a bright flash of a man is no longer in my life.

But I keep putting one foot in front of the other, waiting for the balm of Crompton's consistency to heal me.

Yesterday's call from Sutton had come as a shock. The fact she wanted to stop by today was even more of one. I look up as the bell over the door to the tea shop rings, but it's Viola. She always visits the gardens on Sundays. I don't usually work Sundays, but I've gotten to know her when covering for Sandra.

The bell rings again and this time it's Sutton. I'm a little nervous. I haven't made any new friends since I dropped out of university, but I like this woman. I give her a little smile as she approaches the table and she envelops me in a hug. The tug in my throat catches me off-guard. Sutton is just more evidence of what I'm missing without Vincent in my life.

We swap hellos, order drinks and then come back to our table. As soon as we're seated, Sutton reaches for my arm. "How are you?"

She knows he's gone.

"I'm fine," I say, but the crack in my voice gives me away. "I always knew he wouldn't stay for long."

She sighs. "I thought he might have had a change of heart. Seeing him with you was so...refreshing. I've never seen that sweet side of Vincent. Don't get me wrong, he's amiable and upbeat, but he was so attentive and concerned with your happiness. It was lovely."

I have to take a deep breath. I don't want to lose it in front of people. "He is lovely," I manage to squeak out.

"Have you heard from him?" she asks.

I shake my head, dropping my gaze to my tea. "I didn't expect to. How are you?" I ask.

"Jacob says he'll come around," she says, ignoring my question.

"No," I reply, meeting her eyes. "Don't do that. Don't give me hope when I know there is none. I understand that...the things that went on when he was a child...it's wounded him. I get it. I understand all too well." I let out a shallow laugh. "How ironic that Vincent actually helped me heal some of my wounds." I swallow, blinking back tears. "I'll always be grateful to him for that."

Sutton reaches for my arm. "You mean bringing you to Norfolk?"

"Yes, that was a great example. But just being with him shifted things. I miss him." My voice breaks again and I pause. "I'll always miss him. I just have to get used to it. But now I believe the future can be brighter. I'm not frightened of things shifting and changing so much anymore."

"Have you thought of reaching out?" she asks.

I pick up my cup and take a sip of green tea. "No," I say. "Not because I don't want to listen to his beautiful voice or hear about his day, but because I'm not what *he* wants. It's better if he's free to chase something that will do for him what he's done for me—heal him."

"You might be that person," Sutton says.

But I know I'm not.

She must see the expression on my face because she lifts up a finger to stop me saying anything to the contrary. "Just hear me out. I have a theory. Vincent seems like he has a commitment phobia. We both know that comes from his childhood. But I think he's desperate not to care for anyone in case they leave him. Just like his dad did."

I let her words sink in. "Yes, that makes sense," I say. My heart starts to pick up pace, from a trot to a canter. "But it doesn't change anything."

"Unless he needs some kind of assurance you won't abandon him."

My heart breaks into a gallop. "Assurance. Like a guarantee? Or a pledge or something? How would that work? Even marriages can end in divorce. There are no guarantees in life."

Her shoulders collapse and she sighs. "I know. I don't know how you could convince him you won't let him down."

Is that what Vincent needs from me? Commitment? It always seemed he wanted the exact opposite—his freedom to wander. But maybe what he really craves is comfort and security.

"He left me before I could abandon him." I say it out loud the instant the realization dawns.

"I think so." Sutton doesn't need to confirm it. It all slots into place.

My mind races through possibilities. I don't know how I'll convince him that I'm not going anywhere, but for the first time since he left, hope blooms in my chest.

THIRTY-SEVEN

Vincent

I arrive early for lunch with Jacob and Beau. I flew into London from Tucson overnight and despite my shower, the fog of the red-eye hasn't left me. If I stayed in the hotel, I would have fallen asleep.

My phone buzzes with the arrival of an email. It's the training plan from Olga, addressed to Michael. I'm only copied in and usually wouldn't bother to open it, but there's every chance this email holds some clue to how Kate is doing. I'll take whatever scrap of news I can get.

I open the document and search for her name. Nothing comes up. Then I scan the document for heads of department. I find her new title in a section of the email about Service Experience, which sets out the plan for department heads to travel to London and stay at the Four Seasons—the hotel I'm currently staying at—tomorrow night.

Kate and I are going to be in the same hotel at the same time.

Adrenaline surges in my veins and then my stomach

drops. How will she cope coming to London? She'll be away from Crompton with no way of getting back quickly if she finds she can't manage. A mixture of fear and protectiveness grow in me. I'm no good for her, but that doesn't mean I've stopped caring about her.

I need to do something to help.

Before I can take action, Jacob arrives. "Hey, you look terrible," he says. "You're getting older, can't handle those red-eyes like you used to."

I don't even bother to stand. It's not just the flight that has me tired. I haven't been sleeping. Not properly. Not since I left the UK.

"Great to see you too," I say. "Where's Beau?"

Jacob tilts his head in the direction of the door. I glance around the restaurant and spot him talking to a waitress. Of course he is. He never met a woman he didn't like.

"How was Arizona?" Jacob asks.

"Shit," I reply.

"Not the answer I expected. But I'm not surprised. No doubt you started to enjoy yourself too much with Kate, decided you were getting attached, and split. Now you regret it?"

I swipe my hand through my hair. "Jesus, we're doing the tough love thing already? I haven't even ordered a drink yet."

Just at that moment, the waitress approaches. Before I can say anything, Jacob orders three margaritas.

"Margaritas? We're day drinking?"

"It's my day off. Beau's too. And you look like you need a drink or a good night's sleep. I scanned the menu and of those two things, they only have drinks."

Beau finally arrives at the table and slaps me on the

back before taking a seat. "You look like shit. Anyone up for a beer?"

"Jacob just ordered us margaritas."

Beau laughs. "Happy to go with that flow."

"I was just telling Vincent he's an idiot," Jacob says.

"Just generally or for a specific reason?" Beau asks.

"Because he dumped Kate."

"She was great," Beau says. "Hot. So she's single now?"

"Don't be a dick," I say.

"He's kidding," Jacob says. "But some other guy won't be. She's gorgeous and funny and clever and—"

"I wasn't kidding," Beau replies, but he's grinning. He's totally kidding but it doesn't help move the sludge of dread in my gut at the thought of someone else with Kate. "You shouldn't be so much of a commitment-phobe."

He doesn't need to tell me. But knowing it and doing something about it are two different things. "Kate's better off without me—"

"He's not a commitment-phobe," Jacob says, interrupting.

Beau bursts out laughing just as our waitress reappears with our drinks. We quickly place orders for lunch and then Beau raises his glass. "To the Cove brothers."

The hairs on the back of my neck prickle.

"Come on, brother," Beau says, and despite my frustration and confusion at how this lunch has started, I smile at the address.

We all clink our glasses and take a sip.

"Back to your joke." Beau nods at Jacob. "About how Vincent isn't a commitment-phobe."

Jacob shrugs. "I don't think he is. He's a *creature* of commitment. He's entirely committed to our family. He's always around if we need him. He commits to the businesses he invests in, and you've been working with most of your team for a decade, haven't you?"

"Sure. But that's...different."

"I don't think so. It's not commitment that has you running. It's fear. Some things you're scared of and some things you're okay with. And from what I can see, it goes back to when your dad left. You were forced to leave a home you were happy in and now you're scared to get attached again. You just don't want to commit to living in one place because you're scared it will get taken away—which I don't get. I mean, you could buy most homes in America or the UK in cash, own them outright. Your businesses can't force you out, either. You have the control there. Same thing with your team. Your issue isn't commitment—it's the fear that what you've committed to will somehow get taken away."

Dread slithers down my chest and winds around my ribs. I gave up on Kate because I'm a fuckup. I'm not sure I needed it confirmed, but hearing it doesn't feel good. "Maybe you're right. But knowing the problem doesn't solve it."

"He *is* right," Beau says. "But I think you know that. What you don't realize is that it's bullshit. Like Jacob said, you're completely committed to all sorts of things. Us—your family. Your businesses. I bet in your head you tell yourself you didn't commit to uni. But you only dropped out because you were making so much money doing other stuff. Why would you want to be a medic?"

I don't tell him the reason. I don't say, *because I wanted to be accepted by John and Carole as one of their sons*. It sounds too corny or pathetic or ridiculous. Circle as applicable.

"You also always order ginger beer as your first drink

after getting off the plane," Jacob says. "And you've worn the same kind of underpants since you were at Cambridge."

"It's weird how you even know that," I say.

"You've committed to Calvin Klein," Beau says. "Just not a beautiful, funny, loyal woman."

I groan at the comparison. "Don't say that."

"It's normal not to want to get hurt," Jacob says. "But if you never take the risk, you have to make the sacrifice. Are you prepared to take the risk with Kate, or are you going to be content as a miserable loner?"

"It's one or the other, huh?"

"Sounds about right," says Beau.

"And if she leaves me?"

"Then it will break you," Jacob says. "But mate, you're already broken without her. And you know it."

"Broken" is a good word for how I feel. I haven't had a good night's sleep since I left Crompton; I haven't been able to focus. Even food doesn't taste the same. "But you knew with Sutton that she was...*it* for you, right? That you wanted to marry her and be with her forever."

Jacob nods. "Absolutely. And I think you know that about Kate."

Do I?

"That's why you're back in London so quickly. You've not even been back to New York, have you?" Beau asks.

I take the question as rhetorical. "I've never given a woman a second thought after our time together was over— even if that makes me a bastard. Kate...well, it's different. I miss her. I miss her enthusiasm and her optimism and the way a smile from her is worth every million I've made. And when I think of the future, the thought of her not being part of it fills me with a foreboding sense of dread. Like I will have failed."

"So you know," Beau says. "Because if I ever felt that for a woman, I'd marry her."

My heart has formed a fist and is banging on my chest wall, *boom, boom, boom.*

Marry her?

"Don't *just* marry her," Jacob says. "Love her. Enjoy her. Cherish and nurture her."

"She's not going to want to marry a man like me," I say. "I travel all the time. Even if I was to buy a home and have a base, I'd still need to travel. She doesn't like to leave Crompton."

"Don't make bullshit excuses," Beau says. "You'll find a way if it's worth it."

"When did you become such a romantic?" Jacob asks.

"Just calling it like I see it," Beau replies.

Is it really that simple? Take a risk and find a way? That's how I always approach business, but Kate is more important than anything in my professional life. Jacob talked about risk and reward, which begs the question: What am I willing to put on the line for Kate? And after the way I've fucked up—will it be enough?

THIRTY-EIGHT

Kate

Hi Olga, I think I've got food poisoning. I've been vomiting. I won't be able to make it down with the rest of the heads of department today. I'm really sorry. Best, Kate.

I press send, drop my phone on the sofa and cover my face with my hands.

I've never felt like such a failure.

Food poisoning was only a half lie.

For two days straight, I've been sick at the thought of leaving Crompton to go to London. Literally sick: heaving and vomiting. I have the headache to prove it.

Even though all the department heads will leave Crompton for the station in thirty minutes, ironically, the vomiting has stopped. But the sickness is still there.

I don't think I ever realized the extent of my problems until faced with the prospect of boarding a train to London for what is, by all accounts, a phenomenal opportunity. It's just a train ride. Why can't I do that? I managed a helicopter with Vincent.

Is this my life now?

I want to go to London. I want the job as head of guest relations. I've always thought I don't leave the estate very often because I don't want to, but now? I *want* to leave. I *want* this job. I *want* to share in the excitement of going to a fancy hotel in London and understanding more about the world I'm about to enter.

But the terror? It won't let me leave.

Why was Norfolk so easy?

Vincent.

Everything was easy with Vincent.

I miss him so much. Flashes of our weekend in Norfolk wheel through my brain. The firepit. The party. The beach.

The beach.

I run upstairs and rummage through my bedside table. I definitely put it in here. I feel it before I see it—the smooth, cold edges. I scoop it up and take it from the drawer. That the memento I have to remember our time together is a heart made of stone feels ironic, but I tuck the thought away and instead focus on the weight of it in my palm. How solid it is. I trace the veins of white quartz against the dark gray rock. It's beautiful—the best present anyone ever gave me. The triptych of pictures of Crompton I left beside Vincent's bed the night before he left is a very close second, but this... when we found it, this stone felt like it was made for us. At the time, I thought I was the white quartz that had unexpectedly twined my way into Vincent's impenetrable heart, or maybe it was the other way around.

I turn the heart over and over in my palm.

If Vincent asked me to go to London, I would.

I'd do anything for him.

I managed to go to Norfolk with him and ended up

having the time of my life. Was it just that I wanted to be with him? Or that he believed in me?

If I imagined I was going to London to meet Vincent, would just the thought of him get me on that train?

THIRTY-NINE

Kate

I focus on Vincent and the memories we made—replaying every conversation and kiss—all the way to London.

Walking up to the house with my case to get into the minivan, I thought of the first time he came into the tea shop.

Heading out of Crompton's gates, I remembered him catching me before I hit the ground at the pub.

The train journey down to London was our picnic by the lake.

The tube ride across the city? Him kissing me.

Checking in at the hotel, I replayed the way he looked at me on the beach in Norfolk.

I pretend I am doing this for him.

Maybe I am.

Now, alone in my hotel room, my anxiety levels start to rise again. I look at myself in the bathroom mirror. "You can do this," I say. "It's twenty-four hours and then you're heading back to Crompton." Knowing my fellow department heads are here makes it a little easier to breathe, but only just.

I wipe away the smudge of mascara under my eye and head back into the bedroom to unpack. The porter put my case on the luggage rack and even offered to unzip it. Olga asked us to make notes about what particularly impresses us during our stay. I should write down the detail about unzipping my bag before I unpack, so I don't forget. I kick off my shoes and pull my notebook from my bag. Stepping back, I sink into the comfy navy armchair facing the room.

I scribble down the thing about the porter. How polite he was but at the same time, friendly and warm. He was interested, asking me my plans for the day without appearing nosy. And the check-in experience—they already seemed to know me.

I glance around. What do I particularly like about the room? Something on my bedside table catches my eye—a triptych photo frame, just like the one Vincent gave me on the way to Norfolk.

That's a coincidence. Maybe he got the idea to gift me the pictures from his stay at a fancy hotel?

I stand and cross the room, squinting at the frame. From a distance, it looks like pictures I took of the Crompton Estate. As I get closer, I see it's the *exact* frame, the *exact* pictures I took to Norfolk.

My heart thunders in my chest. Who put these here? Who knew? I pick up the frame and study it closely. There's no doubt—it's the same one. A second frame in the same triptych style stands behind the first.

My stomach swoops then hits the floor. Three different photographs: one of Crompton House, one of my house and one of Granny's.

I collapse onto the bed.

Vincent did this. There's no other explanation.

But how?

I pick up the phone and dial zero.

"Good morning, Miss Saunders, how can we help you?"

"Hi. Thanks. Erm. There are photographs by my bed. Who put them there?"

"Are you a returning guest?" she asks.

"No, this is my first stay."

My comment is met by silence on the other end. "And you're in room four-one-two. Hmmm. We occasionally place photographs in some of our suites for returning guests..."

"You do?" I ask, a little confused, my heart sinking a little. Could this be just another luxury amenity from the hotel? But to have these exact photographs? That's too much of a coincidence, surely?

"We like people to feel they're in a home away from home."

That's one for the notebook. Maybe my team could do some social media sleuthing to accomplish the same thoughtfulness for our future guests.

"But actually," the woman continues, "since this is your first stay— Excuse me while I check something. I have a note on your reservation. Please hold the line."

My breathing is ragged, like I've been running for miles. Could it be Vincent after all? And if so, why? Since my lunch with Sutton, I've been trying to figure out what I can do or say to Vincent to make him feel like he can depend on me to never leave him.

Because he could.

I've come up empty so far. Work has been busy. Now I'm no longer working in the house, I picked up more shifts in the pub and started guest relations training. And of course, I'm still working in the tea shop. During all those hours and the times in between, I've thought about little else but Vincent. But I haven't found a solution. How can I make him believe I won't abandon him?

"Thank you for your patience," the woman on the phone says. "I see those pictures were a special request on your booking. I believe your husband had them sent over to be placed in your room."

Heat courses through my body. My husband.

"Oh. Thank you."

I hang up, stunned. The photographs are Vincent's doing. I guess he's being well-briefed by Michael and Olga; he knew I'd find coming to London and staying away from Crompton challenging.

Vincent is a good man. Thoughtful, sweet and sensitive. The man I want to be with for the rest of my life.

And suddenly, I have it. I understand exactly what I can do to make Vincent realize I want him forever. I just need to work up the courage to leave my hotel room to put my plan in action.

Then I'll be ready.

FORTY

Kate

I come out of the lifts on the hotel's fourth floor and head back to my room, relief coursing through my veins at the thought of being safely ensconced inside. I see him before he sees me. I place my hand on my chest and pull in a breath.

He's here.

And I'm ready.

Vincent leans against the wall opposite my room, staring at the floor. He looks thinner than when I saw him last, even though it's been just a few weeks.

Thank goodness I figured out how to make him stay. At least, I hope I have.

He looks up as I approach. The sight of his handsome face short-circuits my breathing for a second and I have to remember to exhale.

"Hey," I say as I come to a stop in front of him. I want to skip this part and fast forward to the bit where he's holding me, but I don't want to spook him. "You had the photographs put in my room."

He nods. His eyes search mine and I can tell he's looking for clues, trying to figure out what to say. "I was wondering...if we could talk?" he asks.

"Let's do that," I reply. I hope he hasn't come here to apologize and tell me how things would never have worked between us. My agenda looks a lot different. "I've always wanted to go to Hyde Park. I hear it's wonderful."

He narrows his eyes like he's wondering if he misheard me. "Okay."

I turn and head back where I came from. He hits the down button and we wait, both facing the lift doors.

"I'm sorry I left so abruptly," he says.

"I know. I appreciate and accept your apology." I don't feel any anger toward him. It hurt that he left, but I understand why he did.

Before he can respond, the lift doors ping open and we step inside. We join an elderly couple standing at the back of the lift.

"There's definitely the chill of autumn in the air," the woman says.

"Do you want me to go back and get your coat?" the man asks her.

"I was thinking you might want to go back and get yours," she replies.

"I won't be cold, but if you will, you can wait for me in the lobby while I go and fetch yours."

"I think I'll be fine." She scoops his hand up in hers and he presses a kiss to her cheek.

I grin and want to ask them questions. How long have they been married? Where did they meet? Have they always looked after each other like that?

But I don't get a chance because we're on the ground floor and the doors open into the lobby.

"You know when you said *you know*?" Vincent says as we head to the exit.

"Yes," I say.

"The bit where I said I was sorry and you said 'I know'?"

"Thirty seconds ago? Yes, I remember."

He insists on opening the door for me, despite the doorman doing his best to open it for both of us, and we step out into the London afternoon. The woman in the lift was right. The chill of autumn is in the air. My pounding heart does a fine job of keeping me comfortably warm.

"What did you mean?" he asks.

We walk along a little bit and stop at a crossing.

"Just that... I know you're sorry."

"You do?"

I nod, keeping my focus on Hyde Park. I don't really want to have this conversation among the hustle and bustle of traffic and people. I need to find some trees. I'm hoping I'll feel more comfortable. More at home under an old oak.

We cross in silence and make our way into the park, which is bigger than I expected. And less organized. I suppose I've grown accustomed to formal gardens. But this is beautiful, too—this little slice of wild amid the concrete and stone city.

"They were right, in the lift. Autumn is on its way." I bend and pick up a yellowed leaf.

"I really am sorry," he says. "I freaked out and made up a bullshit excuse about work. I flew to Arizona."

I turn to face him under a giant oak. He looks so troubled. I want to reach and stroke his face, comfort him, make him feel better. But I can't.

I need some assurances.

And so does he.

"I love you," I say.

He sucks in a breath and brings his fist to his chest.

After a beat, he responds. "That's not what I expected you to say. But that's part of the reason I love you," He loves me? I want to swallow those words whole. "You never say the thing I expect you to say."

He's in for a wild ride this afternoon.

"I'm happy to listen to the rest of the reasons you love me," I say. "Shall we sit?"

He glances at the grass under his feet. "Here?"

I laugh. "We can find a bench if you'd prefer."

He fixes me with a look that says he accepts my dare and takes a seat.

"You have the kindest heart of anyone I know," he says. "You're fiercely loyal and you are the funniest woman I've ever met. When I'm with you, I don't just want to be a better man, I *am* a better man—and I feel like I'm stealing that line from Jacob, but it's exactly how I feel. I'm happier, more relaxed, more motivated, kinder, more thoughtful when you're around. And that's because *you're* all those things. Not just to me but to everyone you come across. From the moment I met you, you've been completely unconcerned with my wealth or my job. You say what you want and what you need and it's refreshing and...it's also completely terrifying."

I raise my eyebrows. "Terrifying?"

"Because I never want to be without you. I've never felt like this."

His words are fresh summer rain. "Oh," I say.

"When you're near, it feels like I'm home."

My heart stretches in my chest as if it's trying to climb up and out of me and into Vincent's lap.

"I know that feeling," I say.

He sighs and then shifts so he's closer to me. "I feel like a giant chump, but if you forgive me and we love each other, then I want this to work between us. I know you're going to try and tell me it won't. That you won't leave Crompton. But if you don't mind me traveling, then I can base myself there and we can have video calls and phone calls and I'll come home to you as much as I can."

I shiver when he says he'll come home to me. It's such a relief to know he's not trying to walk away. That he understands what's between us is worth awkward apologies and fumbling conversation. I give him a small smile. This man is the best person I know. The best *man* I will ever know.

"You've taught me so many things, Vincent, but the most important of all is that it's not the place that makes me feel safe, happy and loved. It's the people. That's why I enjoyed Norfolk so much. I was with you. You give me roots as deep as this oak. It doesn't matter where in the world you need to be, I'll come with you. And if I'm with you, I'll be safe and happy."

He closes his eyes and I can feel the relief stream through his body.

"But there's one thing we need to figure out before we can be together," I say.

He opens his eyes, gaze narrowing.

"You need to be sure of me," I say. "You need to know I'm not going anywhere. I get that what happened to you with your dad makes you frightened. It's no wonder. But I need to be able to heal that wound for you, Vincent."

"You do," he says, reaching for me.

But I pull my bag onto my knees and bring out the gift

bag I went out for earlier.

"I bought these," I say, handing him the present. "There's one for each of us. Yours might not be the right size."

His frown deepens and he looks at the box, then back at me.

"Open it," I say.

He pulls off the bow and brings out the black box. He shoots me another confused look.

I lift my chin in silent encouragement.

A smile curls around his mouth as he opens the box. Two gold bands sit nestled together on the black velvet.

"We're going to be together forever," I say. "I want to marry you. I want us to be each other's family, each other's anchor in this ever-changing world. The only promise I need from you, is if you think things are shifting between us, you talk to me about it. No running off on a business trip when things get tough or when you're feeling vulnerable. I need a chance to be able to explain how I'm not going anywhere and I never will."

He swallows and nods. "I promise."

I crawl into his lap, my legs astride him so our faces are only inches apart, and wrap my arms around his neck. He doesn't reciprocate, and I pull back.

"Just one more thing." He's fumbling in his pocket. I move slightly so he can access it better. "I bought you something."

He produces another black ring box, exactly the same as mine. "Must be from the same place you bought yours. Beck's friend owns the place, actually. He's a jeweler."

"What is it?" I ask, staring at the box.

He chuckles. "Why don't you open it?"

I take it from him.

"Nothing in there's going to bite you. I promise."

"Pinky promise?" I grin at him.

He shakes his head. "I love you."

This time I get to stroke his face and his skin against mine feels exactly right. "I love you, too."

Finally I open the box to reveal a huge diamond ring. The stone might actually be as big as an acorn. "That's big." I glance up at him.

"If you don't like it—"

"I love it. I mean, I really love it. It's possible I love it almost as much as I love you." He laughs and it warms me from the inside out. I glance from the ring back up at him. "And in case you were wondering, I love you a lot."

He takes the ring from the box, reaches for my hand, then slides the ring on my left ring finger. It fits like a glove.

"So you were planning to propose and I beat you to it," I say, wiggling my fingers, admiring the way the sunlight reflects off the diamond. It looks like it belongs there.

"I wanted a way to show you I'm not going to run again. I realized what a fool I'd been and how I never want to let you go again. I wasn't sure if you'd take me seriously."

"Bribery is always a good option. You know—for future reference." I slide my hands over his hair and press a kiss to his lips. "I've missed you."

He takes my face in his hands. "You never have to miss me again."

We don't need a wedding ceremony to commit to each other, though I'd gladly proclaim my love in front of all our family and friends. Sitting under the branches of an oak tree in Hyde Park, we have the only ceremony that matters. We exchanged promises, swapped I love yous and agreed to spend the rest of our lives together.

Vincent is my home now—and I'm his.

FORTY-ONE

Vincent

How did I get so goddamn lucky? I watch Kate at the window, looking out at the London skyline. I kick off my shoes and go to stand behind her.

"You like the view?"

She turns in my arms so she's facing me. "Yes."

I bend and press a kiss to her neck. "You smell like fresh summer flowers," I say. It suits her perfectly. She's like perpetual summer—all warmth and color.

"I like the idea of never missing you again," she says. "Never missing your body because I get to have it every night." She rounds her hands over my shoulders and down my arms as if she's trying to remind herself how I feel.

"It's all yours."

She trails a finger down the buttons of my shirt.

"And mine is yours."

I inhale, trying to let her words sink in.

"It feels good to be...linked like this." Her gaze flits to

the ring on her left ring finger. "You think people will judge us for moving so quickly?"

"I don't care," I reply. "Do you?"

"I suppose not." She runs her hand around my neck and gazes at me.

Yes, I want her naked right now. Yes, I want to be as close as it's possible to be. Yes, I want to lick, suck, push, pull—fuck. But I also want to stay right here and gaze at this incredible woman for the rest of my life.

"I think we need to try out the bed." She pulls out of my arms and heads around the seating area to the other side of the room, where the bed is. "Olga says we need to understand luxury." She pulls her shirt over her head and unzips her jeans. "That's why we're here. She says we have to make use of all the facilities." She turns as I stalk toward her, stripping my clothes off as I go.

"Sounds like good advice. We can start with the bed. Then the shower. Bath. Sofa. Floor. Maybe even up against the window."

She blushes and it's adorable. "Everywhere other than the window works for me. My agoraphobia is improved but that's a step too far." She's in nothing but her underwear and I don't know where to look. This woman is going to be my wife. She's mine forever, and I'm hers.

"You're beautiful," I say. "And kind and funny and smart and sexy and I'm glad we get to hang out forever."

Her mouth curls up into a smile. "Samesies." I've stripped completely. She steps toward me, rises on tiptoes and links her hands behind my neck. "You're beautiful," she says. "And kind and funny and smart and sexy and I'm glad we get to hang out forever. And I know we've got the rest of our lives, but I'd like the rest of our lives to start now."

I bend to kiss her, pressing the small of her back so we

slot together just like we've done from that first night together. Our tongues slide together and it's so fucking cheesy but it feels like we're moving as one person, or like she was designed just for me. She's fucking incredible and I get to marry her. How the hell did I get so lucky?

I break our kiss to grab a condom.

"Do we have to?" she asks. "I've been tested and...everything. I mean, I'm fine."

"Me too," I say, a little too quickly. She doesn't need to know that I got tested once a month until I met her. Since her, there's been no one else.

There will never be again.

My cock strains at the thought of being inside her soon, but I'm going to force myself to be patient. I want to focus on Kate.

I walk us over to the bed and lay her down on her back. She props herself up on her elbows, releases the catch on her bra and discards it, and I remove her panties.

Smoothing my hands over her thighs, I spread her legs, and lick between them and up, up, up to her clit, over her stomach and between her breasts. She shudders underneath me, her quiet groans seeming to grip and release my cock like a fist. I take her nipple in my mouth and circle and suck. She bucks underneath me, her fingers in my hair, her leg wrapping around mine.

"Vincent," she calls. "I want you. All of you."

She lifts my chin from her breast and we lock gazes. "You're a generous lover, always thinking about me, but right now—this time—I want it to be about us. I want you on me, over me, inside me."

I growl. "Kate." I shake my head. "I don't know how long I'll last if—"

She places her fingers over my lips. "Me neither."

I rub my palms over my face and take a deep breath. "I'm about to lose points here," I say.

"Well, I've already agreed to marry you. And etiquette demands that I give the ring back if I call things off before the wedding, and that's not going to happen, so it looks like I'm stuck with you, no matter what."

I chuckle, circle the base of my cock and anchor my hand on her hip. I press into her, slowly, carefully, trying not to be overawed at how good she feels.

At how good we are. Together.

I start to move. Tentatively at first, because I want to try and make this last, but it's no use.

She feels too good. She's tight and wet and the way she huffs out my name, claws at my chest—I just want to be closer, get closer.

She's fucking irresistible.

I don't know if it's the relentless rhythm, but it's only seconds before I feel her tighten around me.

"Vincent," she cries. "Oh god."

She's close and thank god, because I can feel that rumble of my orgasm in the distance and it's coming for me at speed.

She links her legs around my waist and I fuck and fuck and fuck and as she arches her back, my climax roars into the station like a freight train.

"Kate," I call out. "Kate."

Her hands cup my jaw and I open my eyes to find her gazing at me. I don't need to hear her say it to know she loves me.

I press a kiss to her lips and slump on top of her.

My breathing returns to normal and I shift off her. She rolls and presses a kiss to my stomach.

"Shower next," she says.

I don't know if I can move, but I'm powerless to resist this woman. She takes me by the hand and leads me into the bathroom. "Sit here," she says pointing at the marble bench at one end of the mammoth shower.

Exhausted, I do as she asks. I tip my head up as Kate turns on the water and a warm rain shower descends from across the ceiling.

"Wow. It's like it's raining," she says.

Her body practically gleams under the water. She bends and presses a kiss to my lips. I reach for her hips but she pulls away, instead kneeling at my feet.

I can practically feel the blood rushing to my dick, as if every molecule is racing to be there first.

"Kate," I say, shaking my head.

"I want to. You like giving me pleasure. I like giving you pleasure." She circles my cock in her hand and I groan.

But I don't stop her. She licks, kisses, scrapes and sucks and I can't take my eyes off of her. Her tongue, her hands, the way her breasts move. The water running over her body.

"Fuck," I call out as she takes me deep in her throat and groans.

I'm going to come. Again. I can't stop. She's just too...

I shift, wanting her to move so I can climax. She grips my thighs, refusing to budge.

"Kate," I spit out.

She reaches for my hand and places it on her head and that's it—I'm fucking gone. My balls tighten and I empty myself deep into her throat.

When I regain consciousness, I reach and scoop her up into my arms, pulling her close to my chest. Our bodies fit together perfectly, like two pieces of a jigsaw. Wherever she is, she's my home. And I know I'm hers.

My fiancée.

My wife.

My partner.

Whatever her title, she's the woman I'll spend the rest of my life loving.

EPILOGUE

36 Days Later

Vincent

Despite not needing another ceremony after our exchange of vows in the park, I wanted one. Kate has indulged me and gone along with it. I want all the people I love together in one place so I can celebrate getting to spend the rest of my life with Kate and having a future I'd never thought was possible for me.

And I don't want to wait.

Twenty-nine days after our reunion in Hyde Park, we stand in the Marylebone registry office and take legal vows.

A week after that, all our friends and family gather on the grounds of Crompton for a celebration. We erected a huge marquee, complete with a dance floor and tables for lunch. Despite it being September, we've had a burst of sunshine this weekend and Kate insisted all the sides of the marquee be removed so we could see the grounds better.

The tent overlooks the lake, down to the woods—my and Kate's favorite vista. Flowers festoon the inside of the marquee, winding around supports and dripping off the roof. It's beautiful. There's no other place we could have possibly wanted to celebrate.

There's no aisle, no ceremony, no bridesmaids or groomsmen. Just sunshine, champagne, food, music, dancing and laughter.

It's unconventional, but fits us both perfectly.

"You look so beautiful," I say to my bride, who's dressed in a beaded white gown and a crown of flowers picked fresh from Crompton's gardens. We sway on the dance floor together. "Like a flower fairy."

She grins up at me and fiddles with the pink rose in my lapel she picked from the gardens herself this morning. "How much have you had to drink?"

"You *are* magical," I insist.

"Who would have thought you would have turned into such a sappy marshmallow?"

"That's what you've done to me." I kiss her on the forehead.

Beck and Stella are across from us on the dance floor. He stepped on her toe and she's laughing at him. Kate follows my gaze. "You wondering whether you'll be treading on my toes after a few years together?"

"No," I reply. "I don't plan to dance after tonight."

She laughs and I can't help but smile at her because seeing her happy is my greatest achievement.

"We should arrange dinner with them," she says. "I really like Stella."

"Yeah, let's do that. I also want to hear Beck's story of how they met. Apparently it started with blackmail."

"All's well that ends well, I suppose." She leads me off

the dance floor toward Granny, who's grinning up at us both.

"You make a very fine-looking couple," she says. Kate is pulled away by someone and I take a seat next to Granny.

"She's too good for me," I say.

"She'd say the same about you. That's why you're perfect for each other." She pats my knee. "You just need to make sure you look after each other."

"It's my most important job. Looking after her, making sure she's happy and feels my love. I don't care about much else. Loving her has given me perspective."

"You'll have your ups and downs," Granny says. "You just need to remind yourself it's a long game."

"You think she's really okay about coming to New York?" I ask. I'm going over to close down my office there. I want to tell the staff in person. I'm offering them other jobs, but some of them would have to relocate. There's no point having an office there when my home is with Kate, in England.

"She's fine if she says she's fine. You'll be there, and so will I."

"I hope you'll always travel with us."

"Now and then I will, until these old bones refuse to cooperate." She pauses and shakes her head. "Seeing Kate so happy has lifted a weight off my shoulders I didn't realize I'd been carrying. The worry has gone now. For so many years, I blamed myself. I didn't know what I could do to make her feel okay again."

"She adores you," I say. "You did everything right."

"No one does everything right. But now I see her and I'm so happy—but also relieved—things slotted into place for her. Just do me a favor? So much of her life has been about hiding for Kate. Let her explore her own needs a little. She loves you, and I'm so pleased she's going to be traveling with you on business. She also needs something for herself."

"I agree," I say, just as Kate returns and plonks herself on my lap. "Did you tell Granny about the application you made yesterday?"

Kate glances at me then Granny.

"I think she'd like to know," I say.

"I don't know if it will come to anything," she says, "but I reapplied to Cambridge. I emailed my old tutor to tell him and he replied to say he was happy to support my application. If I get in, I'll start next year."

Granny's eyes go glassy and she grasps both of our hands. "That's fantastic news."

"I'll only travel during breaks from university," I say. "The rest of the time we'll be here."

"In Crompton?" Granny asks.

"We keep talking about it," Kate says. "Vincent wants to take a piece of the estate and build a place for us both, but I'm not so sure. If I'm going to be studying, it makes more sense to be in Cambridge. If I get in."

"Beck is developing some townhouses in Mayfair we're going to look at. It would be good to have a London base too."

"What about Norfolk?" Kate says. "And we want to be close to you too, Granny."

"Lucky for you, I don't have a job," Granny says. "So I can come and visit you wherever you are."

Kate and I share a look. Kate's been clear wherever we go, Granny goes. It suits me fine. Granny's my family now, too.

"The London place has a granny annex," Kate says. "I mean, it *literally* has your name on it."

"Don't fuss about me. I'll just fit in around you. Now, Vincent, introduce me to your brothers."

As if on cue, Beau approaches, wearing a smile as wide as Africa. He picks up Granny's hand and kisses her knuckles. "I'm Beau Cove. Vincent's brother. I take it you're Granny? I've heard wonderful things."

"The charm in your family is quite exceptional," Granny says to me and laughs. "Are you married?"

"Not yet," he replies. "Would you like to dance?"

"Is Beau flirting with Granny?" Kate asks as we watch him escort her to the middle of the dance floor.

"He doesn't know how to turn it off."

"It's going to get him in an awful lot of trouble," she says.

"Beau's used to trouble," I say. I worry about him sometimes. He seems so rudderless—always chasing the next high. I wonder what will be enough for him.

Kate slides her arms around my neck and we look out at our friends and family laughing and dancing and celebrating in this beautiful place.

How did we get so lucky?

"I have a wedding present for you," I whisper in her ear.

"I already have everything I want right here."

I grin because I know she's telling the truth. Kate's made me see that the most important things in life aren't financial. Which is why I'm hoping she's going to like my gift.

I pull out my phone and scroll to the page I'm looking for. "You know whatever I have is yours."

"If you say so." She sweeps her fingers into my hair. She's barely listening.

"But I wanted this to be in your name. The papers are all drawn up. You just have to sign them."

She narrows her eyes at me and glances at my phone, which I have angled in her direction. "What's in my name?"

"This place. Crompton."

She freezes. "You want me to own it?" Her mouth unfurls into a smile.

"Yeah. I mean, you do anyway now we're married, but it's so special to you, I wanted it to be yours specifically."

She cups my face in her hand. "Thank you." She pauses. "You're so special, Vincent. Not because it's such an extravagant gift—which it is. But because you're always thinking about me. You're always putting my happiness front and center. I want to do that for you, too."

I clasp her hand in mine. "You do. Every day. Just by being you."

A few weeks after that

Kate

We all stand looking at Carole and John's house from the driveway.

I keep glancing up at the heavy, gray clouds threatening above. I give it four minutes until it starts bucketing down.

"We've got to have at least four more bedrooms," Carole says.

"Four?" John shrieks. "Do you have a bunch of secret children I don't know about?"

"And a bigger dining room," Carole says.

"We can't just make the dining room bigger," John says.

"Which is why I'm thinking it might just be better to pull the entire house down and build something new. What do you think?"

"What do I think?" John says, his face getting redder by the second. "I think—"

"I didn't mean you, I meant Vincent. And Jacob. Extend or demolish?"

"Nathan has a house just down the road. We don't all need to stay with you every time we visit."

Carole reaches around her back and unties her apron with pictures of Jacob on it. "This is just what I was afraid of. If you all have houses nearby, no one is going to want to stay. And I love it when we eat together, and sit around the firepit and then fall into bed." She screws the apron up in a ball and throws in on the ground. "I want my grandchildren crawling into my bed in the mornings and I want to tuck them up at night."

John sidles up to her and rubs her back. "Hey. Our boys aren't going anywhere, as much as I'd like them to."

I stifle a laugh and shoot a glance at Sutton. John's comment doesn't even register with Vincent and Jacob.

"I have an idea," Vincent says and I squeeze his hand, wanting him to know I agree with whatever he's going to say. "Why don't you add a new house at the front here? You have plenty of space. Then connect it to the old house and convert the old house into a bedroom block that can be used when we're all here. The rest of the time, you can use the new house, which we can make sure has a huge dining room."

"A bedroom block?" John asks. "We're not turning the place into a youth hostel."

"It's a good idea," Carole says. "Because the grandchildren have started arriving and they need space."

"Good grief," John says. "There's never any peace."

"Why don't you go and look at your beans, John? Leave this to me and the boys," Carole says.

John tuts. "Typical. Dismissed from discussing my own house." He doesn't argue and I imagine he's secretly pleased he doesn't have to be involved with whatever it is Carole wants to do with the house. John loves his sons just as much as Carole does. He just has a different way of showing it. "Dog," he screams. "You better not have found any fox shit or I'll skin you alive."

"Don't kill the dog, Dad," Jacob says.

"I'll do what I damn well please," he replies. "This is my house—" Dog rounds the corner from the side of the house and shoots toward us. "Come on. Let's check the beans." John heads toward his vegetable patch, leaving the five of us staring at the house.

"We're always going to come and visit, Mum," Jacob says. "I don't think Sutton would have married me if it hadn't been for the family. You're part of the package."

"It's true," Sutton says. "There's no way we'll stop visiting."

"But when you all have babies, we'll need more space," Carole says. "They're small things, but they take up a lot of room. You'll find out."

"Yes we will," Jacob says. "In about seven and a half months."

I gasp, and Carole snaps her head to look at Jacob.

Vincent slaps Jacob on the back. "Congratulations."

"We were going to do a big announcement at dinner," he says.

"But my soon-to-be husband has the patience of a toddler," Sutton adds.

I wrap Sutton up in a hug and Carole joins us. "I'm so happy for you," I say.

I pull away from Sutton and Carole and glance at

Vincent. He scoops up my hand, then presses his lips to my knuckles.

The pregnancy test I took this morning was positive, but we're not going to spoil Sutton and Jacob's announcement. We'll be back in Norfolk in a few weeks and we can tell everyone then. I called Granny earlier and for at least five minutes, she couldn't speak, then she half-sobbed for the rest of our conversation. She never thought she'd be a great-grandmother. I never thought I'd be a mother or a wife.

But the man by my side changed everything. And I couldn't be happier.

DO YOU KNOW?
>   Jacob and Sutton - **Dr. Off Limits**
>   Zach and Ellie - **Dr. Perfect**
>   Beau and Vivian - **Dr. Fake Fiancé**
>   Tristan and Parker - **Mr. Notting Hill**
>   Nathan and Madison - **Private Player**

FOR MORE OF **Vincent and Kate, sign up to my newsletter for BONUS scenes www.louisebay.com/newsletter**

ALL LOUISE BAY BOOKS **are available for FREE in Kindle Unlimited or on Amazon to buy.**

BOOKS BY LOUISE BAY

All books are stand alone

The Doctors Series

Dr. Off Limits

Dr. Perfect

Dr. CEO

Dr. Fake Fiancé

The Mister Series

Mr. Mayfair

Mr. Knightsbridge

Mr. Smithfield

Mr. Park Lane

Mr. Bloomsbury

Mr. Notting Hill

The Christmas Collection

14 Days of Christmas

The Player Series

International Player

Private Player

Dr. Off Limits

Standalones

Hollywood Scandal

Love Unexpected

Hopeful

The Empire State Series

The Gentleman Series

The Ruthless Gentleman

The Wrong Gentleman

The Royals Series

King of Wall Street

Park Avenue Prince

Duke of Manhattan

The British Knight

The Earl of London

The Nights Series

Indigo Nights

Promised Nights

Parisian Nights

Faithful

What kind of books do you like?

Friends to lovers

Mr. Mayfair

Promised Nights

International Player

Fake relationship (marriage of convenience)

Duke of Manhattan

Mr. Mayfair

Mr. Notting Hill

Enemies to Lovers

King of Wall Street

The British Knight

The Earl of London

Hollywood Scandal

Parisian Nights

14 Days of Christmas

Mr. Bloomsbury

Office Romance/ Workplace romance

Mr. Knightsbridge

King of Wall Street

The British Knight

The Ruthless Gentleman

Mr. Bloomsbury

Dr. Perfect

Dr. Off Limits

Dr. CEO

Second Chance

International Player

Hopeful

Best Friend's Brother

Promised Nights

Vacation/Holiday Romance

The Empire State Series

Indigo Nights

The Ruthless Gentleman

The Wrong Gentleman

Love Unexpected

14 Days of Christmas

Holiday/Christmas Romance

14 Days of Christmas

British Hero

Promised Nights (British heroine)

Indigo Nights (American heroine)

Hopeful (British heroine)

Duke of Manhattan (American heroine)

The British Knight (American heroine)

The Earl of London (British heroine)

The Wrong Gentleman (American heroine)

The Ruthless Gentleman (American heroine)

International Player (British heroine)

Mr. Mayfair (British heroine)

Mr. Knightsbridge (American heroine)

Mr. Smithfield (American heroine)

Private Player (British heroine)

Mr. Bloomsbury (American heroine)

14 Days of Christmas (British heroine)

Mr. Notting Hill (British heroine)

Dr. Off Limits (British heroine)

Dr. Perfect (British heroine)

Dr. Fake Fiancé (American heroine)

Single Dad

King of Wall Street

Mr. Smithfield

Sign up to the Louise Bay mailing list www.louisebay/newsletter

Read more at www.louisebay.com

Printed in the USA
CPSIA information can be obtained
at www.ICGtesting.com
JSHW032155090823
46274JS00001B/4